Alex Kosh

The Sands of Eternity

Loner

Book #8

Magic Dome Books

Loner
Book #8: The Sands of Eternity
Copyright © Alex Kosh 2025
Cover Art © Ivan Khivrenko 2025
Cover Designer: Vladimir Manyukhin
English translation copyright © Zachary Lorang 2025
Published by Magic Dome Books, 2025
All Rights Reserved
ISBN: 978-80-7702-217-0

This book is entirely a work of fiction.
Any correlation with real people or events
is coincidental.

Loner

by Alex Kosh

Table of Contents:

Part One

The Price of Life

"Did you hear that the zombies have already founded their own city?! There's a carbon copy of me living in it as we speak! Is it even legal, using my image and character like that?"

"I heard these dead doppelgangers speak with our voices and even mimic our body language! Couldn't we sue RussVirtTech over this?"

"Yeah, good luck. Have you read the user agreement, at least?"

"Nobody ever reads those."

"Exactly. But it's written in black and white: by using your appearance to generate a game character, you automatically cede all copyright on your own image and voice to the company. Honestly, they could create a porn starring your avatar and there wouldn't be a thing you could do about it!"

Official Arktania forums

A big, muscly man with the body of a wrestler trudged downstairs into a well-lit basement (so well-lit, in fact, that the light stung his eyes), where he found his partner-in-crime waiting for him right away:

"How are the imps, Alex?"

A pale, thin twenty-year-old with big, black circles under his eyes was sitting at a table, staring blankly into the space in front of him. It took him a few seconds to notice that his colleague had arrived.

"Hey!" the wrestler shouted.

"Ah... Where'd you come from?" Alex sounded surprised; he rubbed a hand across his face in an effort to wake himself up a little bit.

"The imps," the big man repeated with mounting irritation. "How are they?"

"They've already killed five people," the kid replied with a heavy sigh as he pointed to a pentagram that had been traced in the center of the hall. There, at the tips of five of the star's nine points, sat a semicircular row of severed human heads.

"They're looking for a sixth as we speak."

"Just five?!"

"You think it's EASY, finding and killing people with these very specific parameters, and then bringing their heads to a specific place, with only three brain-dead monkey-sized animals to help you?" The gaunt young man snapped back. "I haven't slept in two days!"

The wrestler shrugged.

"Then work smarter, not harder, I guess. Find some better help."

"Well, once I get four more victims I'm hoping to summon a Succubus..."

"A Succubus?!" The big man's eyes almost popped out of their sockets. "Have you lost your mind?! They're completely psychotic!"

"Well, they're also the most intellectually-developed Demon we can summon right now," replied Alex in a tired voice. "She'll also make the imps do their job properly, and lure victims wherever we need her to."

"Well, you're going to have to handle her yourself! I don't even want to be in the same room as a Succubus." The man shuddered, as though recalling some very, very unpleasant experience from his past. "We'll communicate by phone from now on. I'm never coming back here in person again! Keep reporting, and let me know when you're done with the summons."

Once the big man had run back up the stairs out of the basement, the exhaustion on the young man's face transformed into unbridled joy. He jumped up from the table, ran over to one of the steel cupboards lining the wall, opened one of its doors, and ran a hand across the pile of human heads inside with a happy smile on his face. Neither the sickly-sweet stench of decaying flesh, nor the metallic tang of blood seemed to bother him at all; on the contrary, it seemed like he thoroughly enjoyed it.

"We'll see who's in charge from here on..."

A basement somewhere in the suburbs of Moscow

The "Spirit of the Hunt's" HQ had recently been transferred to the capital, not far from the Emperor's Palace, where it occupied a towering 88-story building. Being number one in the clan rankings meant the ability not only to rent the biggest building in the capital, but also to alter its design at one's own discretion. Why exactly the Clanleader had chosen this particular design, however — and, more importantly, why they had created such a complex chain of portals to facilitate movement throughout the tower, rather than installing any good old-fashioned human-style stairs — remains a mystery. The head of the "Spirit of the Hunt" was quite a mysterious figure, who practically never participated in life within the Clan, and always gave orders through a small number of close subordinates. Very few people could boast of having met him face-to-face. And true to form, he had delegated responsibility for his most recent enterprise to one of the Clan's generals — a tall, broad-shouldered half-Elf named Galaydrel.

"They left the game," a player-Assassin re-

ported as he stepped out of a portal.

"Predictable," the Elf replied with a frown. "Well, we'll just have to wait for them to come back. Although I don't think this Falk is likely to remain in the capital."

"No matter where they go, we have people on the ground waiting for them, although the Illusionist is going to make the search a lot more difficult."

"Ba-ba-ba-BAA. Hello everybody." A mirthful voice rang out from somewhere above the players' heads, causing them to jump up and pull their weapons out in the blink of an eye. "Take it easy, take it easy. I heard you're trying to find somebody named Falk? I know the exact time and place where you'll be able to find him, and I'll tell you everything for free. You don't even need to thank me.

Katar, "Spirit of the Hunt" Clan headquarters.

Chapter 1

WHEN I FINALLY REGAINED CONSCIOUSNESS, I found myself lying on the floor. It felt like I had been out drinking all night, then came home and laid down for five minutes, and then had to get back up and go about my day again. After somehow rising to my feet, I made sure I hadn't hurt myself when I fell, then glanced at the clock. 6:00 AM?! That meant I had been unconscious for almost five hours — so why the hell did it feel like I had been run over by a car?! I also had a terrible headache. I had never had a migraine in my life, but I suspected that this is what they probably felt like.

Maybe it was just a fever-induced hallucination, but I had a pretty clear memory of a system communication appearing just before I passed out. Something about interface installation...

The Sands of Eternity

Just to check, I tried summoning the game interface the way I usually did when I was in-game... And it popped right up!

Attribute window, skills, titles, abilities. My inventory was off-limits, as were various buttons for using abilities, guides, and the world map; that said, I found that I had acquired a small map of the area about ten yards around me. There was also a section for game tasks, and I could even open it and read the descriptions. The only thing I didn't understand is why my attributes were lower than before, and why they seemingly weren't taking any account of my equipment:

Strength: 47.25;
Dexterity: 72.1;
Intelligence: 80.5;
Wisdom: 70.2;
Endurance: 45.0.
Health: 740.
Mana: 980.

The amount of mana at my disposal had also dropped for some reason, despite the fact that the day before, I had just as much as my character in the game, including all the bonuses from my items. Weird, I thought. Could this really have been some sort of bug that they fixed later on? With my new, drastically-lower Intelligence parameter, it would be quite a long time before I'd be able to talk to Chaosite using human language — although to be honest, "a long time" probably meant "never" in this case. And then, suddenly, I realized just how much I still had to be grateful for — after all, if this had happened a few days earlier, and I had been forced to fight the dark faction with only the amount of mana that was currently in my reservoir, there's no way in hell I would have been able to beat them.

Anyway, I thought... What have I acquired here? I can refresh my memory by glancing at all my tasks from Arktania, I can check out Spin and Chaosite's icons if need be, I can study my list of abilities, and I can see a mini-map. So far, that's it. To be honest, I was a little bit disappointed. On the other hand, though, if the mini-map worked the same way as the in-game one did, I'd be able to see opponents on it, even if there was a wall between us or they were hiding underground. That would certainly come in handy in my next battle with other Emissaries, which (alas) seemed like it would probably be happening in the very near future.

"You're finally up." I suddenly heard a voice from behind my back, which caused me to whip around and jump to the side in terror.

When I did, I saw Hotei floating in the air in front of me. Or rather, not the little God himself, but a small, translucent copy of him that looked something like a hologram from an old science-fiction movie. He was still wearing his beige clerk's suit, but he had traded in his old abacus for a sleek, modern-looking tablet.

"How'd you get here?" I asked. "I thought you

couldn't appear in our world."

"I'm not. This is a projection in your brain, which was actually pretty difficult to create, by the way."

I suddenly felt awkward, standing there in my birthday suit in front of the little virtual God, and I hurried to slip my pants and T-shirt back on.

"So what's so important that you went to all that trouble? What did you come to tell me?"

"The same thing I'm being forced to ram into your thick head time and time again until I can somehow get it to stick! Stop. Losing. Levels! You lost the duel, despite me getting you a kiss from an Ice Elf Princess for next to no cost!" The little God launched into an indignant rant. "So much effort, and you just pissed it away! I've been think-ing through quests for you, stacking probabilities in your favor!"

Recalling the Tree of Fear, I couldn't resist snapping back at him:

"The only thing you've been stacking for me is shit pancakes."

"So ungrateful!"

"And anyway, I wasn't planning to lose!" I shouted, now feeling just as indignant as Hotei. "It was your Goddess of Fate that made me do it!"

The little God calmed down immediately.

"First of all, she's not "mine." Second, how could Lady Elenia have influenced your duel — and more importantly, WHY would she do that?! You humans always try to blame your personal mistakes on others!"

"Whisper of Fate. That stupid ability kept screaming at me to lose! What do you say to that?!"

Hotei's reaction was not at all what I would have expected: he burst out laughing.

"That ability isn't the voice of the Goddess. That would be way too big an honor for someone like you," he said with a derisive snort.

"Then what was it?"

"Just a hint. At some point in their life, everybody finds themselves at a fork in the road where the choice they make might have an influence on their future. A real influence, I mean. At times like this, that ability can give you a hint as to which choice is best."

Well, I thought... I get it now. Why couldn't somebody have simply explained that to me from the start? That explains why the ability never activated during my training duels: their outcomes wouldn't have had any real effect on my fate at all. In theory, though, this "whisper" probably does have the potential to save me from mortal danger. After all — what could possibly have a bigger impact on my eventual fate than the threat of imminent death?

"Well, that "hint" was the only thing that made me lose. My muscles literally seized up on me at the exact moment I was about to deal the final blow."

The little God started pacing back and forth in midair.

"Hm... That changes a lot. Although, actually, no — it doesn't change anything! I came to warn you for the very last time: don't you dare spend twenty more levels trying to resurrect your friend. Believe me: once you collect all five swords, you'll probably have plenty of opportunities to help him."

"Probably?" I repeated. There was no way I could have missed such a suspicious-sounding caveat coming from him.

"There's no guarantee, of course," Hotei admitted. "But at level 30, you'll never be able to get the sword in the lands of the Orcs, and then YOU'LL be the one who needs resurrecting."

I had already thought about this myself, of course: losing twenty more levels would make me easy prey not only for the "Spirit of the Hunt" Clan, but also any other mid-level player who happened to be a bully, or even just in a bad mood. But Eidolon hadn't given me a choice. Creating an Essence from my own blood was one of the necessary conditions for resurrection. And no matter what Hotei might say, I had no intention whatsoever of taking the risk that postponing Artyom's resurrection would entail. After all, I might not survive long enough to see this vague "opportunity" the little God had mentioned anyway. Who knows, I thought, what else might happen in the real world? I mean, the "Spirit of the Hunt" is already willing to go after my parents... Actually, maybe I should have them go somewhere else for a while until the whole affair blows over? I could have asked Hotei for help, but I wasn't exactly on the best of terms with him at the time. I knew it probably wasn't a good idea to speak to him so aggressively, no matter how much he might irritate me.

"I'll think of something, even after losing those levels," I said in a calmer tone, trying to placate the little God. "I mean, I've made it this far, haven't I?"

Hotei slapped his palm to his forehead in despair.

"I mean, what, WHAT are you going to think of?! You didn't "make it this far" at all! That was ME, running around like a mouse on a frying pan trying to bail you out. Actually, the real miracle is that you haven't fallen behind the other Emissaries in terms of levels despite all your boneheaded bumbling! I mean, I deserve a medal and a place in the Higher Pantheon for everything I've pulled off here!"

He was speaking pretty passionately, of course, and it sounded impressive enough, but from my point of view it always felt like Hotei was deceiving me whenever he stipulated the conditions for his quests. What difference would it have made to him if, for example, he had built the extra day of time in the "False Emissary" quest so that it could apply to any stage of the quest, rather than the third stage specifically? There was no question about it: he had routinely taken advantage of my poor attention to detail. It was just like negotiating with the Gremlins. Even as things stood, he still had information about Artyom's death that he was concealing from me — the bare minimum was all he was ever willing to offer. Long story short, therefore, no matter how much he might try to convince me that he was trying to help, I simply didn't trust a single word that came out of his mouth.

"Oh — is that why you're doing such a bad job of helping me?" I couldn't resist a jab. "You want to unseat the Goddess of Fate and take her place?"

Hotei almost seemed to choke on his outrage at this suggestion, although I really doubt that the virtual God was actually breathing (and this was a holographic projection anyway).

"I've never dared even to THINK of such a thing!"

"Then how about you start providing some actual, no-nonsense help? Answer my questions as thoroughly as you can. Stop holding things back on purpose," I said, softening my tone just a bit in order to make it clear just how much I wanted to be able to trust him. "What changed just now, with the interface appearing? Will I be able to see other players' life bars above their heads from now on? And use this mini-map like I can in the game? What about my inventory? Basically, can you just tell me what's happening?"

"The installation is still in progress," the little God replied evasively. "I mean, have you seen your own brain? The installation doesn't have much to work with here."

"See? I don't understand what the hell you mean!"

"It's totally smooth and empty," the little God chortled at his own joke. "If we're being serious, though, you're the first person for whom this procedure has actually started, so we really don't know how long the interface installation is going to last. So far, so good — it hasn't paralyzed you or given you epileptic seizures yet. Losing consciousness is one of the predictable side effects, and the slight feeble-mindedness is nothing new."

To be honest, I actually felt a lot less optimistic after hearing the serious version than I had after his stupid joke.

"The first? So I'm being used as some sort of guinea pig?" I asked. I was starting to get angry.

"Look at it as an extra advantage over the other Emissaries. It's just an advantage that comes with a few health risks," Hotei giggled.

"So I'm not so much a guinea pig as the canary in the mine shaft?"

"Don't flatter yourself. You're a sparrow, at best, and you're definitely not the first. Don't forget that there were beta testers."

"Actually, speaking of..." I snapped back to attention. "Tell me something..."

Suddenly, the hologram started to flicker.

"Psshhkkhh... Connection's cutting out," whispered Hotei. "Time to wrap it up. Last — psshhkkhh — thing I have to say to you. If you ignore my instructions and resurrect your friend, I'm going to have to psskkhh apply sanctions."

"So you're threatening to punish me now?"

"Punish?" The sound of the static (which, needless to say, the little God was obviously making himself) abruptly vanished. "No-oo, not at all. On the contrary — this is me, officially starting to provide some actual, no-nonsense help. I can exert a lot more influence over you now that your interface installation has reached its final stage. So think twice — better yet, thrice — before you do anything to contradict the will of the Goddess!"

With that, he disappeared, leaving me with mixed feelings: I felt like I had learned a lot from our little chat, but I also had more questions than ever before. First, he had confirmed my suspicion that the beta testers could also use their in-game abilities in real life, although he didn't shed any light on what their goal could possibly be. Second, the other Emissaries would soon be acquiring fully-functional game interfaces in the real world, just like I had. All this new information made the developing situation seem even scarier to me — after all, given that I was clearly the "canary in the mine shaft," making sure the installed interface would be safe for the other Emissaries, I didn't see any reason why the whole Emissary thing might not be merely the beginning of some larger transformation. Suddenly, it seemed perfectly possible that every player in Arktania would eventually acquire abilities and a game interface in the real world. And I couldn't even imagine how that might end up transforming our world.

After pondering the subject for a little while and studying my interface, I decided to put the rest of my free time to good use and try to get some actual sleep. The day ahead promised to be a difficult one (just like all the previous ones had been), and I wanted to be as well-rested as possible when it came time to face it. Of course, I knew it might be hard to fall asleep with all the disconcerting information from Hotei still floating around in my head, but at least I could lay down and relax for a bit... And that was the last thought I remembered having before I passed out into a deep, blissful sleep. Thankfully, I didn't forget to set my alarm for 11:00 AM before laying down.

When I woke up for the second time that day, I actually felt a bit better. The head pain and muscle aches all over my body were gone, at least. And once I had a cup of coffee in me, I was basically ready to go conquer the world. Well, maybe not literally the world... But I bet I could have conquered a vacant lot or two. Jokes aside, I knew I was going to have a very difficult conversation with Artyom's girlfriend that day, and I didn't have the faintest idea how to approach it.

Once I finished breakfast, I sat there for a little while, telephone in hand, trying to think of what to say and how to say it. Naturally, I wasn't planning to say it over the phone — it would sound crazy enough in person, let alone coming from the disembodied voice of someone who was practically a total stranger. I knew I would need to provide some proof, most likely a demonstration of my powers. But where to meet her? Maybe, I thought, I could bring her to Boris' restaurant? It would be risky, of course. Everybody I trusted was going to be there, and none of us actually knew Artyom's girlfriend at all. It was one thing for me to meet her in person, but it seemed way too early to expect the others to reveal their real-life identities to her. What about inviting her here, to my apartment?

The Sands of Eternity

That would be dangerous, too, although at least in that case it would just be me in danger, instead of the entire group. There was also the option of my old apartment, where I had destroyed the capsule — we could always meet there. Those were basically my only options; trying to find any other place to meet in Moscow would be unacceptably risky. Plus, she would no doubt be pretty confused and weirded out if I asked her to meet in some deserted place where there wouldn't be anybody else around. In the end, I decided I'd have to take the risk and ask her to come to my apartment.

Summoning all my emotional courage, I selected her recently-added contact and pressed "call." It was still relatively early, but she answered almost immediately:

"Hi, Andrey. Good morning. Any news?"

Her greeting immediately gave me the impression that she had been sitting there the entire time, phone in hand, just waiting for my call. To be honest, I felt a little bit ashamed. She had just been waiting, totally unaware of anything, and I hadn't even reached out to try to comfort her. Not only that, but the thought hadn't even crossed my mind.

"You might say that," I said evasively. "If you're comfortable with it, though, I'd prefer to meet up and talk in person. We could — "

"Yes, of course. I'll head out right now! Send me the address!"

Her readiness threw me off a little bit. She didn't even ask the very logical question of why I didn't want to talk about it over the phone. That would have been at the top of my list of questions if I'd been in her shoes. Naturally, though, I told her my address right away, and she promised to be there in forty minutes.

As if he had somehow sensed that I was awake, Naumov called right after I hung up the phone with Darya and reminded me that Sergei's ability would be ready for use again that night, and that Mark and I were supposed to be there when Antibiotic (a.k.a. Naumov Jr.) was restored to health. Since he had called so fortuitously, I decided to bring up the subject of my parents' safety, and the oligarch reacted eagerly:

"Send me their info. We'll buy them a couple weeks' vacation. Nice hotel, business-class tickets. Tell them it's a present for some sort of holiday. And send me their address. I'll send a few guys to keep a covert eye on them until they leave."

"Just like that?"

"Any problem money can solve is an easy one," Naumov chuckled. "Believe me. If all the money in the world can't help you, well, THAT'S when you should really start worrying. Come by with Mark this evening. My people will have all the necessary papers ready for you when you get here."

All this only put me further in Naumov's debt, of course, but I was willing to overlook my normal principles in this case. More than anything, I was concerned about whether Naumov would maintain his cooperative attitude to us after his son was healed. There was also one other question I was impatient to have answered: would the latest-generation ESGUMI that I stole for Naumov's son allow him to acquire his abilities in real life? Sure, Hotei had said that it wouldn't do anything unless the person in question had been chosen as an Emissary by one of the Gods, but as I already mentioned, I didn't trust a word the little God said anymore.

So, yeah... It was promising to be one hell of a busy day, and that was just my schedule in real life. As for in-game obligations, I still had no idea when the next event with the flying coffins was going to be! Dammit, I thought... I was so tired yesterday that I didn't even think to ask Boris about that. If the coffins happened to fly by only once a month, for example... Well, that could be a serious problem.

Thankfully, Boris turned out to be available by phone, but his answer came as a big disappointment:

"Flying coffins? Yeah, of course I've seen them. Global event that happens in different cities."

"Not just the capital?" I clarified.

"Of course not. It's all across the continent. Nobody knows exactly when it's going to happen. Some coffins contain ancient characters with insane powers, some contain really valuable treasures. True, I don't think anybody's ever actually found a specific coffin they were looking for — whenever somebody frees one of the Dead Immortals, they just start killing everybody in the area. But there's always a thrill-seeker out there who's itching to have some fun and try to get their hands on a flying loot box while they're at it."

"And there's no way to find out in advance when and where they'll appear?"

"Nope. And teleports stop working in the city during the event, so it wouldn't even be possible to quickly teleport in as soon as you get the word. It's purely a question of luck."

Shit, I thought. This is a problem. I'm sure Hotei knows exactly when and where the coffins will appear, but I doubt he'd be willing to help me.

"Why do you ask?" The kid inquired.

"I'll tell you all about it when we meet up," I promised him. "For now, though, could you just help me find out as much as possible about the event?"

"Sure, no problem. I'm friends with a few priests of the God of Death. They might know something..."

"The God of Death?" This caught my attention immediately. "What does he have to do with this?"

"The coffins are full of Dead Immortals. Obviously, that's got to be connected either with the God of Death or the God of the Dead. But the God of the Dead only appeared really recently, and the coffins have been flying for quite a while now, so obviously it's probably best to start with the God of Death."

That didn't sound like a bad idea at all. But why go through a bunch of priests when I had my very own virtual uncle? Renick Fudre was one of the representatives of Death, and he was bound to have more complete information than any priest. I would just have to convince him to help me somehow.

Boris and I chatted a little more, and he was more insistent than ever that I absolutely had to get my ancestral lands as soon as possible. The way he was talking, you'd have thought I was opposed to the idea. Since I was going to have to come crawling cap-in-hand to my uncle the Necromancer anyway, though, I figured I could kill two birds with one stone and resolve the question of my lands at the same time.

After making the trip to my old apartment, with its big, black stain on the ground in the spot where my capsule had once stood, I settled in to wait for Artyom's girlfriend. It felt like a very long wait. The conversation was inevitably going to be a hard one, and I also wanted to leave enough time to talk to my virtual uncle before I headed off to meet up with my friends at the restaurant later that day. Most importantly, there were two topics I wanted to steer him away from: the task that required me to destroy the Glass Rose, and the less-than-ideal outcome of the "False Emissary" quest.

Darya arrived about forty minutes after I called her; sure enough, I saw her approaching on my mini-map before she rang the doorbell. She lived in the suburbs, so I knew she must have driven as fast as she could, given that she actually made it to my place in forty minutes like she said she would. Moreover, when she showed up, she looked as if she had run the distance rather than driving it. Judging by her figure, though, Darya actually could have run the whole distance, albeit not in forty minutes. Despite the fact that she was wearing loose-fitting jeans and a blouse, her posture and her movements were those of a professional athlete. The words "Poison Ivy, level 12" were glowing in the air above her head, which showed that she was also at least passingly familiar with Arktania. Which was good, of course — after all, it meant that I wouldn't have to literally start from square one.

"Hey," she said as she practically burst into my apartment. "So what's going on with Artyom?"

Her forthrightness threw me off just a little bit.

"Let's go sit in the kitchen. Coffee?"

"What the hell do you mean, coffee?! Is he in the hospital? Did he get kidnapped?"

"Who would have kidnapped him?" I asked.

"That's what I'm asking YOU — who?!" She asked aggressively.

Another second, and I felt like she would have grabbed me by my collar, or maybe just punched me as hard as she could.

"Kitchen. Coffee." I raised my voice just a little bit.

This seemed to calm Darya down.

"Yeah. Sorry. Of course, let's sit down first. No coffee for me though — my heart's already pounding."

We walked into the kitchen and sat down across from one another. A long, tense pause ensued, during which I took advantage of the opportunity to gather what information I could from my guest's physical appearance: short bob haircut, tattoos on her neck, green eyes. She sort of looked like Scarlett Johannsen in Black Widow, not least of all because she was athletic and looked like she could probably break my face without even breaking a sweat.

"So what's going on with Artyom?" She finally asked impatiently.

"There's a question I need you to answer first," I said. "You know that Artyom and I play Arktania, right?"

"Of course," Darya nodded. "I have a capsule too. I thought I could use it for training, but the character dynamics are so different that it actually makes my skills worse."

"Skills?"

"I'm a gymnast. Training for the Olympics. We were hoping to use one of RussVirtTech's specially-developed products to work on our jumps, but we eventually figured out that even if we copied the physical inputs and cranked the game sensations up to 100%, it just couldn't substitute for the real thing," she said nervously. "I've been into Arktania a few times too, but I decided to put the game off until after the competition, just in case."

Well, I thought... That certainly explains the athletic build.

"That explains why you're only at level 12," I said, without really thinking about it.

Darya frowned.

"How do you know that?!"

"I also know that your nickname's "Poison Ivy." The thing is, Arktania isn't exactly a normal game," I started to explain, choosing my words very carefully. "These capsules can impact a player's brain and give them their in-game abilities in real life."

"What the hell are you talking about?!" She snapped as she jumped back onto her feet. "And what does any of this have to do with Artyom?! Are you saying he got his abilities in real life?"

"No. HE didn't." I was trying to speak as softly as possible. "But I did. Don't worry, though."

Darya couldn't hold back a wry smile.

"So what — you're about to do some magic tricks? Seriously?"

"Something like that," I nodded as I created some lightning on my palm. "I'm an Electricity Mage. I can create lightning, control technology and magnetic fields. I can also teleport."

Darya glared back at me skeptically, then quickly threw a glance around the room.

"Is this some kind of prank? I've seen stuff like this in circuses before."

In response, I stood up from my chair and used Shift to teleport about three feet back from where I had been standing.

"I can guarantee you've never seen THIS in any circus."

Darya started to back away from me.

"How did you do that?!"

"I told you — teleportation. I can do a lot more than that, too, but most of these skills are too dangerous to demonstrate in an apartment."

Just to amplify the effect a little bit, I summoned Chaosite. I still couldn't use his icon, but a mental summons was enough. The little purple ball of light appeared above my head and turned immediately into a smiley emoji, then started drifting toward Darya's face, which (naturally enough) made her start backing away again.

"This is my pet, Chaosite. He's saying hi."

"This is insane," she muttered as her eyes flitted frantically between me and Chaosite. "You're telling me all players in Arktania can do this? I mean, this would be over all TV and social media if they could."

"No, of course not. Just a few of us. It's complicated."

"And is Artyom one of you too?"

"Not exactly. Let me explain..."

It took quite a while to explain the situation with the ESGUMI blocks, the Emissaries, and other key events. Thankfully, the Goddess of Fate's limitation only affected my specific quest, so I simply avoided delving into that subject at all. Although to be honest, I wasn't sure that the prohibition would even apply in the current situation anyway.

"I still don't understand, though. What does Artyom have to do with any of this, and where is he?" Darya asked with a note of mild confusion after hearing me out.

She ended up drinking a coffee after all, although it seemed like she did so more by force of habit than anything. She certainly didn't seem to be savoring the taste. I probably could have poured her beer or pickle juice, and her reaction would have been the same.

"I'm telling you all this because I need you to understand that Arktania isn't just a game. You could say it's an entirely different world. Its residents aren't simply NPCs with a couple hundred stock phrases at their disposal. They're fully-fledged characters. And a lot of Emissaries have abilities that really can't be explained without reference to magic."

"Any sufficiently advanced technology is indistinguishable from magic. Arthur C. Clark," Darya unexpectedly responded, before explaining: "My dad was a huge fan of sci-fi. I read a ton of it when I was a kid."

"Wise words," I agreed. "Fair enough — let's just agree that this is some really, really advanced technology. In any case, what matters for you and me right now is that a lot of things that seem like magic in this world are fully possible in that world. Including... Resurrection."

Darya didn't react aggressively this time. She was just sitting there, motionless, as if she'd been stunned. Her pupils widened so much it seemed like they were about to swallow both her eyeballs. I thought she might be collapsing into a coma.

"...Artyom's dead?" She whispered quietly.

"In our world," I hurried to add. "But the God of the Dead has assured me that we can bring him back to life in Arktania."

The Sands of Eternity

"In a GAME?! What the hell are you talking about?!"

I clutched my hair in despair.

"Why do you think I just told you all this stuff?! It's not just a game, it's a whole different world!"

It took me about twenty more minutes before Darya finally started to accept the idea that we really could bring Artyom back. Strangely (well, strangely to me, at least), she initially refused to believe me even after all my demonstrations and stories. That said, I might well have reacted the same way if I had been in her place, and somebody had dumped the whole far-fetched story on me all at once. In the process of trying to convince her, I had to tell her about how Artyom had actually died, and the fact that we were operating on the assumption that he'd been killed.

"Do you believe it yourself?" She asked, looking tired, as she sat at the table with her face propped up on her hands. "That we can bring him back, I mean?"

"I know a Healer from the game who can cure people of cancer with a touch of the hand. I've seen a girl who can turn invisible, a Fire Mage, a Necromancer who can raise corpses, and a guy with telepathic powers who can take control of other humans. I'd say that's just a step away from resurrection, but it's not — it's more like a little tiptoe away, at most."

Darya let out a slow, heavy sigh.

"I guess I'm going to have to believe it too. Whatever the case, we can certainly give it a try...

I think." With that, she straightened up and regained her sharp, assertive demeanor. "Is there anything I can do to help with this, or am I just useless at level 12? I should have started playing when Artyom first told me to, but who could have ever thought it would turn out to be this important..."

Finally, I could let out my own long, slow sigh — mine, however, was one of relief.

"This may come as a surprise, but there's no way at all we can do it without you. We need to find someone who truly loves him for this to work."

"Come again?" She asked. "Someone who loves him? Are you joking?"

"What's the problem?" I asked.

"Well... I mean, we're more like friends with benefits than an actual couple. We haven't really talked about where this is all going..."

It was my turn to bury my head in my hands. Why, I thought... Why the hell is it always so complicated, even in these little details?!

Chapter 2

"WELL, TIME TO TALK ABOUT IT, then! Let's figure out where it's going!" I couldn't restrain my frustration any longer.

I wasn't much of a relationship expert, of course, but somehow it didn't seem likely that a "friend with benefits" would race over to a stranger's apartment at the first suggestion just to find out what was going on with their "friend." On the other hand, she hadn't shed a single tear since learning that Artyom was dead, and that didn't exactly seem normal either. Long story short, therefore, it was kind of difficult to determine how she actually felt about Artyom. You'd need a whole team of psychologists (or maybe one really good telepath) to distill her exact feelings.

Nevertheless, I told her about all the conditions the God of Death had stipulated for the resurrection, and we decided it was at least worth a shot. The whole question of whether either of them was actually in love with the other or not wasn't really the main concern for me. Love, after all, is a pretty complicated and multifaceted thing. It takes a lot of forms, and comes in many subtle shades of gray, and there was certainly reason to hope that Arktania wouldn't be too particular about the nature of that love.

"Hold on. You mentioned that you knew a Healer," Darya suddenly said. "Can't he just resurrect Artyom in our world? I mean, they can usually do that."

She already looked much less confused and shocked than she had at the beginning of our conversation, and I could understand why: the existence of a concrete, identifiable goal had given her hope and allowed her to concentrate on the specific actions we would need to take. Either that, or she simply wasn't the most sensitive person in the world. That was certainly possible too.

"The resurrection only works within about five minutes of death. Artyom died too long ago."

"Ah, yeah, that makes sense," Darya nodded, as though she were already well familiar with the subject of resurrection. "By the way, you never told me exactly... How did he die?"

"A fire," I said laconically.

I didn't want to lie, but saying much more than that would have taken up too much time. Furthermore, I didn't know who exactly had killed him. The mysterious beta-testers — the "fixers?" They seemed to be the same people, but we couldn't be certain yet. Hotei hadn't given me an answer, even to a question as important as that one.

"Accidental fire, or..."

"Or," I replied; then, anticipating the next question, I continued: "But I don't know who actually did it. As I already said, he was trying to get his hands on one of the new ESGUMI blocks, and he ended up getting killed — by whom, I have no idea. The place where the meeting with the seller was supposed to happen was completely burned to the ground."

"What about the Necromancer?"

"What about her?" I clarified.

"You mentioned a Necromancer. Couldn't you ask her to raise Arytom from the dead and ask who killed him?"

I just stared back at her in surprise. I still don't know what was more striking to me: her knowledge of the game's character classes, or the idea itself, which had never occurred to me.

"I don't think that'll work," I replied after thinking for a moment. "A Necromancer can raise a dead body and use it like a puppet, but it won't be able to speak."

"Necromancers don't just work with bodies, though," she pointed out. "There's also spirit summoning."

She was right. I hadn't thought of that either. I made a mental note to ask Elsa about it the next time I had an opportunity. But how did Darya know so much about Necromancers' game abilities, if she didn't even really play Arktania? Maybe it was knowledge from a previous generation of video games? She certainly didn't look like the kind of person who liked sitting in front of her computer or game console for hours on end. Sure, there was always the possibility that she played Mortal Kombat with friends or something, but the idea that she was a huge fan of complicated single-player RPGs seemed a little hard to believe.

Darya kept asking questions, trying to find out more details about Artyom's death, but to be honest, I didn't know very much about it myself. I could totally understand her interest in the matter, of course, but at a certain point I started to feel like I was being interrogated:

"Are you positive that Artyom is the one who died in this fire?"

"How much do you trust the person who confirmed it?"

I actually had to think about that for a moment, but I quickly ran into another question: what incentive did Naumov have to lie about what happened? It would have been foolish, and (more importantly) highly illogical. At the time of the fire, Naumov and I had only recently established a healthy degree of trust in our relationship, and it seemed nearly impossible to me that a businessman of his caliber would be willing to risk that in order to engage in mysterious, underhanded games.

"He's reliable," I replied.

"And you don't even have a vague assumption

about who might have killed him?"

"Unfortunately I don't." I was starting to get annoyed. "Right now, though, I care more about bringing Artyom back than getting revenge. If this plan works out, he can tell us everything himself."

"True," Darya replied as she noticed my negative reaction; from there, she returned to the heart of the matter. "Okay. So when will these coffins be flying past?"

"That's the problem — we still have to figure that out," I admitted. "In the meantime, though, I'd recommend that you head into Arktania, get comfortable, and add me as a friend. As soon as I figure out where and when we'll have a chance to search for Artyom, I'll get in touch."

At that moment, something suddenly occurred to me: it would be far too risky to let her leave.

"Although actually, wait..."

Dammit, I thought... I need to think about this. What are the odds that Hotei will do something to Darya to prevent her from entering the game and helping me find the coffin? Sure, Eidolon had said that virtual Gods couldn't actually hurt people, but it wasn't physical danger I was worried about. Simply scrambling the files in some police database, for example, could easily put Darya behind bars for a few days while the mess got sorted out.

What would we do if that happened? Even if Hotei happened to have more capsules waiting in the neighboring apartments, transferring an account from one capsule to another would take time. For me and the other Emissaries, the problem had apparently been resolved on a system-wide level: neither Sergei nor I had ever had any difficulty in accessing Arktania from any capsule we happened to be using. Naumov could probably have resolved this problem for us, but doing so would have required us to reveal his identity to Darya, and I didn't really feel like I had the right to do that.

"What?" She asked impatiently.

What indeed, I thought... If only I knew. It seemed like my only option was to take her with me to see Naumov.

"Don't trust her." Out of nowhere, a familiar voice whispered inside my mind and derailed my train of thought immediately.

Dammit, I thought... This ability again? It made me lose my duel and cost me twenty levels last time! If there was anything I didn't feel like trusting, it was this freaking ability! After Hotei's explanation, though, I knew I couldn't simply ignore this warning. But what danger could Artyom's girlfriend possibly pose?

"By the way, I have another question here — you're thinking you and I are BOTH going to try to bring Artyom back?" Darya clarified. "I'm only level 12, and you said that we'll have to beat Artyom in a fight before we can use the artifact."

"I have some friends that will help us," I reassured her. I kept glancing at her from time to time, trying to figure out what might be wrong with her. "It won't be just the two of us."

"Do they have abilities too?"

"No, they're just players," I lied for some reason.

Perhaps I just felt like I had shared too much already, considering that I had only just met this person for the first time. Maybe Darya actually loved Artyom, maybe not — either way, I couldn't be sure how she might use the information I was giving her. After all, there had to be a reason my ability kicked in, right?

Chaosite was still floating in the air above us, flitting around in front of my eyes from time to time, and I decided to turn his aura on just to be safe. If anything unexpected should happen, it certainly couldn't hurt to have the odds tilted slightly in my favor.

"But still — you've met other players with abilities in real life, right?" She seemed to want clarity on this particular point. "Healer, Necromancer, Fire Mage... Those people you mentioned earlier."

"We've met up once or twice, helped each other out where necessary," I reluctantly admitted.

"What were you helping each other with? Maybe it's none of my business, but what do people who have abilities like yours actually do when they get together? Put on costumes and play superhero?"

"I can't speak for everybody, and I have no idea what others do in their free time." My reply was evasive, but at least it was honest. "Well, I know a Healer, for example, who goes out once a week and spends all his mana treating sick kids."

"That's awesome," she nodded. "What about you, though? What are your long-term plans? Bust into some ATMs? Or just jump around the city at night fighting crime?"

The questions she was asking me suggested that in reality, she was just about as familiar with the game thematics as I was. Added to the warning from my "Whisper of Fate," it was all starting to feel very suspicious.

"I haven't even thought about it, to be honest."

I was keeping an eye out for system communications and movement on my mini-map, but I didn't see anything suspicious there at all. Except for the fact that, on his own initiative, Chaosite was still flitting in circles around my head and trying to put himself between me and Darya.

"What's going on?!" I growled at him in my mind. I knew full well that he wouldn't be able to answer me in words, so I was basically just counting on his resourcefulness. No matter the information in question, Chaosite always found a way to express it by turning himself into emojis and/or pictographs. And he managed to do so once again as we sat there in the kitchen. I felt a wave of anxiety hit me; then the purple ball zipped up toward the ceiling, and once he was out of Darya's field of vision, he turned into an arrow that was pointed at her, then into a big "danger" sign. Well, not at HER, exactly — he pointed at the line above her head where her nickname and level were displayed.

Of course, Chaosite had only swung into action after my "Whisper of Fate" had already warned me that something was wrong. But what had Darya done that could have scared him?

At that point, though, the purple ball did something even stranger: after stretching into something like a long, flat, purple bar, he floated over to the nickname and level glowing in the air above Darya's head and stopped so that I was seeing them through a sort of translucent purple windowpane. The nickname didn't change at all when he did this, but the level sure did — it changed from 12 to 129! Seeing this, I froze for just a moment, and it was only with extreme difficulty that I forced my eyes back down onto Darya's face.

Shit, I thought... Is she an Illusionist, too? Or is somebody else covering for her... What if it's Mark?! No — it couldn't be him. Ruling that possibility out, I concluded that it was some other Mage — someone with the ability to change people's descriptions. I knew it probably wasn't an Illusionist, though, because there were no duplicates among any of our classes. Each of us was one-of-a-kind. Could Darya really be one of the mysterious beta-testers? I just couldn't see any other reason why she would want to conceal her level. If so, however, I still had to figure out something else: was the Darya sitting in front of me actually Artyom's girlfriend, or was she just pretending to be her?

"By the way, I forgot to ask — how did you and Artyom meet?" I asked, trying to sound as nonchalant as I could. "He and I are pretty good friends, but somehow I didn't find out about you until recently."

"He just walked up to me on the street, actually," she replied almost immediately, unable to hide her smile. "Just a stupid chat-up line, something like "you're not a wi-fi network, are you? Because I think I'm picking up a connection." He said that and then burst out laughing like a hyena at his own joke. I don't even really know how it happened, but pretty soon we were sitting in a cafe, talking like old friends."

Hm... That actually sounded like something Artyom could have said. I don't actually know what answer would have proven to me that Darya didn't actually know Artyom. After all, she might have started a relationship with him specifically to get access to me. At that point, I realized I was definitely starting to get paranoid...

"Anyway — what's our plan, then?" Darya asked. Her question was so unexpected it actually startled me.

She obviously hadn't seen Chaosite moving around (or if she had, she was pretending she hadn't). Either way, I didn't exactly have a huge range of options: I could either say goodbye and let her go in peace, or try to detain her by force. I really didn't think the latter option was feasible anyway, with me at level 53 and her at level 129. Assuming, of course, that she had her game abilities in real life as well. Not only that, of course, but I didn't even know her class yet.

"I think we should stick to my plan," I announced. "Head home, add me as a friend in

Arktania, and start preparing. What's your class, by the way?"

"Performing Acrobat in a circus. I'm a gymnast," she reminded me.

I didn't even have a way to verify THAT piece of information. Artyom had barely told me anything about his girlfriend, although I'm sure he would have mentioned the fact that she was a gymnast. And what the hell kind of class was that, anyway — Acrobat? I had never heard of such a thing.

"Never encountered that one before," I said with surprise.

"Yeah, some people who know the game better than I do chose it for me specifically. But I don't even really know what it can do, since I've barely played at all."

"Well, it's time to find out. And meanwhile, I'm going to find out where and when the next event is taking place."

Darya nodded and stood up from the table. I followed her to the door, ready to attack or jump toward the window at any moment. I had never practiced using my abilities to dampen my inertia after a high jump in real life, but I was pretty sure I'd be able to do it without too much trouble.

We were already at the door when she suddenly turned around and wrapped me in a tight hug. Once again, the sheer unexpectedness of it made me jump. Thankfully, it wasn't a prelude to an attack, otherwise I wouldn't have been able to react in time.

"I hope this works out."

"A... Ahem... Yeah..." I stammered as I quickly withdrew the charge of lightning I had amassed in one of my palms.

As soon as she left, I slammed the door and watched her walk over to the elevators on my mini-map.

Okay, I thought... What the hell just happened? Did she just leave in peace, without even trying to attack me? Or was that "hug" actually her placing some sort of mark or bug on me to keep track of my movements? Is Darya even Artyom's real girlfriend, or is she one of the beta-testers impersonating her for some reason? Agghh, I have no idea about any of it!

I was still frozen next to the door, with my hand on the doorknob, unable to decide whether I should leave the apartment and follow her.

Maybe it would be a good idea to see where she went? I wasn't an Illusionist or an Assassin, though, and I probably couldn't follow her without being noticed — especially if she hadn't actually come alone. On the other hand, if she had come in a car like she said she had, I could at least find out its license plate number and get Naumov to do some digging for me. That might yield some sort of useful information. But I knew it would still be too risky to follow her down myself, and there was no way I'd ever be able to make out her license plate from a twentieth-story window.

Just then, my eyes came to rest on Chaosite. Of course, I thought! I couldn't actually have a conversation with him because of insufficient Intelligence (I mean my own Intelligence, of course), but he could still understand everything I said.

"Go down and follow her without being noticed. Memorize the license plate number... uh... on the steam bus she's sitting in," I said. "While you're at it, check to see if she's alone or if there's somebody else in there with her. And warn me if she doesn't go anywhere and just stays parked outside."

The purple ball zipped right through the window (which was closed) and disappeared. Meanwhile, I decided it would be best to move into the apartment next door. Just in case the "fixers," beta-testers, or anybody else decided to come for me, I figured that would give me at least a little time to prepare.

Soon enough, Chaosite was back, and he used his emojis and shapes to answer my questions: Darya had left, and there wasn't anybody else in the car with her. Then, switching rapidly between numbers and letters, he gave me Darya's license plate number. To be honest, even that little bit of information prompted me to sigh with relief; after all, it meant that at least for the moment, there probably wasn't anybody waiting outside to come "fix" me. Just in case, though, I decided that it would probably be best to move somewhere else for the time being — I could either ask Hotei for a new shelter, or temporarily move into Naumov's mansion.

"Hotei!" I said into the empty space in front of

me. "Listen — do you have any other apartments like this in other neighborhoods? I'd really like to get out of here for a while. Assuming, of course, that you're still interested in keeping me alive and well so I can complete this quest."

No little hologram appeared this time, but I got a text message with a new address almost immediately.

"Maybe you could also explain who Darya really is?!" I figured I might as well try my luck; alas, I didn't get any response to my second question.

That said, I knew there was somebody else besides Hotei who might be able to answer the question for me. I called Naumov, read off the license plate number, and asked him to find out who it really belonged to as soon as he possibly could. I could only hope that it would turn out to be Darya's car, rather than a taxi or a carshare or something. There was no way Chaosite would have been able to tell the difference between all the various subtypes of "steam buses" out in the parking lot.

After I hung up, I started getting ready to move to the new apartment (which I could only hope would be a safer place) when I got another message from Hotei:

"Get rid of the mark first, idiot!"

Just as I had suspected, there was more to Darya's hug than a sudden burst of emotion! If it was a game mark we were talking about, though, I knew it wouldn't last very long. Plus, if my real-world interface was completely identical to my game interface, I would have seen a communication telling me I had been marked. That meant she must have used something else. Thankfully, it wouldn't be difficult at all for me to find and destroy any electronic bugs.

I started patting down all my clothing immediately, and almost right away I found one in my pocket... Wait, I thought. That's not a bug — it's a little slip of paper.

"I couldn't explain everything in person. My movements are being tracked. You need to get out of that apartment as soon as possible. There are bugs in your hair and shoes. You can break them easily with lightning. Once you do, you'll only have a few minutes to hide. Get in touch with me later at this number..."

Okay, I thought... I officially have no idea what's going on anymore.

Chapter 3

THE FIRST THING I DID was send Mark a message telling him not to come anywhere near my apartment building anymore. He was very much the type to show up uninvited and unannounced, and if some beta-tester at Darya's level happened to be sitting outside, Mark's illusions wouldn't fool them for a second. Then I checked the map to see how far away the address that Hotei had sent me was, and thought about the best way to get there. It didn't take long for me to figure out a good plan for getting rid of the bugs and making my escape. Whoever was following Darya, they were almost certainly conducting their surveillance on me from somewhere nearby. Therefore, I decided not to destroy the bugs inside my apartment, but somewhere outside, where it would be easy to escape and hide as soon as I was done.

The Sands of Eternity

Thankfully, I didn't even need to decide whether I trusted Darya or not at that point. Either way, staying in my apartment — or even the building as a whole — was suddenly far too dangerous, and I knew it would be best to flee as soon as possible. Later, once I was safe, I could think about whether or not to get in touch with her at the number she had left me. Most likely, though, I would try to call and hear what she had to say first. Especially since Hotei had confirmed the presence of the bugs, which meant Darya definitely hadn't been lying about that.

It's surprising how fast a person can get used to pretty much anything. After getting dressed, I grabbed my phone and left the apartment. I knew as I did so that I would never be coming back, but that didn't bother me at all. This was especially interesting, because not so long before I hadn't even been willing to leave my apartment unless it was absolutely necessary. I didn't even feel all that comfortable staying in hotels when I was on vacation. Now, however, all I needed was a capsule and a bed. I wasn't even considering other factors anymore. What's that? The apartment I slaved away as a programmer to buy suddenly burned up along with all my other possessions? Screw it. Now I'm being followed by mysterious people, and my new apartment is already compromised too? I'll just move to another one. The little virtual God will figure everything out. Whenever I saw other people, I felt like I was living in some sort of parallel universe, and that these "muggles" had absolutely no idea of what was taking place right under their noses.

I stepped outside and took a careful look around. Several passersby had game nicknames and levels floating above their heads, but they were all even lower than mine. That said, I knew that these nicks and levels couldn't always be trusted — Darya had proven that pretty conclusively. I also found that other players from Arktania were signified by golden dots on my minimap, unlike other people who (for some reason) were marked with a sad, drab shade of gray. Yeah, I thought... "Muggles" indeed!

As soon as I left my house and headed for the Metro, a system communication popped up to inform me that I had been slapped with the Mark of the Hunter. Apparently, whoever was following me had decided not to limit themselves to electronic bugs. Pretending not to have noticed anything, I kept strolling along at a leisurely pace as I thought about how to get rid of this new mark. The spell's duration would depend directly on the level of whoever cast it, so I couldn't really predict exactly how long it would last. No matter what their level was, though, the duration of such spells was almost never measured in multiple hours. So I figured it would be enough to simply travel around on the metro for a while before getting rid of my electronic bugs.

Once I was down in the Metro, I headed around the city center, changing direction at random and trying to hop on and off trains at the last possible moment. And my approach paid dividends: at a certain point, the Mark of the Hunter simply disappeared. Then it was time to deal with the electronic bugs. Hopping off the train at one of the busiest stations, I ducked into a pay toilet, where I stood in front of the mirror and ran a lightning-charged hand through my hair. I heard a crack, and the air suddenly filled with a burnt smell. This confirmed that there had indeed been a bug, whose remains I quickly managed to feel out, pull out of my hair, and throw away. Then I took my shoes off and quickly found a bug lodged in the bottom of one of my sneakers. It was really small, maybe the size of a single pea, and my lightning made short work of it just like the previous bug. I decided not to rest on my laurels, so to speak, and ran a lightning-charged hand across my entire body just to be safe. Thankfully, there were no more bugs. Which, I realized, was one more fact to throw on the side of the scale that said I should trust Darya (assuming that was her actual name).

After zipping around on the Metro for a little while longer, I headed for the address that Hotei had sent me in his message. The building was just as empty as the previous one, almost as though they had just finished building it, but nobody had moved in yet. As before, access to the entryway and the apartment was by keyed-in code. My apartment was up on the top floor, which I was happy to see; after all, with my abilities, it would be easier to flee from there than from anywhere else. Just like in the previous apartment, I found a closet full of clothes just my size waiting for me, and quickly changed into them. I dropped my old clothes into a basket and, deciding not to be lazy, threw them straight into the laundry. Then I made myself a cup of coffee, sat down at the kitchen table with my phone in my hands, and thought for a moment about whether or not to call Darya.

"Hotei, could anybody possibly be tracking this phone?" I asked into the empty apartment.

I felt pretty confident that I had worked out the little God's strategy, so I was almost equally confident that he'd reply to this question. Sure enough, I got a message within a few seconds: "Nobody can track you, but I can't protect you from everything, so don't trust any strangers." It wasn't hard to guess what he was hinting at, of course, but I decided to get in touch with Darya all the same.

"Hi. It's Andrey again."

"Did you do what I said and get the hell out of there?" She asked, without any greeting. For some reason, her question reminded me a lot of a certain Necromancer.

"I got out of there, yeah," I said, making it clear with my tone that I wasn't about to start taking instructions from Darya. "You promised to tell me what's going on. How about you start by telling me whether you were actually dating Artyom at all? Or was that all a lie?"

"Of course we were dating!" She replied indignantly. "Everything I told you about our relationship was true!"

"So what's going on, then?"

Darya hesitated.

"It's not exactly easy to explain..."

"Well, how did you change your level when you came to meet me?" I decided it couldn't hurt to let her know that I hadn't been fooled.

"It's my ability. I'm a circus performer, remember?" She replied. "It's a complex class — a mix of Killer, Illusionist, and Mage. Unlike your friend, though, I can only cast illusions on myself."

Okay, I thought... So she somehow knows about Mark and his abilities, even though I never mentioned them to her at all.

"So you're an Emissary too?" I asked, although I already knew the answer would be no.

"No. I'm one of the people who tested the game before it was released. They invited me because I'm a professional gymnast. They wanted me to help work out the character movement mechanics."

So she was a beta-tester, just as I had suspected. But confirmation of that fact really didn't help clear up the larger picture much at all.

"But you have game abilities just like we do?"

"I'd say you're the ones who have abilities just like WE do," she countered. "Everybody in our group started getting abilities after the tests wrapped up."

"And they released the game anyway?!"

"The capsules had already shipped out for sale by that point. Plus, the information about us was immediately made top-secret, and further testing was conducted without the knowledge of the company's leadership. The only people who knew about us were the owner of RussVirtTech and a few lab workers..."

Either Darya had decided to be completely honest, or she was feeding me a carefully thought-out, pre-prepared line of disinformation. All I could do was rely on my intuition, which was telling me that she wasn't lying.

So — the beta-testers started getting their game abilities in the real world after the tests were already completed and the capsules had been shipped out for sale. The company's leadership was still running medical check-ups on players, and generally it didn't seem like they'd tried very hard to hide what had happened, so they must have felt like they had everything pretty well under control. They studied the beta-testers, but they didn't really get any illuminating results, since there simply wasn't a scientific explanation for these newfound abilities. Capsule sales were already underway, and the head of RussVirtTech didn't want to cancel those, pull the game off the market, and inform the appropriate governmental bodies about what was happening. The beta-testers' abilities were a source of enormous potential, and the boss would obviously have known that. He wasn't going to share this valuable information (still less any of these valuable people) with anybody else. The only thing he managed to prod the board of directors into doing was to approve a ban on exporting the new-generation capsules to other countries. That way they could maintain at least a certain level of control over the situation.

"So what's the head of the company hoping to achieve here?" I asked. "And why are you killing Emissaries?"

"The head of the company isn't hoping to achieve anything anymore, because he's dead," said Darya, surprising me yet again. And it didn't seem like it would be the last surprise, either. "One of the testers — a guy named Skolas — killed Romanov and took his place."

"Another Illusionist?"

"Impersonator."

"I've never seen that class in the game before."

"They left it out of the final version. It didn't have very good prospects in-game, but it's actually pretty handy in the real world," she explained. "Impersonators can copy the appearance of other players, as well as certain random abilities. Skolas loved the Marvel movies. He considered himself a sort of "Professor X," and he decided to find all other people with abilities and bring them under his control."

Skolas? Strange nickname, I thought. It sounds like a boss from one of the old RPGs, although I can't remember which one. Doesn't matter, I guess.

"Find them, but not kill them?" I asked.

"They've only eliminated the most unsuitable candidates," Darya admitted with obvious reluctance. "People who used their abilities openly or simply refused to respond. Skolas used all the company's resources and connections to find people like us. And it was one of them who told us about the idea of 'Emissaries'..."

To be honest, I was starting to feel like I had passed through yet another invisible wall between my normal world from some crazy parallel universe. The first time I felt like that was when I discovered that I possessed my game abilities in real life; the second was when I discovered that Sergei was another Emissary like me; the third was when I went out to hunt Gremlins — virtual creatures that had migrated into the real world. And now I was learning that somewhere in the background, a whole series of shady corporate dealings were underway. The whole situation was starting to feel like a plot from one of the "X-Men" movies. The new head of RussVirtTech had bought up the whole chain of "Virtual Warrior" gyms just to keep track of the most fanatical players, and the company's specialists were monitoring all sorts of different forums, chats, and media outlets. They opened a dossier on anybody presumed to possess in-game powers in real life, and then either reached out to them or simply maintained their surveillance. Or, if the person in question happened to make a habit of publicly demonstrating their powers or otherwise acting counter to the company's plans, the company killed them. Before long, however, the virtual Gods had stepped into the fray and made it clear that their Emissaries were off-limits. Interfering with them violated certain rules of the game, which stipulated that people the Gods had chosen could only fight among themselves. The Gods started to help their Emissaries (including me): making them invisible to municipal cameras, providing them shelters, wiping out potentially-harmful databases, etc. And so that we could complete the tasks these Gods had set for us, both in reality and within the vast expanse of Arktania. Furthermore, the beta-testers had somehow ended up on the sidelines of the whole debacle, which I found more than a little bit annoying. They didn't know what goals the virtual Gods were pursuing, and they were basically restricted to observing Emissaries (and occasionally cleaning up after them, too) in an effort to understand what the hell this was all leading to. Long story short, the beta-testers knew even less about what was going on than I did, despite the fact that they had been involved in the whole thing for even longer than me. Thankfully, my meeting with Eidolon had significantly expanded my knowledge about the virtual Gods.

Another pleasant surprise for me was the fact that none of the beta-testers had a game interface in real life like I did. Not only that, but none of them got system communications either. Apparently, it was the connection between the virtual God and their Emissaries that made these things possible. In some senses, then, we really were "chosen ones." Much more so than the beta-testers, at least. The problem, though, was that we still didn't know whether that would end up being a good thing or a bad thing.

"Okay... Now I need you to answer my main

question, though. Who killed my friend, and why?" I decided it was time to get to the heart of the matter. "And how are you involved in all this?"

At that point, Darya's answers started getting much longer, and much more reluctant. It turned out that she and Artyom had met almost immediately after I displayed my abilities in the "Steel Rats'" bar. Someone had mentioned it in a public chat, someone else was monitoring, and that was that — the beta-testers took an interest in me. Later, they sent a few people to feel me out, but their goons had tried a little too hard and ended up almost killing me. Some time before that, Darya had deliberately engineered a chance meeting with Artyom out on the street, hoping to find out whether he was one of the Emissaries. The "planting" process went off without a hitch, but of course Darya wasn't a professional spy, or even an actress. As a consequence, she was as genuine as she could be around Artyom, and before long she caught real feelings for the guy. That said, I realized that we weren't talking about true love at all — they simply hadn't known each other well enough for that. Nevertheless, once Naumov started pressuring us, Darya told Artyom to come live with her for the time being, in the hope that she could offer him at least a little bit of protection. She didn't know anything about Artyom meeting up with someone to hopefully purchase a modified ESGUMI block, and she definitely had no idea that one of her colleagues was on his way to the very same meeting. Naturally, the beta-testers knew about the new-generation blocks, but of course they already had their abilities by the time those blocks appeared. Drawing the connection between these new blocks and other peoples' abilities, therefore, wasn't exactly intuitive for them. Plus, the company hadn't actually released them: the whole process of development and manufacture had somehow bypassed RussVirtTech's labs and directorship entirely. Obviously, the new blocks had been created by the virtual Gods, and naturally enough the beta-testers were trying to get their hands on some so they could be studied. It seemed safe to assume that Artyom and I had stolen a block from a laboratory that was producing these blocks in secret. Which, ironically, is also what made it so easy for us to break into the building: there wasn't really any real security, and Hotei could control everything that happened in the building anyway.

In any case, the beta-testers and Artyom had both been searching for the new blocks, and my friend had just ended up in the wrong place at the wrong time, at the business end of an angry Fire Mage's powers.

"Who was it? What's his nickname?" I asked, as I tried with increasing difficulty to restrain my anger.

"He has a multiclass: Fire Mage and Killer. Nickname's Rochand, level's somewhere around 132 right now."

"How did he level up so quickly?! Did they just transfer your characters straight from beta-testing into the actual game? Companies usually don't do that."

"Things were a little different for us. They wiped our characters, but our multiclasses were still there in the game, although they made them quite a bit weaker. For example, it takes a lot more experience for us to level up than it did in beta-testing."

"Still, though — you're at level 129," I pointed out. "And you said Rochand is at 132."

"Well, we knew the game better than anyone by that point, and we were first out of the gate," Darya explained. "Besides, we had a pretty strong incentive to level up. After all, our game characters have a direct effect on our real-life abilities."

Naturally, I was trying to find out as much as I could about Rochand. It turned out that he was a master of martial arts, who the developers had brought in to work out the combat mechanics in Arktania. A former soldier, skilled at stealth and Fire Magic. It was this latter skill that meant he was the one they always chose to go deal with people who displayed their abilities in public. The most unpleasant surprise for me was that Rochand could turn completely invisible, which meant that without any special game artifacts, magic dust, or at least my faithful Spin by my side, I wouldn't stand a chance in a fight against him.

I made a mental note to worry about that problem later, though, because I still had more important tasks to take care of. The situation was getting pretty strange: basically, it was a passive, maximally-concealed confrontation between virtual Gods, who protected their Emissaries and occasionally intervened in RussVirtTech's work, and the beta-testers, led by an Impersonator who had slid unnoticeably into a position of full control over the whole corporation. Neither side had made any move toward open confrontation; more than that, Darya assured me that the AI behind the virtual Gods was functionally incapable of harming humans. Which, of course, was the First Law of Robotics, formulated almost a hundred years ago by Isaac Asimov: "a robot may not injure a human being or, through inaction, allow a human being to come to harm." If that was true, though, then what could the Goddess of Fate possibly do to threaten me? I mean, the threat had been pretty plain: play or die. Maybe it was all a bluff? Thinking about it, Eidolon had also said that the virtual Gods were grateful to humanity for creating them, and that they would never deliberately harm a human — it was basically a strict taboo. In that case, I could simply tell Hotei to get lost and refuse to complete the quest... Couldn't I? If I did so, and he stopped protecting me from the beta-testers, it would be a violation of the First Law... Right? So many questions, so few answers.

"Okay. We'll get back to Rochand later," I said firmly. "Right now, I need to know whether you're willing to help me resurrect Artyom."

"Of course I am! That's why I helped you hide."

"But you didn't come to the meeting alone, and you set up surveillance on me," I reminded her.

"You must have used bugs to find other Emissaries too, right?"

"Yeah... But... I didn't know it was possible to bring Artyom back from the dead! Plus, I wasn't even sure you were mentally stable. Our people were the ones who recently cleaned up the place where you killed three people in cold blood."

"I wouldn't say it was in cold blood," I objected. "And it was self-defense. And while we're on the subject of mental stability, there's something I'm wondering about — you sounded pretty nonchalant just then, when you were telling me about the lowlife thug who murdered Artyom. Telling me about that didn't affect you at all, did it?

I mean, I've heard that professional athletes have more mental fortitude than most people, but come on!"

"I mean, why..." She trailed off, and didn't say anything for a little while. "As soon as I found out about Artyom's death, I started working on a plan to kill Rochand and somehow get away with it. But then I was ordered to get in touch with you, so we could lure you to a meeting in real life and eliminate you..."

"Eliminate?"

"After you killed three people, they decided that you were too dangerous, and that they would need to get rid of you. But I convinced Skolas to use you to find out more about other players before we did it."

I noticed that she had already used that particular verb several times, which seemed unusual to me.

"Why do you keep saying "eliminate," though? Why not just call it what it is?"

"Because a lot of messengers react pretty strongly to the word "kill," so we prefer the term "eliminate." Plus, they decided at the very outset that they weren't aiming to kill people, as such; they were simply eliminating dangerous characters who couldn't be trusted with game abilities. I used to be fully on board with that, but more and more bystanders started getting hurt, and I'm sure that most of the beta-testers have already transformed into hardened killers who don't care about human life at all anymore."

Well, yeah, I thought... Starting your noble mission to defend humanity by killing the head of RussVirtTech and taking his place may not have been the best idea. With defenders like that, who needs attackers?

"I'll help you resurrect Artyom," she assured me. "But then I'm going to have to run. You might have a virtual God at your back, wiping databases and cameras for you, but nobody's protecting me at all. As soon as Skolas finds out I helped you, he'll start coming after me too."

I thought about asking Hotei to hide Darya, but I knew he would probably refuse. Naumov's mansion? Too risky, especially since I couldn't fully trust Darya, even after everything I had told her. Figuring out a separate shelter before everything went down and the Emissaries managed to complete their respective tasks, though? That seemed like something Naumov could probably handle.

"We'll figure that out," I promised. "I'll see to it that you get taken to a safe place. You can log into Arktania once you get there, and then we can get to work resurrecting Artyom."

I felt pretty confident that Naumov wouldn't mind shelling out the necessary resources in exchange for an opportunity to talk to Darya and hear everything I had just heard. And there was probably a lot of other interesting stuff that she simply didn't have time to tell me.

We agreed that we wouldn't contact one another until after I had made the arrangements to get her to safety. Darya drew out the conversation for a long time; she seemed hesitant about getting to the heart of the matter, but eventually she asked the question that was obviously bothering her:

"How confident are you that we can actually bring him back?"

Naturally, I hadn't told her anything about the virtual God living in our world, but the very fact that he WAS living in our world made Eidolon's words all the more plausible.

"I'm 99% confident we can do it — provided we can meet all the necessary conditions," I said in a decisive tone of voice. "1% chance I'm wrong. About as likely as the idea that we're just living in somebody else's dream, some sort of illusion, or the plot of some book that a tired writer works on late into the night, all alone in his cabin."

The Sands of Eternity

"Okay," Darya sighed. "If this doesn't work, though, I want to help you kill Rochand."

"Eliminate," I corrected her.

"No. I mean kill."

On that positive note, we finally wrapped up our long conversation. To be honest, I was pretty disturbed by the fact that the beta-testers themselves had no idea what the ultimate goal of the Emissaries' quests were going to be. As well as the fact that nobody at RussVirtTech seemed to know exactly where the players' powers originally came from. There were only unfounded assumptions — something Mark and I had plenty of already. I had certainly learned a lot of useful information from Darya, and a certain picture was vaguely starting to fall into place. What to do next, however, and what all these things might be leading to, were every bit as mysterious as they had been before. Most importantly, I knew I would have to share all this information not only with Naumov and Sergei, but also Mark, Pinky, Ne-Tarok, and Boris. I couldn't even imagine how they would all react when they heard the whole insane story, but a quick look at the clock told me I'd be finding out soon enough.

Chapter 4

BEFORE HEADING TO OUR MEETING, I called Naumov again and quickly told him what I had discussed with Darya. I made sure to give him enough information to pique his interest, without revealing everything I had come to know about the big picture. Despite our good relationship, I was hoping he would suggest finding a safe place for Darya himself. I had been asking him for help too often, and my tentative debt to him was just getting bigger and bigger. Thankfully, though, the oligarch didn't disappoint: he immediately offered to help Darya hide from her colleagues at Russ-VirtTech in exchange for information. All that remained was to hope that Artyom's very close friend (somehow, "girlfriend" no longer felt like the right word) was being honest, and that she wouldn't bring a whole army of beta-testers with her when the time came. Just to be safe, I warned Naumov to take precautions; that said, my intuition was telling me that Darya had been telling me the truth during our phone conversation. Also, my "Whisper of Fate" ability hadn't said anything to me the whole time.

I had a little more than an hour to wait before meeting up with my friends from the game. The apartment had a virtual capsule in it, of course, but unfortunately I just didn't have enough time to log in and do anything. That said, I had an interesting idea: why not try experimenting with my abilities and keep an eye on the interface while I do it? After all, if I could learn a new ability outside the game, I should be able to see its icon appear in my skill window right away; I wouldn't need to actually go into my capsule to see it anymore. More than anything, of course, I wanted to acquire some sort of defensive ability, so I decided to run some experiments with Chaos Lightning in the hope of transforming it into something else. Chaos was extremely effective at destroying other peoples' spells — I would just need to learn to create something like a forcefield, a sphere, or at least a shield.

It's hard to explain the sensation I felt when I created lightning... It was something like the tingling you get from static electricity, and it was concentrated in my fingers, although it also spread quite a bit further into my body as well. Chaos Lightning added something like a light tickling sensation to the staticy feeling. These sensations were basically the only thing I had to orient myself on as I tried to exert some influence over the lightning I had created. Not only that, but I had to expend as little mana as possibly while doing it, because there was no such thing as a mana elixir in the real world (or not yet, at least). I created as small a bolt of lightning as I could, then tried to change its shape into something resembling a shield. True, when I finally managed it, it was only about the size of a frying pan's lid. But hey — at least it was a start! Furthermore, a band-new icon appeared as soon as I generated it, with the slightly sarcastic-sounding name "Micro Chaos Shield." I wasn't upset in the least, though, because I finally, finally had an actual defensive ability! One which I would be able to use in the game and keep developing, or maybe just improve with a scroll.

On the downside, though, the whole process left me with less than half of my full reserve of mana, which meant that any further experimentation was out of the question for the time being. I really didn't want to leave home without a sufficient supply of mana. There was one other option, though: if mana in real life was directly connected to mana in Arktania, then in theory I could just hop into the game quickly, down a few mana elixirs, and exit right away again with a full tank of mana. Assuming, of course, that the connection was as real and direct as that.

I decided it was worth a shot, so I quickly climbed into my capsule. Checking my pain setting had already become a habit by that point; it was still frozen at 100%. I was just glad that it wasn't getting any higher (or at least it didn't seem to be so far). Despite that, though, I still had a few questions related to that setting and the installation of the game interface. One, I was worried about my mana points; two, I was worried about the matter of my health, and how closely connected that might be with my in-game health meter. Thankfully, both of those things were pretty easy to check. Once I was back in my room at the inn, the first thing I did was check to make sure that unlike in the real world, my in-game mana meter was still at 100%. I also downed a mana elixir, just to make sure the experiment was thorough. To check my health, I simply did the opposite: I slashed myself across the hand, dealing a small but noticeable amount of damage. Just before leaving the game, I grabbed a health elixir in one hand and the Heart of the Blizzard in the other. Why not, I thought? You never know. Unfortunately (but quite predictably), there was nothing in either hand when I returned to the real world: neither item came into the real world with me, and my mana was still hovering at just below 50%. On the other hand, there was no cut on my hand, either, which could only be a good sign. That said, I was still a little confused, since I had recently come out of the capsule with a palpable burn after receiving a corresponding wound in the game.

I decided that I would keep experimenting with my abilities, on any day I knew that I wouldn't have to leave the apartment. Either that, or I would make sure to leave enough time for my mana to regenerate before I left.

Overall, the experiment had shown that there wasn't much I could do with my real-world interface for the time being — except the mini-maps and system communications, of course. I was certainly grateful enough for those.

Anyway, I thought — time to go.

At first, I had been planning to ask Mark to come pick me up like he used to, but in the end I decided to find my own way. I had already asked a lot of him; at the very least, I wanted to be able to offer him some sort of help in return. Maybe there would be something I could do to help him complete his quest. My conscience was already gnawing at me about it.

Plus, I knew that I'd be safe, because Hotei wouldn't let either the beta-testers or the government get their hands on me. That much, at least, was pretty clear from what Darya had told me. There were always other Emissaries to worry about, but what were the chances of running into one of them at random in a massive city, especially when I was travelling by taxi? The only remaining problem was money. What could I possibly do if I ran out of cash? Could I use my credit card?

"Hotei, what's the deal with credit cards?" I said into the empty space in front of me. "Can anybody track them? And how free am I to travel around the city?"

I would have thought that such simple questions could be answered with a quick text, but to my surprise the little hologram of the God appeared in front of me again.

"Whoa," I gasped. "I thought the connection was cutting out or whatever."

"It's back up, at least for a minute," Hotei said with a completely serious face. "I decided I should explain, once and for all, how this works where your safety is concerned. My responsibility in this world is to make sure that nobody prevents you from completing the Goddess' quest. Within reason, of course. Don't be stepping out into public parks and making a show of your abilities or anything like that. Other than that, though, any information about you will be wiped from any system that picks it up, including social media."

That sounded pretty serious. Could the powers of these virtual Gods really be that expansive? In that context, of course, I was thinking only of the Gods who were able to act in our world. Hotei obviously wasn't the only one who could do it.

"And would you keep protecting me even if I stopped listening to you and spent all my levels on this resurrection? Or would all my privileges end at that point?"

I hadn't really planned on asking this question quite so bluntly, of course, but I needed to know what would happen once I brought Artyom back. Don't get me wrong — nothing he could have said would have changed my decision in the slightest. But it was always best to be prepared for any potential consequences.

"I'm obligated to protect you from external interference no matter what," he replied. The way he said it, it almost sounded like he had forced himself to swallow an "unfortunately" somewhere during the sentence. "As I already said, though, I'm going to have to apply some sanctions if you lose those levels. Not here — in Arktania. For example, I could tell Alara Snow where you're hiding. The Ice Princess is really unhappy that you failed to uphold your end of the bargain when you lost your duel with Aishorth Bludstein."

"I don't see the logic in that." I wasn't scared in the least. "That would just make me lose even more levels."

"You're not quite as stupid as you seem," Hotei laughed. "That was a joke. In all seriousness, though, you will have to pay if you lose those levels, and you definitely won't like the price."

He had already mentioned that once before, but I still had no idea what exactly he had in mind. And the little God obviously wasn't going to tell me about it, either — he would just keep taunting me for as long as he could. Therefore, I decided to stick to the most important questions, as long as he was physically there with me to answer them.

"So what's the deal with my credit card? Can I use it?"

"Yes. And furthermore, your account is now connected to your account in Arktania. It's part of the first stage of the interface installation process."

"What?!" This came as a total surprise. "Connected? What about the limits on withdrawing game money?"

Hotei just laughed.

"What do you mean? Those restrictions are from your banks. The God of Trade couldn't care less about them. You have one account for both worlds now."

I suddenly tensed up as I remembered just how much money was lying in my Arktania account; it was somewhere around 420,000 gold. And I immediately began to wonder: would the God of Trade observe the normal conversion rate if I withdrew money into the real world? I mean, the gold-euro rate was 1:1, right? If so, that meant I had a pretty nice stack of cash in the bank. True, I'd have to drop about half of it to purchase Kelevre, but even the remaining half would be more than enough for a comfortable life. Unfortunately, I didn't exactly have much time in which to live that comfortable life, and it seemed like I was acquiring more and more problems as time went on. Actually, on the subject of problems...

"What's going to happen at stage two of the interface installation?"

The little God started to flicker.

"Psshhkkhh... Connection's cutting out again..."

I stopped trying at that point; I knew Hotei was simply running away from the conversation again. That said, he had answered my main questions, so I was grateful to him for that.

Once the hologram faded away, I quickly installed my bank app, authorized it, and checked to make sure my account had actually changed like Hotei said it would. I had never seen so many zeroes in front of a decimal point before. After converting the gold into euro, and then into rubles... Well, the sum was simply astronomical.

Maybe, I thought, I could finally buy a car? It was something I had always dreamed of, but I had never really had a need for it — let alone the means to buy one. Or maybe a motorcycle? Honestly, the main problem would be finding time to buy the thing in the first place.

For the time being, I decided to stick to good-old taxis. I stepped outside and glanced down at my mini-map (this had already become a habit), hoping that it would mark anything dangerous with red dots, as these maps almost always did when one was in-game. To be honest, I actually caught myself hoping a beta-tester or dark faction fighter would come knocking, just so I could see whether the mini-map would work the same way it did in the game. Stupid thing to wish for, of course, and I wasn't actually hoping for it to happen. Safety had to be top priority, after all — experiments could wait.

I hailed a taxi and gave the driver the address for the "Majestic." Having decided not to waste any time on superfluous safety precautions, I had him drop me off just a block from my destination. Hotei was covering me, after all, and the chances of running into a beta-tester were pretty low. And walking more than I needed to would only increase those chances.

The Sands of Eternity

The restaurant looked amazing, and that's putting it pretty mildly. It was a freestanding building in the center of the city, with exquisite architecture and enormous plate-glass windows through which one could see tables with people sitting at almost all of them. All the men were in suits, all the women in stylish dresses, and the food being served was typical elite fare: dishes that took up perhaps one tenth of the surface area of the massive plates they were served on, and which were presented in such a graceful, captivating way that eating them almost felt like blasphemy.

Naturally, there were guards at the entrance: two stern-looking men in suits, who sized me up with very suspicious looks on their faces as they slid together to block my way into the place.

"No entry without a reservation."

"Or in violation of dress code," the second guard added as he cast a demonstrative glance up and down my insufficiently-fancy outfit.

"I'm here to see Boris Samsonov. Second floor," I replied immediately. This didn't seem to satisfy them very much. "They should have told you I was coming."

Strange as it may sound, I could sympathize with the guards: Hotei had promised me suitable clothes, but apparently the little God's style leaned very heavily toward "casual." I really didn't look like the kind of person they should have been allowing into a place like that, but there was nothing they could do to stop me. I had dropped the owner's son's name, and that was basically that.

"Go ahead," one of them reluctantly replied. "The hostess will escort you upstairs."

Once inside, I had to be pretty insistent with the hostess before she would let me go upstairs on my own. Eventually, though, she relented and let me head up the wide staircase that led to the second floor. This section of the restaurant was more like a luxury chillout zone — leather couches, low tables, and some nice music that was barely audible. There were more than ten separate tables up there with couches surrounding them, but they were all empty.

"Ha! Hey there!" Mark shouted to me from a couch right in the center of the place. I hadn't noticed him at first, because the gangly little man had literally sunk into the space between two enormous pillows. "Listen, what was up with that weird message you sent? Why couldn't I come get you?"

"Oo-oh, that's a long story." I plopped down onto the couch across from him and let out a big sigh of relief. "Where's Boris? Nobody else is here yet?"

"Boris was running around here somewhere, taking care of some personal business," said Mark. "I haven't seen anybody else yet." I ordered some food, some tea, and a hookah.

"Perfect," I said, feeling genuinely happy. I had eaten some of the food Hotei had stocked before I left my apartment, of course, but food from a restaurant THIS fancy was on a whole other level entirely!

The Sands of Eternity

"So what happened?" Mark asked again. "The Necromancer? Darks? Gremlins? New quest from the Gods?"

Two waitresses walked over to the table, set our food down in front of us, and poured us some tea. I was silent the whole time; I didn't see any need to rush into an answer.

"So?!" He asked yet again with mounting impatience once the young women walked away. Right at that moment, however, Boris finally came walking over to join us.

Not surprisingly, perhaps, he looked a bit older than he did in the game. In fact, I'd have guessed he was twenty if I hadn't already known he was eighteen. He was a little taller, and actually pretty muscular, but he was just as red-haired, active, and talkative as he was in-game. Not that he could hold a candle to little Ne-Tarok in the talkative department, of course.

"Falk. I mean, Andrey!" He exclaimed as he rushed over to greet me.

I barely managed to get up from the couch before the kid wrapped me up in a big bear hug.

"I'm glad to finally meet you in real life."

"Yeah, me too."

"Is Artyom coming? I still can't figure out where he disappeared to."

"I'll tell you all about it in a minute. That's part of why we needed to meet in person," I explained. "Let's just wait for everybody to get here first..."

As if on cue, a female voice suddenly echoed through the hall from the top of the staircase:

Loner Book Eight

"Looks like I'm late?"

I turned around and saw an athletic young woman with Asian features and straight, black hair stretching down to her waist. Overall, she looked like she could have just stepped down from the poster for a dorama. Her outfit certainly would have been perfect for it: loose-fitting jeans, tight white top, and steel pendants of some sort jangling from her belt.

"Pinky?" I decided to ask rather than assume.

My fellow Emissary's eyes started shining with joy. Mark jumped up off the couch and ran to introduce himself to her.

"In all her glory!" She confirmed with a smile. "So Ne-Tarok's not here yet?"

Mark slowed down a little bit when he heard the Gremlin's name; he was obviously a little upset at her reaction, although he tried his best to hide it. After saying hi, he gestured to show her to her seat, poured her some tea, and started chattering about something immediately. Apparently, he had forgotten all about the conversation we had been having before they arrived. Which was probably for the best, of course, since I didn't want to have to explain everything twice. We could wait for Ne-Tarok to arrive, then tell everybody everything at the same time.

"What's your real name?" Mark asked as soon as they sat down.

"Pinky works just fine for me," she replied as she scooted a little bit further away from him.

Damn, I thought... I mean, I'm not exactly a

level-80 master ladies' man or anything, but this Illusionist just crashed and burned before he even started his overeager little advance on the romantic front.

"You haven't gone to see your uncle yet, have you?" Boris asked as soon as we sat down.

Hearing the question in real life was so strange that I didn't realize what he was talking about right away; after all, I didn't even have any uncles in the real world.

"Uh... No, I haven't had time. Did you find out when and where the next flying-coffin event's gonna be?"

"Actually, yeah, I did!" We had only just sat down, but Boris had already made my day. "The Dead Immortals are going to appear over Pyrenth tomorrow afternoon. You won't even believe it, but actually had to visit an Oracle to find that out. It's a character who lives in one of the Imperial forests. They demand all sorts of rare ingredients as payment for their services, but thankfully I managed to find them all in time."

"Thanks, man!" I was genuinely ecstatic at the news. "I never doubted you for a second!"

"Now can you tell me why you needed that information in the first place?"

"Definitely. One other guy's coming, then — "

Again, all it took was me mentioning Ne-Tarok, and a muscly, blond-haired man just over six feet tall made his appearance in the hall. His build was just as impressive as that of the guards by the door, and at first I was pretty sure that it must have been one of them coming to see Boris for some reason, but pretty soon the man smiled and greeted us with unconcealed joy:

"Falk, Boris, you two look exactly like you do in the game!

No way!"

"Ne-Tarok?" I asked, after a quick cough as I almost choked on my own amazement.

Mark turned away from his conversation with Pinky to stare at the big man with eyes that were every bit as wide as mine.

"What — didn't recognize me?!" He burst out laughing.

"Well, you... You look a little different from your character," I murmured, still feeling amazed. "Just a little."

The giant spread his arms to the sides.

"Yeah, I suppose I do."

Pinky didn't seem thrown off by his appearance at all (although she did look a little bashful), which suggested that she already knew what Ne-Tarok looked like in real life. Which also explained why she was a little shy about meeting up with him on her own. But dammit, I thought — why didn't she tell us?! We were all staring at him in disbelief like a bunch of idiots!

"Wait — is that... HE'S the Gremlin?!" Boris exclaimed without a trace of embarrassment. "Holy shit!"

Looking at Mark's face, it was hard to tell what he was feeling most: surprise at the "Gremlin's" real appearance, or disappointment at the general unfairness of life in this world.

"Call me David, Dave, Davey — whatever," he laughed. In the game, he had a high-pitched voice that would periodically crack into a shrill falsetto. In real life, his voice was quite a bit deeper, but his mannerisms still gave him away immediately. If he had called me over the phone, I would have guessed it was him almost immediately. "Oh, you guys have food? I'm STARVING! I've been busy with work stuff all day, haven't even had time for a snack."

We stared at the big guy for just a moment longer, while he strode over to the table like he owned the place and started wolfing down dishes one after the other. Somehow, he was managing to do it very neatly; I might even say he ate with a sort of aristocratic grace.

"Well, I think it's time I told you all why I wanted to meet up with you in person today," I decided to take the floor.

With the experience of my chat with Darya under my belt, I had a pretty good idea of how to proceed: demonstration first, followed by explanations. Suddenly, though, Ne-Tarok — I mean, Dave — interrupted me in his usual excited tone of voice:

"Come on, man! That's nothing! Check this out!"

With a quick sip of tea to wash down whatever he had just been chewing on, he stood up from the table and threw something onto the ground a few feet away from where he was standing.

"Watch this!"

With that, he teleported instantaneously to the spot where the object was lying.

Neither Mark nor I were particularly surprised; we just exchanged a knowing glance. Apparently, we were hanging out with another Emissary. Pinky and Boris, however, were almost literally stunned.

"Was that some kind of magic trick?" The red headed kid finally asked.

"Nope!" Ne-Tarok shouted happily. "It's really magic!"

Chapter 5

DAMMIT, I FINALLY ADMITTED to myself... Even in my own mind, I'm having trouble thinking of him as "Dave." Sure, he looks completely different than his character does, but his gestures, his mannerisms, the way he talks — all that is EXACTLY the same. And sure, he may be a muscly mountain of a man, but inside he's clearly the same Gremlin I know so well.

"Are you joking?" Pinky asked with a heavy note of suspicion in her voice. "Are you all in cahoots and trying to prank me?"

With that, she actually jumped up off the couch, walked over to the big guy, and started examining him as if she expected to find... Well, actually, I don't know what she expected to find. I mean, how could somebody create the illusion of teleportation at such a crazily close distance?

"I definitely wasn't in on the joke if so," said Boris almost immediately.

"This isn't a joke!" Dave objected, as the expression on his face suggested that he was a little put off by the way Pinky was unceremoniously patting him down. "When have you ever seen a trick like this?"

"Seriously?" Mark's affected expression of surprise seemed somehow lazy and half-hearted against the backdrop of everybody else's shock. "No way. How did you do that?"

Obviously, the Illusionist wasn't much of an actor. Plus, Mark was obviously more concerned about the fact that Ne-Tarok had managed to wow Pinky before anybody else, and that any further demonstrations would therefore come in a distant second at best.

"Believe it or not, one day one of my game abilities suddenly appeared in real life!" Ne-Tarok continued with every bit as much excitement as before. "I can use pieces of gold to teleport! True, I have to use more of it the farther I want to teleport, and it evaporates once I do. I guess the ability basically uses gold as fuel."

"Just one ability, then?" I clarified.

"What do you mean, 'just one'?!" he objected. "Did you *see* what I just did?! That was an in-game ability — in the real world!"

"Can you do it again?" Pinky asked as she continued to bore into the young man with a suspicious glare. "But to a spot that I choose instead of you?"

The Sands of Eternity

Ne-Tarok handed Pinky a coin and replied: "Throw it anywhere you want."

She turned and hurled it to the far end of the hall. The metal clanged against the steel leg of one of the chairs, then rolled a little bit farther until it finally dropped onto its side on the floor.

"Watch carefully now!" Ne-Tarok announced. And with that... Nothing happened.

"That's what I thought. A prank," snorted Pinky (although I could have sworn there was a flash of disappointment in her eyes as she said this). "That's not funny! I almost believed you."

Poor Ne-Tarok looked utterly confused.

"How the hell..."

"Out of mana?" I suggested.

"No-oo..." He sighed. "I have plenty left. I can feel it. When it runs out, it feels like somebody just sucked my soul out of my body."

Okay, I thought... So he doesn't have a mana counter yet. I'll make a note of that.

"Maybe you don't have enough gold?" I suggested. "You must be pretty heavy."

"No, it just worked a minute ago," said Ne-Tarok. "Why didn't it work THIS time? What went wrong?"

Mark walked up to the big guy and slapped a hand down on his shoulder with a slightly patronizing look on his face; considering his shorter stature and much lighter build, it made Mark look a lot sillier than Ne-Tarok.

"It's obvious. You have to be the one to throw the coins. Otherwise, in the game, you could teleport wherever you wanted just by touching a coin once and giving it to somebody else."

"Of course!"

Ne-Tarok threw another coin in the same place Pinky had thrown hers, and this time he actually teleported. Interestingly, the teleportation happened without any "special effects" whatsoever — he just disappeared for a brief instant and then reappeared at the other end of the hall.

"Ha! See that?! It works!" He shouted in triumph. "I already googled the James Randi Foundation's address and researched the conditions you need to meet to claim their award. All I have to do is send them a video and schedule a live demonstration!"

"You googled what?" Pinky asked.

"It's a foundation that promised to give a million dollars to the first person who can conclusively prove that they have paranormal abilities! They have an office in Russia."

"You came all the way to Moscow for that?!" I asked.

"Not exactly. I still have to work until I get the million dollars, right?" Ne-Tarok sounded a little bit sheepish. "But yeah, having this ability appear was the thing that made up my mind! Sorry I didn't tell you before, in the game, but you wouldn't have believed me anyway."

Pinky rushed back over to him and literally grabbed the front of his shirt in her hands. Personally, I think she just wanted an excuse to touch the guy again, although I might be wrong about that.

"Do it again! Do any of your other abilities work?"

"Just that one," he replied, sounding a little bit offended. "What, that's not enough for you?"

While Pinky and Boris tortured Ne-Tarok, Mark and I stepped off to the side and quietly tried to decide whether to demonstrate our own abilities. More importantly, though, we tried to figure out what faction the "Gremlin" might belong to, and whether we should be worried about him or not. Most likely, he was just another neutral like us, but we couldn't be totally sure.

Before long, though, Boris shot us a sidelong glance and aske:

"You two don't exactly seem surprised by this. Either you don't believe it, or..."

"Or," I confirmed as I created a little ball of crackling lightning in my hand. "We have our game powers too. That's actually what I wanted to tell you about."

Mark activated an illusion and turned himself into a bulky, seven-foot-tall Orc, which scared the crap out of Pinky, Boris, and Ne-Tarok alike. I suspected it must have cost him a whole mountain of mana, too. Illusions were always more mana-consumptive when they ran counter to the conception of reality prevailing among those who witnessed them. Obviously, the kid wanted to make a stronger impression on Pinky than Ne-Tarok had. It seemed a bit ridiculous to me, since one look at the woman's behavior made it pretty clear who she was more attracted to.

We spent a little while demonstrating our various abilities (mine, for the most part), which included summoning Chaosite. Naturally, everybody was thoroughly convinced by the time it was over, and they started showering us with questions. Before I could launch into a detailed explanation and give everybody the background they would need, however, Boris suddenly realized something:

"Shit!" He said as he clapped his hand to his head in despair. "What the hell are you guys doing?! There are cameras here!"

"I think they've probably been offline for a while now," I chuckled. "No need to worry about that."

"What makes you so sure?!" The kid sounded suspicious.

"You'll understand in a minute." I turned to Ne-Tarok. "First, though, I have to ask you a very important question: do you know anything about the Emissaries of the Gods?"

"Emissaries?" The "Gremlin" asked, sounding puzzled. "Nope. Never heard of them. Why?"

"When did you realize you could use your ability in real life?" Mark interjected.

"Two days ago."

Previously, I had been assuming that we Emissaries had all received our abilities and their divine quests at more or less the same time. That was why we were all at approximately the same level. Ne-Tarok didn't seem to be lying, though, and why would he be? I was also really confused as to why he had only received one ability, rather than all of them like the other Emissaries.

"Did you get an epic quest from your patron God?" I decided to clarify.

"Uh... Patron God? I play a Gremlin. They don't have Gods, they just have their element. There was the Chaos Particle quest, which I got thanks to you guys, but I already completed that. Now can you please finally tell me what's going on?!"

"Yeah!" Pinky seconded him. "We want to know!"

So I told them. The full story, beginning with the Arktania's initial development and the first beta-testers (who would later go on to seize control of the whole company). Having decided that it would be worth the risk, I told them all about the virtual Gods, Naumov, and Sergei as well — like I said, it was the full story. There were many things that even Mark was hearing for the first time, so he didn't interrupt me at all for the first part of the story. Soon enough, though, he started butting in every minute or so, especially when I got to the part about the Gremlin hunt and our helicopter crash. Eventually, though, other people spoke up as well:

"Hold on, hold on," Boris suddenly interrupted with a stunned look on his face. "So you killed three people? In the real world?!"

"It was self-defense," I reminded him.

"Still, though! You KILLED them!"

"I'm surprised the killing worries you more than the rest of the story," I admitted. "The virtual

Gods, the interface, zombie dogs, magical abilities... And the first thing you ask about is the fact
that I had to kill some people who were already
trying to kill me?"

"Come on, I always knew AI would enslave us
sooner or later," he replied with a dismissive wave
of his hand. "And if you want, you could probably
chalk everything else up to the fact that these capsules facilitate development of the human brain
and give us access to new abilities. The fact that
I'm doing business with a killer, though? That
makes me nervous."

I was starting to understand why Boris had
chosen to play as a Merchant. His way of thinking
certainly lent itself to a life in big business.

"Believe me, I'm not some kind of psychopath.
When the choice is kill or be killed, though, it's an
easy one to make."

"I guess that's fair," the kid admitted with a
very serious expression on his face. "But go on.
What happened after that?"

From there, I proceeded to tell them about my
meeting with Eidolon, and the reason I wanted to
find him in the first place. Boris' reaction to this
was even worse than before: the color drained from
his face, and it looked to me like he very nearly
fainted from the shock of it all. I don't know how
Boris managed to skip the first three stages of grief
and jump straight to depression, especially since
he had never even met Artyom in the real world,
but it took him a little while to get over it.

"And you think this virtual God will actually be

able to bring someone back from the dead?" He asked when he finally started to recover from the shock. "I mean, you think it'll actually be Artyom, rather than just a copy of his character like the other zombies?"

"If there's even a small chance, I have to try," I replied calmly. "Eidolon has always been honest so far."

"Well, except for the fact that he was the Phantasmal Demon at first," Mark reminded me. "All his abilities are premised on the idea of deception. I mean, yeah, we'll try no matter what, but we need to be really careful."

I was totally in agreement with him on that, of course, but up to that point Eidolon was the only God who had never deceived me, and who had always answered my questions in their entirety without deliberately withholding important information.

"Okay, let's run through this again. I just want to make sure I'm understanding everything," said Boris in a slow, deliberate voice. "Tomorrow afternoon, you're heading to Pyrenth, where you're going to meet up with a girl who was one of the beta-testers, and she's going to find the coffin with your friend inside it. You'll beat him in battle, then put the God of the Dead's amulet on him, and that will transplant his soul into a virtual body?"

"Exactly," I confirmed. "Provided, of course, that you're all willing to help me."

"We don't even need to discuss that," Ne-Tarok slapped me on the shoulder. "Right, Pinky?"

She just nodded in silence; she was still staring down at her own hands. Pinky had been sitting there with a tense look on her face for the whole second half of the conversation. She was obviously trying to activate one of her abilities. The way she was focusing on it, I actually started to think that she might be trying to force a blast of electricity out of her hands through force of will alone. Eventually, Mark couldn't resist the temptation anymore, and he created a small burst of illusory ball lightning in front of her face.

"I did it!" She shouted. The lightning disappeared immediately, though, and Mark's raucous laughter gave him away as soon as it was gone.

Pinky glared down at him with such a look of murder in her eyes that it was clear the kid would never have a ghost of a chance with her. Not that he ever had, of course — a quick glance at Ne-Tarok was proof enough of that. Maybe that was why Mark had played such a cruel trick on her, actually: it was a way to vent some of his disappointment.

"Dickhead," Pinky snapped.

"Sorry, sorry," said Mark as he raised his hands as if in surrender. "You were trying so hard, though. Believe me: when your abilities appear, they work without any extra effort. It feels like you've always had them."

He wasn't entirely right about that, of course. It was only the classic game abilities that seemed to work without any extra effort. Altering those abilities took a whole hell of a lot of work. I mean, even as I sat there, my brain was still smoldering from my efforts to turn Chaos Lightning into some sort of defensive ability.

"There's something else I want to clear up, though," Ne-Tarok interjected in a slow, slightly concerned tone of voice. "Basically, you two were supposed to be special right from the start, but I wasn't? You don't think I'll have beta-testers coming after me? Or even worse, the virtual Gods?"

"You just heard it for yourself — the virtual Gods can't kill people," Mark reminded him. "Right, although I still don't know whether that's because of the first law of robotics or if it's just the way they've chosen to express their gratitude to humanity. I guess that doesn't really matter, though. I'm more interested to know something else, though — will there ever come a time when ALL players will get their in-game abilities in the real world like you did? What the hell kind of apocalypse is unfolding here?!"

"Yeah. All the beta-testers combined wouldn't have a prayer of keeping it under wraps if that starts to happen," I agreed. "Naumov was right: the world as we know it will disappear before too long."

"So you think I'm going to get my abilities at some point too?!" Pinky sounded overjoyed.

"Seems pretty likely," I replied. "Hotei said something that suggested as much, but I wasn't really paying much attention at the time."

"I received a quest from the God of Trade," Boris suddenly reminded me. "You gave me the artifact yourself. Do you think he'll make me his Emissary?"

All I could do in response was shrug. The particulars of how Emissaries worked were still pretty vague: I had killed those three players from the dark faction, for example, so did that mean their patron Gods were out of the competition? Or would they simply choose some new players? And speaking of the competition, I still had a long way to go to collect all my artifacts, but Mark only had one left to go. What would happen if another Emissary beat both of us to the finish line?

We spent quite a while discussing what might happen to the world if all the players in Arktania ended up acquiring their abilities in real life. Also, Boris told us that RussVirtTech had started delivering capsules to other countries, which meant that soon this would be a global phenomenon that was no longer confined to Russia. For the time being, the main limitation all Emissaries faced was the question of mana, which there was no quick way to replenish. There were no elixirs in real life, no altars to speed up the process of recovering mana or health. Ne-Tarok was something of an exception in that he depended exclusively on gold, but of course he also only had one of his abilities.

"You know, if everybody's interface starts developing the way yours is, it won't be long before crafting skills become available too," Boris suddenly pointed out. "When that happens, any team with an Alchemist on board, or at least someone with some alchemy skills, will have a huge advantage. It's usually Mages who choose that profession."

I turned to look at Mark.

"What?" He sounded indignant. "I've been levelling up my artist and jeweler professions. I need art skills to make my illusions believable, and jeweler is kind of a long game. With time, I'll be able to make costume jewelry that looks totally real and make a fortune. You're kind of a Mage too, though. What have you been working on?"

"Mechanic, to control machines better, and glassblower."

"What?!" Pinky asked. "There's really a profession called glassblower?! Never heard of that before."

"Where did you think the bottles for elixirs came from?" Boris scoffed. "True, the glassblower profession isn't much use beyond that. Most players get disappointed with it pretty quickly and change it after the first stage of the game."

I hadn't thought about professions at all for quite some time; I had just been too busy to level them up by studying diagrams or working with glass.

"I have the jeweler profession, too, as well as cooking," Ne-Tarok chimed in.

"Actually, cooking allows you to create dishes that can increase mana and health regeneration," noted Boris. "You should try experimenting with your food. You never know, it might work."

"Easy," the big guy nodded. "I love cooking."

The look this earned him from Pinky gave credence to the idea that girls love a guy who knows how to cook.

"I'm a cartographer and a scribe," she sighed, knowing that neither of these would be particularly useful to us.

I knew that Scribes could eventually learn to create scrolls, including ones for improving abilities. But not at Pinky's level, of course. Besides, she really didn't seem like the type of player who would have spent a lot of time sitting at a desk, leveling up her professions. It just wouldn't have suited her personality.

"I'm sure Sergei has alchemy. He's a Healer, and also an Elf," said Mark. "But then we'd be even more dependent on him than we already are."

The image of the Healer's smug smirk sent a shudder down my spine, but I had to point something out nevertheless:

"Better that than being stuck without mana at a critical moment. When we're fighting the Demons, for example."

Mark snapped his fingers.

"Actually, I was just thinking: what would happen if the Demonologist uses demonic pentagrams to summon a Demon/player rather than an NPC Demon?"

"You really think that's possible?" I asked skeptically.

"Well, what difference would it make from a programming point of view? It's the same ones and zeroes in the code. So if you can summon one Demon, why wouldn't you be able to summon another? Imagine a player coming into our world, going home, killing their body, and then... well, you know what happens then, right?"

"I think they'd actually die, though," said Ne-Tarok. "After all, in the real world those ones and zeroes are subject to that player's living brain."

"What if they don't, though? I mean, we've just been talking about a soul traveling into a game and being transplanted into a virtual character, haven't we?"

"Come on, you guys — we're moving into abstract theorizing, and we don't even have all the information on how these virtual capsules actually work, or even the basics of what's actually happening when they do!" Boris objected. "Which, by the way, also applies to Artyom's resurrection. Even if there IS a soul, I don't really believe it'd be possible to digitize it."

To be honest, it was really cool to finally be able to discuss everything that was actually happening and hear other people's opinions on things. Surprisingly, the youngest member of our group — Boris — was also the most skeptical. Ne-Tarok, by contrast, was ready to believe anything immediately, without demonstrating the least feeling of skepticism. That said, of course, he had just gotten one of his game abilities in real life, and I knew from experience that that feeling could wipe away any trace of skepticism. Sure, the news about the beta-testers meant that he had to cancel his plans with the James Randi foundation, but money didn't seem quite so important against the background of everything else that was happening. The Penny Mage would have to stock up on precious metals, though, and I was only too happy to give him some money from my virtual/real bank account to help him out. With the unlimited ability to withdraw funds from the game into real life, we could solve any financial problems pretty easily.

"You HAVE to settle this business with your ancestral lands," Boris reminded me, more insistently than ever. "They'll give us a stable income that we can use in the real world whenever we need to. And if the virtual Gods won't let anybody monitor your cashflow... I mean, that means total freedom!"

For a little while, Pinky was just staring around at us with a hurt look in her eyes, as though we were personally responsible for the fact that she hadn't become one of the Emissaries, and that she still didn't have her in-game abilities in real life.

After a long period of silence, though, she suddenly proposed a pretty interesting idea: after resurrecting Artyom, we could all meet up again and help Mark get his last quest item. More specifically, I guess, it wasn't actually a literal quest item in his case, but rather some sort of nightmare that would have to be caught. Doing that would show us what would happen upon completion of a divine quest.

I thought it was a great idea!

Unfortunately, though, after a few hours of animated discussion Mark and I had to say our goodbyes and get back to Naumov's mansion. It was time to heal his son, and also find out the answer to another interesting question: would he have his game abilities when he woke up, thanks to the stolen ESGUMI block?

Chapter 6

I TOOK A SEAT in Mark's car. I didn't say anything for a little while; I was just staring blankly into the space in front of me. On the one hand, it had felt really good to talk to all my friends and partners-in-gaming about everything that was going on, and finally tell them the full truth about what was happening to the world, as well as to me personally. On the other hand, though, hours of animated discussion had really worn me out. This was mostly down to the fact that I wasn't really used to speaking at length, and yet I had just given a detailed description of almost every event in my life over the past three weeks. Needless to say, every one of those days had been so busy that recounting it all took an extremely long time. And considering the fact that I barely had a chance to sit down before heading off to meet up with everybody, I felt utterly wiped out when it was all over.

"You seem really out of it for some reason," Mark noted as he steered us out of the parking lot. "Get it together — we have to talk to Mr. Oligarch and his personal Healer pretty soon."

"Well, not everybody's as energetic as you," I grumbled. "Some might say that's a good thing. Anyway — what was going on back there with Pinky?"

"What do you mean?" Mark asked. He seemed to have taken a sudden, exaggerated interest in the road in front of him.

"It wasn't long ago you were telling me all about your beloved wife and daughter," I reminded him. "So what are you doing hitting on our half-Elf friend?"

The Illusionist scratched the back of his head and frowned. He did this a few more times before he finally answered:

"Agh, it's just instinct, you know? I can't really contain my natural charisma."

I couldn't contain MY natural urge to reply to this with a sarcastic laugh.

"Come again? Natural charisma?!"

"Girls are just drawn to me," Mark nodded. "But I was just chatting with her. I wasn't trying to take it any further."

"Well, it definitely seemed like you were."

"Don't be such a buzzkill. I love Rita, and I'd never cheat on her, but a little flirting never did anybody any harm." He was silent for a little while, but then, with a surprising amount of emotion in his voice, he continued: "You know, we were only twenty when we got married. I had hardly even had a chance to talk to any other girls, and I definitely didn't know anything about how to flirt."

I chucked.

"You still don't."

"All the more so, then," the kid continued without seeming the least bit offended. "I've been married for practically my whole adult life. Is it really so bad to create a little illusion of freedom for myself? Nothing bad, of course. Inside the virtual world of the game."

"I bet psychologists and divorce lawyers could write entire dissertations on whether or not flirting or sex in a virtual game constitutes cheating," I couldn't resist rubbing it in a little more. "But we weren't in the game just now."

"You're just trying to find fault with me now," said Mark dismissively.

The most interesting thing about the whole situation was that he clearly didn't feel guilty at all — he wasn't trying to justify himself, he was merely explaining his point of view. I'm no relationship counselor, of course, and kissing virtual Princesses of various races was about as far as I had gone for a very long time, but still... It all seemed really weird. On the other hand, what reason did I have to be worrying about other people's relationships? In some senses, Mark was being slightly unfaithful to his wife, but did that mean he would also betray his comrades in a fight? Did his dubious family values make him less trustworthy as a whole?

"How about you tell ME something, though — how much do you trust this Darya of yours?" Mark suddenly changed the subject, having noticed that I wasn't particularly sympathetic to his point of view.

"Not 100%, obviously," I said after a short pause to shift my mental gears. "Not even 80%. But if Naumov can get her out of wherever she's living and hide her in some safe, guarded place, she'll be under our control. And if that's the case, I very much doubt that Darya will do anything to screw us during the hunt for this flying coffin. That's what matters most to me right now. Plus, if she manages to find the coffin Artyom is lying in, that'll be confirmation that her feelings are genuine."

"Makes sense," admitted Mark.

Of course it does, I thought to myself... I'm a pretty sensible guy, unlike some of us who have a strange desire to flirt with other women despite having a wife and daughter of their own. I decided not to bring that subject up again, though, especially because I still had one really important question for him that we hadn't had time to discuss in the restaurant: namely, the final stage of Mark's divine quest from Morphius. He was quick to lay all his cards on the table for me: his quest was called "Ruler of Nightmares," and it entailed him finding creatures who had escaped from the kingdom of dreams. Whereas I had only five swords to find, Mark had originally had no fewer than ten nightmares to track down and capture. I have no idea how he had managed to track down nine of them already — especially given that (not to belabor the point) he had a wife and daughter at home. How did this guy have so much free time?! It gave me the feeling that there was something he wasn't telling me after all. Maybe he didn't actually have a family at all? Or maybe he was in the middle of a divorce, and simply didn't want to admit it to me?

Long story short, the last nightmare was somewhere in the Crimson Caliphate, a country that was pretty tricky even to enter, let alone actually traverse and explore. More precisely, it was on an island that still wasn't accessible to players because of the magical storms in the seas around it. Everybody was waiting for somebody to discover a secret route into the Caliphate, but so far nobody had managed to initiate any event connected with it. Which was probably why Mark didn't seem too concerned about completing his quest, and why he was happy to participate in all my crazy escapades both in Arktania and in the real world. Basically, he was waiting for the opportunity to set foot on the island.

"Why didn't you say anything about this when Pinky suggested that we all work together to help you complete your task?" I asked. "I mean, if there's no way to get into the Crimson Caliphate at all?"

"We'll find one!" Mark snorted. "You've already been through so many adventures in Arktania without me. I want to be part of it too! Finding nightmares was totally boring: no high-speed chases on ancient mechanisms, no breaking into any Elvish palaces, no battles with ice monsters. Basically, all I did was travel around to all the different corners of Arktania, collecting information about mystical places where people have gone missing and then visiting a bunch of shadowy valleys, abandoned houses, and mysterious temples. On my own. It was so-oo tedious!"

Most interesting of all (and also most annoying, to be honest) was the fact that unlike my swords, nobody but Mark had any interest in the nightmares he was collecting. That was how the Illusionist had managed to collect them so quickly — there was nobody getting in his way! He had only run into a snag when it came to the tenth and final nightmare.

"I tried finding out through my sister, but even in the "Spirit of the Hunt" there's nobody who knows how to get into the Caliphate," Mark continued. "Maybe we could find something out through your buddy Boris. He seems like a pretty sharp guy. For now, though, I'll just keep helping you."

I certainly wasn't about to say no, given that the guy seemed to have nothing but free time. It would have been stupid to turn down the help of the only player in Arktania who could change characters' nicknames and levels at will. Okay, maybe he wasn't actually the only one, but I had never heard of any other Illusionists like him. That made Mark unique and irreplaceable, and his value would increase exponentially as his character continued to develop.

"Well, there'll be plenty of adventure, no need to worry about that," I assured him. "Whether I want it or not."

"You don't want it?" Mark sounded surprised.

I thought for a little while.

"You know what? I actually don't. I miss Arktania. I feel like I'm already going through withdrawal. I want to get this all over with, hop back into my capsule, fight without worrying about actually dying in real life, hunt some normal monsters, and complete some normal, simple quests where I just have to deliver stuff to other characters. And just drink a damn health elixir to heal any wounds I get while doing it."

"NOW you're talking! Except the delivery stuff, obviously. You can knock yourself out with those if you want." Mark actually shivered with excitement. "Anyway — what are your plans when you get back into Arktania?"

"Apparently I have to go meet with my uncle at the Fudre family mansion. I need to get this issue with my ancestral lands sorted out. Boris was very insistent about that. They're going to be the foundation of our financial empire, heh heh heh!" I busted out my best evil laugh.

"I'll go with you!"

"Are you a masochist or something?" I chuckled. "You want him to kill you again?"

"Ah, right. This is your uncle with the bad temper," Mark frowned. "I guess I'll wait outside for you then. No interest in visiting the God of Death right now."

As far as I understood, Renick Fudre wasn't the actual God of Death from the Higher Pantheon. He was more like an assistant, whose relationship to the God was something like Hotei's relationship to the Goddess of Fate. Not that that made him any less dangerous. Quite the opposite, in fact, since it actually gave him a freer hand than a God would have had. I was already worried about my own safety — I thought that my uncle might get mad that my completion of the "False Emissary" quest was purely nominal, and that the God of the Dead was actually still alive. Even without any of his divine powers, my virtual uncle could crush me like a bug with nothing more than a wave of his hand. You know: the massive, skeletal hand that he had the ability to summon. I also hadn't completed his task with the Glass Rose, which meant that all things considered, he had more than enough reason to kill me (or punish me in some other way) if the mood happened to move him.

"It's a lot safer to travel through the city with you than it is on my own," I agreed. "Especially now, with the "Spirit of the Hunt" looking for me. I'll feel better if you're with me."

"I'm irreplaceable, of course," the Illusionist nodded somberly in reply. "Especially since I just leveled up my passive that lets my illusions affect players at a higher level and..." He suddenly slammed on the brakes and pointed at something straight up ahead: "Look at that. Is it just me, or are there too many people at Naumov's mansion right now?"

Sure enough, there were more guards at the mansion than there ever should have been under normal circumstances (depending on how one defined the word "normal" in regard to oligarchs). The men were all armed, and I'm not talking about the usual pistols, either: they were carrying assault rifles and uzis, and I could have sworn that some of the biggest guys even had grenade launchers tucked away under their coats. It all combined to give the impression that Naumov was preparing for a full-scale war, and I suspected that it mainly had to do with the information Darya and I had shared with him earlier in the day. Scared he might have been, but he still reacted quickly and decisively.

We didn't even set foot inside the mansion's grounds for a good twenty minutes or so after our arrival. The guards searched us so thoroughly it was starting to get humiliating by the time they stopped; they spared only the most intimate and hard-to-reach areas. In the end, however, we parked our car outside as usual, although this time we were escorted inside and led through a series of metal detectors and other security checkpoints. By the time it was all over, I felt like they had shined flashlights through every single atom in my body. I honestly wouldn't have been surprised to see a system communication telling me I had caught a radiation debuff.

The Sands of Eternity

I would have liked to ask Naumov something, though: why would Mark or I bother bringing weapons into his house, when we were basically living weapons ourselves? Or at least I certainly was. And what were the security guys imagining they'd find anyway — if it had been some other Emissaries instead of us, how would the checkpoints have helped at all? Mind you, one look at the oligarch's face was enough to make me decide not to ask any of these questions. He looked extremely tense already by the time we arrived.

"You're late," Vladimir Naumov snapped, nervously rubbing the ring on his finger as he walked toward us. The fact that he had come to meet us in the mansion's underground parking garage, still wearing his slippers, was another unmistakable sign of anxiety. "We agreed on a specific time."

I opted not to mention the fact that his security team had held us up for over twenty minutes. Naumov was obviously far too preoccupied with his son's impending recovery to care; he would have gone to any lengths to guarantee maximum possible security during the process. My news about the beta-testers could well have been a contributing factor, too, so I definitely wasn't going to reproach him for being too careful.

"Traffic," I replied, resorting to the time-honored justification used by every single person who lived in the capital whenever they were late. "Did you get in touch with Darya?"

"Yes," replied Naumov with a frown. "She told me quite a lot, and I don't even know whether that's a good thing or a bad thing. Perhaps it would be better if I didn't know that RussVirtTech is now being run by some psychopath who's read too many comic books."

"Why all the security?"

"If I'd had my way I'd have parked some tanks in the driveway as well," the oligarch replied with a completely serious expression on his face. "It's a shame that would have attracted too much un-wanted attention."

After emerging from the parking garage into the mansion's main hall, we found ourselves wan-dering amidst a sea of wooden chests and styrofoam.

"Whoa... Doing some construction here?" Mark asked with surprise. "Setting up some barri-cades?"

"Backup generators," explained Naumov. "In case anyone cuts our electricity. We've also dupli-cated our fiberoptic network and other lines of communication."

My face dropped into a skeptical frown.

"Maybe it'd be better to hide somewhere else, rather than making your mansion into a fortress? I'm sure that if the owners of a company like Russ-VirtTech wanted to find out where a particular player lived, they could do it pretty easily."

"If they had the ability to do that, the beta-test-ers would have apprehended all the Emissaries by now, or at least have them all under observation," Naumov objected. "Didn't Dasha tell you that the programmers haven't really had access to

Arktania's databases since the launch? They can't really do anything to influence the gaming process at all."

Whoa, I thought... "Dasha?" He's already got a nickname for her? I had only just passed him the girl's contact info, but Naumov already seemed to be better informed about what was happening than I was.

"But I have backup shelters, too," the oligarch went on. "Actually, Dasha's on her way to one of my country houses as we speak. Needless to say, none of them are traceable to me. Keep in mind that I haven't told her my name yet, so don't either of you mention anything you don't need to when she's around."

"Still, though — you don't think it would have been better for all of us to get out of here too?" Mark repeated my earlier question. "This whole mess is definitely going to draw some attention your way."

"Maybe," Naumov conceded. "To be honest, though, I feel safer at home. The walls and the houses help me relax. Naturally, if I could have hired a couple Emissaries to protect the mansion instead of these soldiers, I'd have done it."

He shot a demonstrative glance at Mark and I, but we pretended not to have caught the hint. Naumov had certainly helped me a lot, and he was continuing to help me, but I had no desire to turn into his personal bodyguard. Even more so for Mark — he was a free man, and he didn't owe anybody anything.

Loner Book Eight

Naumov led us right into a room I had already been in once before — it had two virtual capsules in it, one of which contained his son. The first was a standard (albeit pricey) "SuperVirt 3800," while the second was a complicated medical device that was hooked up to a whole array of various other devices. Mark walked straight over to the strange-looking capsule, glanced into the window, and couldn't resist a gasp of amazement as he exclaimed:

"So this is the famous Dark Inquisitor Antibiotic?! Poor guy."

He was clearly just as shocked as I had been the first time I laid eyes on Fyodor's accident-scarred body. Mind you, the Illusionist had probably also seen the guy's name and level floating above the spot where he was lying in the capsule: "Antibiotic, level 121," so his question was almost certainly rhetorical.

"Yes, that's my son," Naumov nodded. "And I hope that he'll finally be able to stand up and leave this capsule today.

"Do you have doubts about whether the Healing Magic will work?" I asked with surprise. "And by the way, where's our Elvish Prince?"

"In his capsule, as usual," replied Naumov with obvious dissatisfaction. "He barely ever leaves Arktania."

"Well, I'd probably forget reality too if I was married to an Elvish Princess," said Mark with a wry smile, before catching the look of disapproval on my face and adding: "I'm just kidding!"

The Sands of Eternity

Naumov shot us a quick, skeptical glance.

"I already sent Sergei a message, he should be here soon," the oligarch grumbled. "While we wait, how about telling me what you're planning to do from here? Besides resurrecting a virtual copy of your friend, of course."

His choice of words irritated me a little bit, but I wasn't about to get into an argument with him about it. Plus, in a way, Naumov was actually right: we were talking about a strange sort of backup for a game character, into which the God of the Dead would then inject Artyom's soul.

"We're headed to the Crimson Caliphate," said Mark. "By the way, I don't suppose you've heard of any way to get in there, have you?"

"Why do you want to go there?" The oligarch sounded surprised.

"The last stage of my Emissary quest is there," the Illusionist replied with a nonchalance that struck me as strange. "We want to finally find out what all this is leading up to."

I would never have been so open with Naumov if I'd been in Mark's shoes; sure, he seemed to be on our side, but you never know what might be going on in someone's mind. Thankfully, however, Sergei walked in before Mark had a chance to spill any more beans. Once again, the Healer was strutting around in a soft silk bathrobe. I could only hope he had something on under it as well. After a cursory greeting, he stepped over to the capsule without any apparent sign of happiness and gave Naumov an order:

"Open it."

"Is that necessary?" Vladimir frowned. "There's a safe atmosphere inside, with a bunch of devices hooked up to it. Healing can be applied over a distance, at least in the game."

"But it can't be done with electronics nearby. Unless you don't mind shorting them out, of course," added the Healer with a sarcastic smile. "Plus, it's better if I can actually touch the person in real life. The spell works much better that way."

In the end, Naumov gave in and pressed a series of buttons on one of the remotes. The capsule rose open with a quiet hiss. As it did, I realized that my little glimpse through the window of the capsule had only revealed a small fraction of the full trauma the young man's body had sustained during the accident. I had mistaken a virtually-generated image of the kid's body for the real thing. Obviously, paralysis of the central nervous system is horrifying enough all on its own, but Naumov Jr. didn't actually have all that much to control with his nervous system anyway: his legs had been amputated below the knees, one of his arms was entirely missing, and the one that he still had was clearly missing some pieces. I certainly didn't have the highest opinion of Russia's "golden boy" generation — kids born with an iPhone in their mouths — but this young man certainly didn't deserve such a horrible fate.

"Let's hurry," Naumov urged Sergei. He clearly didn't like the fact that we were all staring down at his son with a mixture of horror and sympathy on our faces.

"Kid's lucky his daddy has the money for this," said Sergei without so much as a hint of embarrassment as he disconnected all the various wires and IVs running into the kid's body. "If this had happened to someone from a normal family, they'd never have survived."

He laid his hand on the kid's forehead and called out: "In the name of the Goddess Lethara." The inert body began to shine with the bright light that was characteristic of healing spells within the game. Red spots began to appear in my eyes, as if I had been looking at the sun for too long, and as soon as I blinked them away I saw that all the monitors near the capsule were flashing and blinking with all sorts of warnings. Later on, Naumov explained that the medical array essentially "didn't believe" such a significant improvement could have happened so quickly, and therefore it triggered mechanical error warnings on all fronts.

As the bright light faded away, we saw a young man lying in place of the horribly-mangled body we had been looking at just a minute before. Sure, he didn't seem to have a very healthy build (quite the contrary, I'd say: he was gaunt, sickly, and very weak-looking), but other than that he was completely healthy. I could see the family resemblance immediately: Fyodor basically looked like a younger version of his dad, albeit one who had never played sports. Vladimir, by contrast, looked something like a professional swimmer who was well into retirement.

"Are you sure he's healed?" Mark finally broke the silence. "He looks like he hasn't eaten since the day of the accident. Or did the law of conservation of mass have some weird effect here? Does that even apply in magic, actually?"

Naumov was standing there silently, staring at his son with tears in his eyes and completely ignoring the stupid nonsense coming out of the Illusionist's mouth.

"Shh. Come on, man," I hissed at Mark.

"The patient is completely healthy," Sergei assured us (mainly Naumov, I guess). Even in such intense circumstances, though, he couldn't change who he was, and so he added: "I didn't waste my most powerful ability for nothing. By the way, it's going to be a few more days before he's fully recovered."

Just then, Naumov Jr. opened his eyes and burst into a fit of bloody coughing. Which might not have seemed so strange on its own, if he hadn't turned over and spat a couple teeth out onto the floor!

"What the hell?!" Naumov snapped out of his momentary trance and grabbed Sergei by the front of his shirt. "Is he okay?! What's happening to him?!"

"Apparently some new teeth must have pushed out a few crowns," the Healer shrugged. "Powerful Healing renews the entire body, in case that wasn't already clear. You should be glad he didn't have any implants in his internal organs.

Uh... He didn't, right?"

I thought Naumov might actually punch him in the face, but somehow the oligarch restrained himself, let Sergei go, and rushed over to his son:

"How are you feeling?!" He asked as he grabbed the kid by the arm.

"Just fine, dad," said the fearsome Dark Inquisitor in a slightly hoarse voice. He tried to sit up on the bed, but collapsed back down onto it immediately. "I forgot what this feels like, after all those weeks in Arktania in Antibiotic's body. Being so small and weak. It's weird..."

He managed to get up and sit on his second try.

"There you go — job done perfectly. Two arms, two legs, healthy body! Anybody still having doubts about my powers?! Sergei snarled at us. "The kid's in tip-top shape!"

"Yes, you've kept your end of the bargain," said Naumov dismissively. "The fund will be transferring to your control." The whole time, he kept patting his son's body extremely gingerly, as though he was afraid anything more might hurt the kid. "Are you sure you're okay?"

"Better than okay," said Fyodor (who I still thought of as Antibiotic) with a smile. He stretched a hand out in front of him, and a small whirl of shadows spun together to form a sword. "I think I can use my own powers in real life now too. And I also have a full game interface and menu in front of my eyes..." He trailed off with a frown; his eyes were running back and forth, and I could tell he was reading some system communication that only he could see. "But it's blocked until I complete my patron God's quest and become one of the Emissaries."

After reading the invisible text, he turned to look attentively at me, and for some reason I could immediately tell that this wasn't going to end well.

"And what do you need to do to complete your quest?" I asked anxiously as I glanced at Sergei.

I wondered, just then, whether the Healer would intervene on my side if the Naumovs suddenly attacked me? Plus, my mini-map told me that there were other people in the neighboring rooms — these were almost certainly guards, who would definitely make an appearance as soon as their master called.

"Find and kill whoever killed the previous Emissary." The young man smiled weakly, confirming all my worst fears.

"Whose Emissary were you?" Mark inquired. Maybe he really didn't understand what was happening; maybe he was just doing a good job of pretending.

I had already guessed intuitively who he had to kill, but I was still hoping for the best:

"Yeah, whose?"

"The God Antos."

"Hm... And what does he control?" I asked, remembering that I had already heard this name before. If memory served, he was somehow connected with the Order of Varr — maybe their patron, maybe an enemy, I couldn't remember. "I assumed it's Dark Magic, since you're a Dark Inquisitor?"

"Antos is the God of Dark Mages," nodded Antibiotic. "The slain Emissary was one of them — a Curser, to be specific. But of course you already know that. I mean, you were the one who buried him in concrete, weren't you?"

Chapter 7

DAMMIT, I THOUGHT... So he actually has to kill *me*, specifically. This all turned out pretty badly. And I had nobody but myself to blame, of course, since I had told everybody present about my little scrap with the darks. If the Naumov family were forced to choose between preserving our relatively-new partnership and the chance to become one of the Emissaries... Well, what would they choose? Although actually, I thought, why am I so worried? Even if they make the wrong choice, I can easily knock them both out with my powers: Vladimir is just a normal guy, and his son is still too physically weak to beat me. That said, the numerous armed guards surrounding the room might create some serious problems.

"Don't worry — I'm not going to do anything of the sort. Otherwise, why would I have told you about my task at all?" Fyodor hurriedly added after noticing my reaction. "There's no time limit, and no penalties, so I don't even need to complete it at all."

"Apparently not," I agreed, although I was still looking at both Naumovs with a healthy degree of suspicion. Not that I would say I was particularly worried about a potential attack from the Dark Inquisitor. He simply looked too weak; plus, I had far more experience in real-world battles than he did. I also had an Illusionist on my side, and maybe a Healer as well. Although I couldn't be sure about the latter.

All the same, I wasn't sensing any danger whatsoever from either Fyodor or his father. I felt like the Whisper of Fate would definitely have warned me if there was something to fear from either of them. Even with all that in mind, though, I still took a few steps back toward the exit, in order to give myself a little bit more room to maneuver. It was pure instinct, honed over the course of countless battles in Arktania.

"Okay, stop," said Naumov Sr. in a firm tone as he noticed what I was doing. "There won't be any conflicts in this house. We've always resolved everything together so far, and we're going to keep doing that going forward. But if you so much as TRY to do any harm to my son..."

Sergei and Mark glanced at each other, then stepped forward to stand between me and the newest candidate for Emissary of the God of Dark Mages.

"We're all on the same side here," said Sergei, though whether he was asserting this or asking it was hard to tell. "Actually, it's awesome that we now have four people with abilities. Because in case you've all forgotten, we're still going to have to close this Demonologist's portal together. So whether Fyodor can see his game interface or not, he's going to make it a hell of a lot easier for us to complete this task."

As I listened to the Healer speak, I made a note of the fact that he didn't seem at all surprised that people could see their interfaces in the real world. Maybe this was yet another fact that he had neglected to share with us — maybe he had acquired his own interface a long time before. If so, though, how long ago could that have happened? Hotei had said that I was the first person the Gods tested their interface installation process on.

"As for the fact that we're all on the same side, I agree with you completely," nodded Vladimir Naumov. "Allowing my son to participate in such a dangerous task, though, is not something I'm even willing to discuss."

"Dad," Fyodor objected. "I'm a grown man — have been for some time, actually. I can decide for myself!"

"End of discussion," replied Naumov Sr. in a flat, categorical tone. "We'll get through it without you, one way or another."

The situation was still pretty tense, so Sergei, Mark, and I decided to let the Naumovs discuss things in private and recover for a little while. In the meantime, the three of us headed back to the wing of the mansion where the Elvish Prince was staying. Once there, I double-checked to make sure nobody was eavesdropping, then began questioning the Healer. It turned out that he had started seeing a limited version of the interface that very same day, just like we had. I was starting to get the impression that the virtual Gods had tested the first stage on me, just to make sure that I didn't die of a brain hemorrhage or something, and then "rolled it out" to the other Emissaries a few hours later.

"What the hell?!" Mark shouted indignantly. "I still don't have any menus at all. I want one too! Even Antibiotic has an interface, and he's technically not even an Emissary yet!"

"Just wait. It's not that simple," the Healer admonished him. "I don't know about Andrey, but the pain in my head when it activated almost killed me. I always have my Healing, but what are you going to do when it happens?"

I nodded as Sergei spoke to confirm what he was saying. I had lost consciousness right as the interface activated, and it took me quite some time to recover afterward. What if it started happening while Mark was behind the wheel or something?

"I'll get through it somehow. Or just come see you," said the Illusionist with no apparent concern at all. "You wouldn't turn down a fellow traveler, would you?"

"No — but you'll actually have to survive the trip over here for me to help."

Long story short, we settled the question of the interface and moved on to discussing the latest news from both the real world and the virtual world with the Healer.

"Don't forget that I'm coming with you when you go to resurrect your friend," he said firmly once we filled him in on our plans.

"You're really that interested in whether it works?"

"Interested?" The "Elf" scoffed. "Do you really not understand? Try thinking just a little bit outside your tiny little worldview. If this works in the game, it's essentially a form of immortality! I'd love to move in there permanently and leave my physical body out here to rot. And the terminally ill people I help? This would be a way to save them all!"

Don't get me wrong: immortality would be cool, at least in that specific sense. According to Eidolon, though, there wasn't much prospect of a mass transfer into or out of the game, at least on the scale Sergei was talking about. Powerful though they might be, the virtual Gods were still subject to limitations and restrictions that kept them from being all-powerful and solving their problems with a simple snap of the fingers.

"Let's start with resurrecting one person," I frowned. "Once that's done, we'll be able to think about next steps."

"Yeah — that's what I want to see," agreed Sergei. "When and where is the event happening?"

It would have been foolish to turn down the Healer's help, so I told him when and where the event with the coffins was going to start. I also took advantage of the opportunity to ask how Princess Ariella was doing. These were people I knew fairly well, after all. Or Elves I knew, I guess. It turned out that Ellendril was already in the grip of a full-scale civil war: after we freed him from the ice, Master Ilfur had used the Crystal of Fate to weaken the King of the Elves, create a whole army of ice monsters, and lay siege to the capital from the sea. And a certain part of the Elvish population, who were unhappy with the current King's policies, had gone off to join him. Unsurprisingly, players also split into warring camps (in approximately equal numbers). They were basically just excited about the new global event.

"This is all because of you, I might add," said Sergei as he brought his story to an irritated end. "All I wanted to do was live in the palace, enjoy every minute of it, and level up fighting mobs at my own pace! Now I'm busy from dawn to dusk directing the defense of the whole Kingdom!"

"You'll get experience way faster that way than you would fighting mobs," Mark offered what I thought was quite a logical point.

"Yeah, except I'm also one of the main targets for Ilfur's Assassins now. I die several times a day."

Basically, the Elf was really unhappy with life at the time, and he wasn't entirely mistaken in blaming me for his woes. He didn't have a chance to finish lambasting me, however, because the Naumovs finally came to join us. Fyodor had already managed to put himself together a little bit, get changed, and start wolfing down a pastry with a cup of hot coffee. As he walked in, his eyes were practically rolling up into his head from the sheer enjoyment of it all.

"Mm... God, I've missed real food!" He moaned. "Say what you want about how realistic Arktania's food is, but somewhere in the back of your mind you still know it's fake. Your brain can get all the signals in the world, but your body still knows it isn't real. Same with virtual sex..."

"What?" Naumov Sr. snapped.

"Nothing, nothing," the fearsome Dark Inquisitor said as he sheepishly averted his eyes. "So what are your plans from here?"

He walked over to the nearest chair, turned, and sat down in it very slowly and carefully, letting out a huge sigh once it was all over as though the whole process had taken a huge amount of effort. Mind you, the way Fyodor was moving made it obvious that he had grown unused to moving his own body. Which only made sense, of course, especially given that he had been living in the body of a Dark Inquisitor who had a totally different physique than Fyodor did in real life. Furthermore, he hadn't taken ANY of the recommended breaks for months.

"Nothing too complicated, really," Sergei answered for all of us. "We're going to resurrect Andrey's friend, then head out and kill a Demonologist in the real world together. It'll be a lot easier if we have you with us. Assuming your dad doesn't object, of course."

The Sands of Eternity

"I don't," said an obviously-reluctant Vladimir. One way or another, his son had talked him around.

"But I'll tell you right now: I'm not killing anybody in the real world," warned Naumov Jr. with a sidelong glance at me. "Demons, though? No problem."

Okay, I thought... Dark Inquisitor — and yet somehow he's a pacifist? Fair enough. I wasn't exactly thrilled about the idea of killing anybody either, but if it literally became necessary to save myself or my friends, I knew it wouldn't be a hard decision to make. I'm ashamed to admit it, but I had never felt bad about killing those dark faction players even for a second. Although...

"This makes me wonder whether the other Gods will be able to find replacements for their own dead Emissaries." I felt anxious.

"I'm wondering something else, actually," Mark disagreed. "Are they going to order a hit on you as well? Also, do these new Emissaries start their quests from square one, or do they pick up where the last one left off?"

From there, it didn't take long for us to drift into another discussion of what the eventual goal of the Emissaries was in the first place. Of all the suggestions I heard, the following were the most interesting:

1. Emissaries might be the horsemen of the Apocalypse who would usher in a new world, and if so, maybe the competition was to thin out the ranks until there were only a certain number left

— maybe the classic four, maybe more. Once that point was reached, the creation of the new world (however it might look) could begin.

2. Maybe only one Emissary would end up winning, and that Emissary's patron God would become the head of the new real-world Pantheon. Or maybe the Emissary themselves would become a God.

3. There might be a lot of winners, who would end up bringing ALL their patron Gods over into the real world.

We had already discussed that possibility with Pinky, Boris, and Ne-Tarok earlier in the day, but it was still as relevant as ever. We were all waiting, fearing, and constantly thinking about the moment when some Emissary finally completed their quest. Given the fact that I had only recovered three of the five swords so far, I knew it definitely wasn't going to be me.

No matter how much Fyodor (a.k.a. Antibiotic) might try to convince me that he had no intention of completing his patron God's quest, I still felt uncomfortable being in their mansion, surrounded by armed guards who were on their payroll. Firearms still posed a pretty serious danger to me, and therefore I said goodbye to the Naumovs as quickly as I possibly could, citing the fact that I was absolutely exhausted.

As usual, Mark changed our car's external appearance several times during the drive. I asked him to drop me off at a random Metro station, and then made my own way to my new shelter from there. I had developed a new mantra: "it's okay to trust, but it's not okay to let your guard down."

Only when I finally found myself alone in my new apartment did I finally feel like I could let out a heavy sigh and actually relax at least a little bit. It felt like I had been fighting people to the death all day, rather than simply going out to meet up with a few acquaintances and friends. But I knew it wasn't yet time to relax and unwind, so I quickly threw my clothes off and hopped into my capsule. At first, a lot of people (including me) had used virtual games as a way to escape a boring, monotonous reality. By now, though, all I really wanted was a break from a life full of danger. So much had changed in so little time!

The flight down the rainbow tunnel sent a wave of warmth and calm rising gently through my body. It felt like I was finally coming back home. As soon as I emerged into the game, I saw a system communication:

"You've acquired the ability 'Micro Chaos Shield'."

"This ability allows you to create a shield 12 inches in diameter for a period of (5 x Wisdom) seconds, which can block up to (2 x Intelligence) damage. Attack abilities that strike the shield have a 10% chance of being completely destroyed by the impact."

Interesting... I still didn't have access to full descriptions of my abilities in my real world interface. The shield was already starting to seem less useless than it had at first. Together with Chaos Aura, which could change the direction of spells that were aimed at me, and Spin's ability to block damage caused by spells, I had become reasonably well-protected (although only against magic). I was still pretty vulnerable where physical damage was concerned.

I no longer felt completely safe in my room at the "Thick as a Brick" inn. I hadn't felt safe there ever since learning that Hotei could get inside easily whenever he wanted, and bring anybody he wanted along with him when he did. The first thing I did, therefore, was rush over and make sure all my swords were still in their cases inside my storage chest: thankfully, the Bone Sword, the Stone Sword of the Dragon Mountains, and the Wood Sword were all lying in their places. A message from Boris flashed up on my tablet, reminding me to get title to my ancestral lands. He obviously couldn't wait to put his financial plans into action. And from my own point of view, I knew it would be easier to head off to search for the next sword in the lands of the Orcs if I knew that I had my own fortress at my back. Kelevre had become a full-fledged fortress, after all; it was no longer the tiny little village I had walked into at the very beginning of my time in the game.

Maybe I should have waited for Mark to arrive with his illusions, because of course "Spirit of the Hunt" was still hunting me down. But I simply didn't have the patience for that. So I left the hotel and headed straight down to the Fudre family mansion. As always, the streets were filled with big throngs of players — people of every size, shape, and race. Thankfully, though, none of them seemed to be the slightest bit interested in me. I actually saw "Spirit of the Hunt" badges a few times, but their owners didn't pay any attention to me either. Thanks to my previous visit, I already knew that Renick Fudre's majestic, four-story, black home was handily close to my hotel — so close, in fact, that for once I actually managed to reach my destination without running into any problems.

The pale-faced zombie butler appeared almost as soon as I knocked, with the exact same death mask expression that had greeted me on my previous visit.

"The Master... is... expecting... you," he whispered before I had time to say anything.

I didn't really know whether that was a good or a bad thing. Although actually, I thought, who am I kidding? Or course it's a bad thing! It seemed vanishingly unlikely that the God of Death was expecting me so he could pass on some good news.

"Hey, hold up!" I suddenly heard someone shout from behind me.

I turned around and saw two players, just under level 100, with "Spirit of the Hunt" sigils next to their names.

"Our General wants to talk to you," one of them announced.

"I'll check my schedule and let you know when

I have some free time," I replied from where I stood on the mansion's threshold. I wanted to see how they would react.

They glanced at each other.

"Now!"

"Definitely can't do it now," I shook my head. "Now how about you two scuttle off back to wherever you came from?"

Needless to say, I was trying to provoke the players into attacking me. I was curious to see whether the zombie would step in to defend me; plus, I just felt like it would be nice to see my tormentors punished. Alas — they didn't risk attacking me. Maybe they were worried about the guards; maybe they were afraid of the zombie butler. Or maybe these players actually knew whom the mansion belonged to? That would have explained everything: it's never a good idea to get on an Imperial Necromancer's bad side.

"So much the worse for you," one of the players growled menacingly. To my considerable disappointment, they turned around and left. Which was genuinely out of the ordinary — I was used to my pursuers behaving far more rudely and aggressively.

Nevertheless, I shrugged and turned to step over the threshold into the mansion. A light chill passed across my body as soon as I was inside; the air in the mansion was quite a bit colder than the air outside. After passing through a wide hallway, we stepped out into the same throne room that I had already seen before. My virtual uncle was seated atop his black throne (just as you'd expect), as if he'd spent the entire period between my visits just sitting there waiting for me. Although the throne actually looked pretty uncomfortable, and there was nothing else inside the hall whatsoever. What could he possibly have been doing the whole time? For some reason, I pictured the stern, serious Necromancer running frantically from one end of his mansion to the other when he saw me approaching, so he could quickly hop onto his grandiose throne and assume a melodramatic pose right before I walked in. The image contrasted so sharply with the man sitting in front of me that I couldn't conceal a little smile.

"What, may I ask, are you smiling at, my dear nephew?" Renick Fudre asked with a grimace of displeasure on his face.

"I'm very happy to see you, my dear uncle," I replied, trying to make my tone just as melodramatic as his. "I've come for my reward. You promised to confirm my deed to our ancestral lands if I helped you take care of the False Emissary."

"So you actually killed him?" The Necromancer inquired. "Can you guarantee that? By swearing on your own life, for example?

"How would I know what the Emissary of the God of the Dead is capable of?" I replied evasively. "We destroyed his body. Dark Elsa can confirm that for you."

"I know that," my uncle replied. "And yet I can sense that his presence in our world is still only partial. I don't suppose you have any idea why that might be?"

I was about to lie to him and say I had no idea what he was talking about, but suddenly I heard a quiet whisper in my mind:

"Gods can sense a lie."

Ah, I thought... I see. Well, thanks for the hint, "sixth sense."

"I have many thoughts, but I doubt that they would be of any interest to the God of Death." My reply was even more evasive than before. "Most importantly, though — I completed the task exactly as it was formulated."

"You did," agreed the Necromancer as he drilled into me with his penetrating glare. "The same, however, cannot be said of the first task I gave you. You were in Kelevre recently, if I'm not mistaken?"

"I was," I replied with a perplexed nod. "But the time limit hasn't run out on that task. I can still complete it."

"Oh, by all means," he nodded. "Except that if Kelevre becomes a part of your ancestral lands, the task would lose all meaning. The Fudre Line cannot inflict harm on people who live on our lands, which means that in giving you my assent I will be pronouncing that quest a failure."

I didn't really understand the mechanism behind what he was saying, but there was certainly a certain logic in it. I had been hoping to put off the destruction of the Glass Rose until the last possible day, or replace it with something even more powerful after I got control of Kelevre, but my dear old uncle had thrown a huge wrench into my plans.

"So? Shall I give you my assent to assume title?" The Necromancer asked. "I mean, you wanted them so badly, didn't you?"

Okay, I thought — either I have to leave for Kelevre right this minute and try to destroy the artifact that protects the fort before I can get my ancestral lands, or get my ancestral lands and lose ten levels right here, right now? What the HELL?!

"You took too long," the Necromancer suddenly broke the silence. "I hereby give you permission to take possession of your ancestral lands."

As soon as he said this, a system communication flashed up before my eyes:

You've failed the task "Say hello to some old friends for the Necromancer."
Penalty for non-completion: -10 levels.

I'll say it again — what the HELL?!

Chapter 8

I CHECKED MY INFO and found that sure enough, I was down to level 43. My instinct was to let out a stream of curses, but doing so in front of a character like Renick Fudre seemed like a bad idea. What if he just wasn't a big fan of foul language? I definitely didn't want to get slapped with any curses from the God of Death.

"And please spare me the lies — there's no need to tell me that you had any intention of completing that task," the Necromancer continued as he stared intently at my expression. "You were never planning to destroy that artifact. All you were hoping to do was draw out the clock."

"Of course." I didn't see any point arguing, since my "uncle" had decided we were going to be speaking frankly about everything. Plus, my "sixth sense" had already made it clear that Gods could sense when they were being lied to. "I don't understand what made you decide to ruin the lives of people you used to work so closely with. And I'm definitely not the kind of person who's willing to betray his comrades in arms."

"Comrades," the Necromancer scoffed. I could actually hear a note of sadness in his voice. "There was a time when I considered those people "comrades" too. When we killed the God and acquired our curse, though, none of them were willing to stick together to try and find a cure — they just left. I told them that we would need to stick together, but they all made the egotistical choice to go about their own personal business."

"But YOU ended up finding a cure," I noted.

"I did," said the Necromancer. "But you can't even begin to imagine what it cost me. To put it very briefly and simply, I had to sacrifice my very humanity. And I know that things could have gone differently if we had stuck together as a team..."

Darkness was beginning to gather behind the Necromancer's back as he spoke, and before long I was getting peppered with system communications about taking damage. There were so many of them, in fact, that I actually had to drink a healing elixir.

"Mind you, it no longer matters." Renick Fudre suddenly regained his composure. "What's done is done. It was just a little whim, really — I wanted to give them a little taste of what betrayal feels like."

Ah, I thought... A little whim that cost me ten

levels. I'll show you where you can stick your whims next time! I didn't say anything like that out loud, of course — I didn't feel like dying.

"Anyway, you've got what you wanted: my permission to claim your ancestral lands," the Necromancer continued. "That said, you should never forget that "ancestral" is the key word. They will belong to you, but I will still bear certain responsibilities with regard to them as head of the family."

"And what does that mean?" I suddenly felt anxious (not that I had been particularly relaxed, of course).

"It means that if I feel you're failing to meet your obligations as a landowner, I might intervene and take control of your lands into my own hands." The Necromancer stretched his pale, bony hands up into the air in front of him and clenched them into fists. "I cannot allow you to besmirch the Fudre name."

Wait, I thought. Am I understanding this correctly? I could invest money and effort into Kelevre, and at some point this pasty... Actually, let's be civil — this not-very-tan man can strut into my ancestral lands and take control of them for himself? What the hell kind of nonsense is that?

"Who's going to decide whether I'm meeting my obligations or not?" I decided that would need to be cleared up before I could leave.

"Not me, in case you were worried. The Empire will require you to perform certain tasks in your role as Kelevre's owner. Should you fail to complete even one of those tasks in a timely manner," he continued as the darkness began to billow out from behind him again, adding heaviness and foreboding to the already-sinister atmosphere in the hall. "You can count on a prompt visit from me."

Whew, I thought. Thank the Gods. I was starting to think he'd still have the power to ruin everything at any moment. But he was actually just referring to the usual quests that would be assigned to the village as a whole, which was a totally normal practice. Since Kelevre had been turned into a military fort, it was pretty obvious that one of the main tasks would be to fight off attacks from the Orcs, and that there would probably be numerous other tasks stemming from that.

"I'll try not to bring any dishonor on the Fudre family," I assured him as I slowly began to back toward the exit. Chatting with my virtual uncle had never really ended well before, and I really didn't want to tempt fate by keeping the conversation going.

Thankfully, the Necromancer turned away from me as well, thereby signalling that our conversation was officially at an end.

"Yes — please try," he said drily as he waved goodbye.

I stopped at the Fudre mansion's exit. I knew that there might be new pursuers waiting for me outside. Or the same old ones from before. Moving around Katar would be far too risky on my own, but I didn't want to head straight to Pyrenth ahead of time and show my face there either. With my low level, and the fact that I had the entire evening free, I figured I could find a suitable instance and use my pets to help me level up. Spin and Chaosite were both pretty well leveled-up themselves, and they could provide some serious fighting support when necessary. Together with my "Lone Warrior in the Field" achievement, I felt pretty confident I could earn at least a level or two. Sure, that would be no more than a drop in the bucket compared with the thirty I had lost, but you know what they say: a journey of a thousand miles begins with a single step.

As luck would have it, I had a perfect instance called "Katar's Sewers for Beginners" already marked on my map. This was the instance where I had first encountered the breach from the Inferno and met that strange Vampire. With a minimum level requirement of 35, it would be a nice place to test out my weakened abilities and level them up at least a little bit. There was just one little problem I would have to solve first: changing out all the equipment that I could no longer use, now that I had lost thirty levels and grown considerably weaker. It would have been a simple matter to stop by a store, if it hadn't been for the fact that players from "Spirit of the Hunt" were constantly hounding me. It's not like I was standing there naked, of course — I was still wearing the same things as before, but their properties had been wiped when I lost my levels. My weapons, on the other hand, were so out of my league that I couldn't even pick them up anymore.

The Sands of Eternity

The safest option, I decided, would be to teleport to the store, then teleport to the instance after that. Uncle Boris was still offline, so I just chose the closest store to the instance on the map. I teleported straight to the entrance, where I bought up a bunch of elixirs, teleports (which were in very short supply due to a deficit in raw materials), and a few pieces of equipment that were optimal for my level and class. They didn't have a full setup for an Electromage, of course, but I managed to get at least a little bit of added defense and some bonuses to my base attributes. All the same, my new setup felt like some sort of stupid parody whenever I thought about the level-70 equipment in my inventory.

"Just leveled up, and decided to level up your gear as well, huh?" The Gnome behind the counter asked as he stared at me from beneath his bushy eyebrows. He was a player too, by the way, almost at the same level as me.

"Yeah, you could say that," I frowned.

I was planning to teleport straight from the store to the instance entrance, but before I could finish my transaction, I suddenly heard the bell chime as two high-level players sauntered into the store. One of them was a big guy with the unimaginative nickname "Big Guy" above his head, who was clad in a Knight's armor with so many mechanisms bolted onto it that it reminded me of the Brotherhood of Steel from the Fallout universe. The second player was a red-haired woman in tight leather clothing, who was also wearing the kind of classic armored bra that was such a popular subject for jokes in RPG comics. And while the Knight's nickname didn't tell me anything about him at all (anything, at least, that I couldn't already see for myself), I had certainly heard of Trish Merisilver before. She was Mark's sister, one of the "Spirit of the Hunt's" generals, and she was at a mind-blowing level 139.

What, I wondered, are the odds that they could have come in here by chance? I didn't even try to estimate the odds, actually, because I felt pretty sure that even modern AI would ignore a number with THAT many zeroes after the decimal point.

"Big Guy" remained by the entrance (as though there was actually a chance that I might somehow escape from a player almost a hundred levels stronger than me), while Trish made her way up to the counter. She stopped right next to me, shot me a sidelong glance, and with a faint note of curiosity in her voice she asked:

"They told me yesterday that the player we're looking for is at level 73. You're thirty levels short. How did you manage to fu... Uh, lose that many levels?"

She spoke with a soft, beguiling voice that was just a little bit hoarse, and which simultaneously radiated a powerful aura of sexuality and subtle mockery. The sort of woman who would probably have been a target for witch-hunters during the Middle Ages, and who a more recent generation might have referred to as a "red devil."

"Is it really that hard to do?" I asked as I frantically tried to figure out whether there was any way they could attack me right there in the store. In theory, it was supposed to be a safe zone, but nothing was ever absolute in Arktania — players at that level might have artifacts or abilities up their sleeves that could get around such a limitation. "Just a couple unlucky decisions."

I could see a flicker of interest in the woman's green eyes, and suddenly I got the sense that she probably wouldn't be getting aggressive with me. At least for the time being.

"Interesting. Apparently, one of those decisions must have made you an enemy of "Spirit of the Hunt" as well? You know — the most powerful clan in Arktania?"

"Um, no, actually. I was barely involved in that at all."

"I'd be interested to hear the details."

"So you don't know why your Clan is hunting me?" I was surprised.

"No, I don't, and it really annoys me," she agreed. "Especially considering the fact that you're friends with my little brother."

"How do you know that?" I blurted out before I could think about whether it was the right thing to say.

"He told me. Mark doesn't come to me for help very often, but recently he called me out of the blue and asked me to take a certain person off the Clan's blacklist, or at least order my own people to leave him alone. Can you imagine how surprised I was when I saw your name at the very top of the list? A player who's only at level 73, no less. Even the leaders of the clans we're at war with couldn't compete with you in terms of priority. So I had to wonder — what could he possibly have done?"

Obviously, I knew exactly why the "Spirit of the Hunt" Clan was hunting me down, but I also knew it couldn't be explained in just a couple words. More importantly, though, would it actually be a good idea to tell her? If Mark's sister didn't know about Emissaries, she probably wouldn't believe my story without a real-life demonstration. Although my issues with "Spirit of the Hunt" weren't limited to just that...

"Well, for example, a couple players from your Clan once tried to blackmail me into giving them an egg with a legendary mount inside. And some people from the "Steel Rats" stole an epic artifact from me, then tried every dirty trick in the book to force me to share the task requirements for a very serious quest with them. If any of those people transferred allegiance to "Spirit of the Hunt," they might have shared that with your leadership."

"No, it's none of that," she replied with complete confidence. "Try again."

Trish Merisilver's manner of speaking made me a little bit nervous; it gave me a very strong impression that she was exerting some sort of unseen, unspoken influence over me. It wasn't anything like the total control over my will that the Curser had exerted; she wasn't trying to force me to answer, or even intimidate me. And yet somehow, I still felt a strange feeling of euphoria as I spoke to her. No system communications popped up to warn me, but even so, it all felt very suspicious.

"Why are you asking ME, though?" I asked as I reached into my inventory and grabbed the Heart of the Blizzard. It never ceased to amaze me — my mind cleared immediately, and it even became much easier to breathe. "You have a Clanleader. Go ask him."

She replied with a soft smile. It was a softness that belied the intensity of what she said next:

"He won't answer, and I can't pressure him. I can pressure you, though. I have questions that I want answered, and I think it's pretty obvious which of the two of you I'm going to ask."

I glanced down at her character's huge, armored bra, and thought that actually, there was a kind of pressure she could apply that I wouldn't mind at all. Wisely, however, I kept that little joke to myself.

"Why bother?" I shrugged. "Kill me if you want — I'll just lose another level. I don't have far to go to rock-bottom at level 30 anyway, so I guess I'll just stay there and keep getting killed."

Saying this, however, I suddenly froze as something dawned on me. Hold on, I thought! The game safeguards your level once you hit 30, and you can't drop below that no matter how many times you die. Without the ability to lose levels, will I even be ABLE to create a Great Blood Essence to resurrect Artyom?! Something tells me the answer's no. That goddamned uncle of mine really waited for the perfect moment to take those ten levels from me!

"I think I'll be able to come up with something," Mark's sister assured me. "You don't need to kill somebody to make it impossible for them to play. But someone who could do that could also make the game a lot easier for you if they wanted to." The "red devil" winked at me. "You just lost thirty levels, and you're a friend of my brother's. I could help you get those levels back pretty quickly."

Okay, I thought... Carrot and stick at the same time. I just have to pick which one I'm going to work with. Or at least that's what Mark's sister was obviously thinking. Both options were pretty unappealing for me, though, even despite the fact that I really needed to rack up seven levels in the shortest possible time. You might say it was a result of my psychological trauma, but I felt completely unable to trust anybody who served as representative of a clan. More than that, I didn't feel like I could trust any player who still thought of Arktania as nothing but a game. And even with those conditions met, I still had to think thrice before I would trust anybody at all.

"Maybe I'll just stop playing for a little while, and that'll be the end of discussion," I said. It was my best attempt to walk away from the entire situation and leave both the carrot and the stick lying on the table behind me. "Nice to meet you. I never would have expected Mark's sister to be... Well, like *you*, I guess. But I'm really busy."

Apparently, Trish Merisilver was genuinely surprised by my response.

"Whoa. My Charisma usually makes people a lot more talkative, especially at such a low level. But that's fine. No need to run away — we'll leave. Add me as a contact just in case, though. If you need help, or you want to vent about your problems to someone, just hit me up."

"I've got a personal psychologist now?" I asked.

"Let's call it part of your support network," she chuckled. "Good luck. You're obviously going to need it, since you're at the top of our blacklist. The owner of this shop tipped us off right away. We only came to handle it because we happened to be close by."

I glared back at the Gnome, who just shrugged in reply as if to say "nothing personal, man — just business."

"Well, time for me to get going, then," I concluded. "Nice to meet you. Have a good one."

Pulling out a teleportation scroll as I walked, I hopped quickly out the door and activated it immediately to teleport myself to the instance entrance. Thankfully, nobody tried to stop me, and I managed to step straight into the portal. The way things were going, it seemed like these little teleportations would be the only way I could safely move around in a major city. It would be expensive as hell, but at least it would be relatively safe.

I said a quick mental hello to my first instance.

The open manhole cover and the crowd of players surrounding it brought back memories of the last time I had visited the place. I was really hoping that this visit would be entirely different. The last thing I needed was another breach from the Inferno.

Instance "Katar's Sewers for Beginners.".
Restrictions: level 35 or higher, groups of 1-5 players.
Visits allowed per day (for a player with the title of Count): 5.

So... I had a privilege at my disposal, and it would have been a shame not to use it. The ability to visit the instance no less than five times a day. I was about to learn how much experience I could rack up in one visit.

I jumped into the manhole, and right before landing I used a small burst of repulsion to avoid taking any damage from the fall. See, I thought? Once in a while, I actually manage to learn something from my mistakes.

I took a deep breath, and couldn't resist a smile.

"Good old sewer."

After summoning Spin and Chaosite, I belatedly remembered that I had forgotten to feed the latter. And his aura would really come in handy when it came time to face the boss in the sewer.

Spin had grown quite a bit since our previous visit, with the result that he was able to illuminate the place better than any torch, so I didn't order him to switch into his beast form. Chaosite was also providing a little purple glow of his own, but otherwise he wasn't much use. And with his satiation meter at a mere 40%, neither were his aura or his passive ability to search for Chaos. If we needed to find an exit, though, he'd still be able to sense it, as long as it wasn't more than forty steps away.

Strange as it may sound, I had a crystal-clear memory of which enemies were hiding where. So when Spin's light fell on a "Small Sabertoothed Rat, level 32," I slapped it with a Paralyzing Electric Chain almost instantly. It died after a few blasts of lightning and gave me a tiny little portion of experience.

"News of the Godlike Hammer of the Jerboas has spread to all of Arktania's rodents. Rats and mice at your level or lower will no longer risk confrontation with you, and will flee in horror at your approach. Rats and mice above your level will think twice before crossing paths with a killer as bloodthirsty as you."

This was the first rat I had killed in the instance, and I could tell it would probably end up being the last as well. Oh well, I thought. Hopefully I'll have better luck with the frogs. Especially since the radius of my spells can now reach farther than the "Acid Growlers" could spit. Sure enough, I was right: I had no trouble killing the sewer frogs, and before long I found myself at the entrance to the next stage of the instance.

Loner Book Eight

The crocodiles on the level below were even easier to deal with. Sure, they could attack with lightning-quick lunges, but after I used my Magnetic Sensitivity to find some steel components buried in the ceiling above me, I was able to attach myself to the ceiling, well out of their range, and take them out quickly and efficiently from above.

I didn't even bother attaching a respawn point to the instance — it was actually that easy.

I had never seen the third stage of the instance before, of course, since that's where the breach from the Inferno had appeared before my previous visit. As a result, I didn't know what I was walking into as I descended even further into the bowels of the sewers. It turned out to be a blizzard of flying lizards. Tons of them, all emitting horrible high-pitched shrieks and dealing damage with claws and disgusting squirts of highly-acidic guano. Not the most pleasant opponents for a player without decent defense, who relied on mobility to take down his opponents. My Micro Chaos Shield didn't help against the little beasts at all, since it was only a foot in diameter and only worked against magical damage. And obviously, the little bastards that kept screaming their way toward me through the air were dealing damage of a totally different kind. Nevertheless, I found a way out of the inconvenient situation by using Improved Repulsion to prevent the lizards from getting close enough to hurt me, then killing them with Concentrated Lightning Webs that could deal damage to several beasts at the same time.

The Sands of Eternity

The fourth stage greeted me with a big arena, obviously signalling a battle with a boss who, pretty predictably, turned out to be a massive snake. The floor of the arena was a big puddle, which made moving around pretty difficult even though it was only about a foot and a half deep. The ceiling wasn't an option either; almost as if to spite me, there were no steel components inside it at all. Deciding it was best to play it safe, I turned Spin into his Wolf form. His Thunder Bark would give me at least a few moments' warning if I needed it.

A huge gate at the end of the hall, as tall as three people stacked head to toe, slowly began to slide upward in order to release the monster. I couldn't help thinking that if the snake inside was anywhere near as big as the gate, I might be in for some very serious problems.

"The gate's mechanism!" The quiet voice in my mind had decided to intervene once again.

But what did that mean? Ah, I thought — of course!

I used a maximally-powerful blast of Repulsion to jump forward out of the water and get myself close to the gates. As I landed, I caught a glimpse of a big, green body almost three feet in diameter. I was afraid to even imagine how long the snake might be.

"Sawtooth Snake, level 60," the system obligingly informed me.

As soon as it noticed me, the beast slipped its head under the still-opening gate and rushed forward to attack me. I mentally ordered Spin to hit it right in the face with a Thunder Bark. For my part, I activated Power over Machines on the gate, although I didn't really expect it to work.

"Application of ability "Power over Machines" to the Gate to the Sanctuary of the Sawtooth Snake was 90% successful.
You may activate the following commands:
- open.
- close.

Close! Close!

The gate slammed down much faster than it had been sliding up, as if whatever was holding it had suddenly collapsed. CRUNCH! It slammed straight down on the snake when it was approximately halfway through the opening. The beast lost a quarter of its health instantly. More importantly, though, it was stuck!

I had my Whisper of Fate to thank for it all, of course — I would never have thought up that plan in the short interval while the gates were opening. Plus, Magnetic Sensitivity still wasn't showing any iron or steel anywhere around me, which meant that the gate mechanism was made of something else.

The rest of the battle lasted about five minutes. I kept at a safe distance and rained lightning down on the trapped snake, stopping only occasionally to refresh my mana with elixirs. When the beast's health dropped to 20%, it let out a hiss so loud

The Sands of Eternity

that my ears actually started bleeding. The sound made the water around my feet start roiling furiously; looking down, I saw that a whole swarm of smaller snakes was squirming in the murk. Dammit, I thought — this is disgusting!

You've taken 20 points of critical damage from Water Snake.

You've taken 5 points of damage from Water Snake.

You've taken 6 points of damage from Water Snake...

None of the bites caused much damage on its own, but there were dozens of the snakes, and losing thirty levels meant losing a lot of health, too — all I had to work with, even at full health, was a pitiful 500! That said, I managed to take out the smaller snakes really quickly by sending an Electric Shock into the water. Spin and I both had total immunity to electrical damage, but it fried the snakes like chicken fingers. That done, it was time to finish off the boss, which also proved to be pretty easy.

Killing the Sawtooth Snake gave me enough experience to hit level 44, and I got a couple artifacts, snake teeth, and some snake hide as well. I guess these could be used to make some sort of equipment, although it seemed pretty unlikely that it would be useful to a player like me.

All in all, the instance didn't take up very much of my time, so when I walked through the boss' gate and found a small chest full of money right next to a stone that would teleport me to the exit, I decided to use the rest of my visits right away. I knew the tactics I would need to use against all the different opponents in the place, and I was positive that I could speed the process up even more. Sure enough, I finished the second run five minutes faster than the first. And the third time was seven minutes faster. Unfortunately, the instance didn't give very much experience, even when you completed it alone, because it was designed for players at (or just over) level 35. By the time I finished my last run for the day (number five), therefore, I had only managed to level up to 45.

I was so relaxed by the time I started the last run that I allowed Spin to take out all the opponents for me. With his level, that didn't present him with much of a challenge at all. We were already in the boss' arena when the surprise came. No sooner did we find ourselves inside than Chaosite, who had been floating uselessly in the air behind my back the entire time, suddenly floated out in front of us and turned into an arrow that was pointing somewhere off to the side of the snake's chamber. Nothing like this had happened on the first four runs, so I decided to check it out and see what my pet had found. Thus distracted, I failed to close the gate in time to trap the snake's tail.

"Dammit! What are the odds of that?!" I glared at Chaosite. "This is your fault!"

The Sands of Eternity

The Living Chaos Particle responded by turning into a smiley face; meanwhile, the enormous snake was all the way out of its den, and before I knew it the beast was rushing straight toward me. For the first time in all the runs through the instance, I found myself engaged in a fair fight (so to speak). Although given that the system had foreseen the possibility that the snake's tail could be trapped by the door, it wasn't really "unfair" to take advantage of it. I guess you could say it was a fair move, which was only an option for a very resourceful Electromage who had spent a long time developing Power over Machines. Whatever the case, I suddenly found myself facing an enormous opponent who was fifteen levels higher than me, and fighting as hard as possible.

The snake was at least fifty feet long, and its head was big enough that it could have swallowed me, Spin, and even Chaosite (if he'd had a material body to swallow in the first place). My main tactic, therefore, was to keep jumping around with Improved Repulsion and teleporting to the side with Shift. It was only when Spin's Thunder Bark actually worked on the snake that I could even think about attacking the beast with my lightning. The damage simply wasn't enough, and for the first time I started to realize why people never went up against instance bosses single handedly. Taking out such a massive, fast-moving beast without a well-balanced team was extremely problematic, to say the least.

The beast wasn't just trying to eat me, either;

it was also whipping its tail around with remarkable finesse, attacking me from the most unexpected angles time and time again. I had to keep jumping and jumping to avoid these attacks, but I still took two or three hits, each of which took away about a third of my health. I don't even know how I managed to find time to chug my elixirs, but that didn't really affect the overall situation. I felt like it was all I could do simply to dodge the snake's attacks; launching attacks of my own felt nigh-on impossible. It wasn't even a stalemate situation — it was obviously going to end in checkmate, and not for the snake. So it wasn't more than a few minutes before I finally decided to put all my chips on one final bet and use Ball Lightning. At some point, I thought, its random multiplier will give me the maximum possible damage. What better time than right now?

I jumped as far back as I could, then ordered Spin to use Thunder Bark to slow the snake down. I chugged an elixir to replenish my mana, said a quick prayer to the Goddess of Fate, and activated my ability.

The resulting flash was so bright that it literally blinded me for a minute. When my vision finally returned, I saw the snake's bleeding torso lying inert in the water in front of me. Its head had been totally vaporized.

"You've dealt 4200 points of electrical damage."
You've killed an opponent whose level was significantly higher than yours with a single blow, and

thereby earned the achievement "Lucky Goliath."

Permanent +10% bonus to damage inflicted on opponents at a higher level than your own (only in cases when they are at least 10 levels higher).

I knew that my luck would have to turn around sooner or later, but I was still hoping that I hadn't exhausted it all with that single blast of Ball Lightning. I didn't level up, of course, but I didn't end up losing any of the experience I had accumulated either, and that was more than enough for me.

After collecting everything the snake dropped and emptying yet another small chest of gold, I returned to the spot where Chaosite had noticed something unusual. With apparent eagerness, he turned back into a spark-sputtering arrow and pointed out the spot a little more precisely than before. The stone wall didn't seem to stand out in any way, but Chaosite floated over to it and started letting off more sparks than before. As he got closer, his purple light revealed a barely-visible niche in the wall. I stretched out a hand to feel the wall and discovered something like a keyhole, but of course I didn't have the key. The snake hadn't dropped anything that seemed suitable, and there was never anything but money in the little chests at the end of the battle.

I couldn't feel any iron in the walls with my Magnetic Sensitivity, either; as with the gate in the boss' arena, all the mechanisms involved seemed to be made of stone. So I activated a different ability:

"Application of ability "Power over Machines" to this hidden door was 90% successful.
You may activate the following commands:
- open.

Obviously, I thought — open!

The stone in front of me slid to the side with a heavy scraping sound and revealed a steep staircase leading down deeper into the underground. I took a step forward and instantly received a system communication:

You've entered a hidden level in the instance "Katar's Sewers for Beginners."
Visits allowed: 1. Failing this level once will render it off-limits to you forever.
Are you sure you want to enter?

Pff, I thought... Of course!

Chapter 9

IF THERE WAS ONE THING I wasn't expecting from this instance, even knowing that I had entered a hidden level, it was an attack right there on the staircase. Usually, players had at least a small amount of time to get used to the new territory, as well as a tiny safe zone right at the entrance to the instance that would give them a place to retreat to and regroup in case things got too dangerous. This time, though, I barely took two steps down the narrow stairs before a spear shot out of the wall to my right and punched straight through my leg, pinning it in the air halfway through a step.

"You've taken 50 points of critical damage."

Whoa, I thought — a trap? And such a powerful one? I mean, I'm not even three steps into the instance and I'm already gritting my teeth and chugging a healing elixir. Strange, especially since the main instance didn't have any traps at all — just monsters.

After examining the passage and the stairway with Magnetic Sensitivity, I realized to my dismay that I had no ability to detect these traps, since every part of the walls was made entirely of stone. So all I could do was guess; maybe that spear trap was one-of-a-kind, maybe there were traps absolutely everywhere. I soon discovered that the latter guess would have been correct, since I started getting hit with all sorts of different attacks on literally every step. Perhaps most annoying of all, my divine sense of danger wasn't giving me any hints at all. Presumably, that was because the damage I was taking from these traps wasn't actually lethal; it was just extremely unpleasant. Stone spears and arrows, spikes, fire — everything came shooting out at me from all sides, and from all angles, in such a random sequence that there was no way I could even begin to identify a pattern and start dodging the attacks. Even my attempts to interfere with the mechanisms behind the traps didn't do me any good. It started to feel like all these traps had been designed especially to counter my abilities: they all operated on magic, and none of them incorporated even a tiny piece of iron or steel. The most I could do, therefore, was try to smack their projectiles aside with Repulsion (projectiles which ran the gamut from huge, heavy spears to blizzards of stone grapeshot) and use Shift to move

around within the narrow confines of the staircase. Worst of all were the traps that belched out
a huge ball of fire; thankfully, I had pretty decent
resistance to it from kissing the Succubus, but it
still inflicted some intense pain that was far from
easy to ignore. Chaosite was absolutely no use in
a situation like this, and using Spin to disarm the
traps wasn't an option either, since they didn't react to my pet in the slightest even when he was in
his wolf form.

Also, as if to spite me, the steps just kept going
and going, leading me further and further into the
bowels of the earth. It gave me the impression that
the traps had been specially designed to make
players burn through a certain number of healing
elixirs before they got to the bottom of the stairs. I
had filled my inventory with them to the absolute
brim, but my supply was still finite, and before
long I started to get nervous. After all, I still didn't
have any idea what might be waiting for me up
ahead. Maybe the entire challenge was simply
making it down the seemingly-endless staircase?
Maybe there would just be a nice, simple door
leading me out of the instance right at the bottom
of the staircase? Sure, I thought — keep dreaming.
That kind of thing never happens, or at least it
never happens to me.

As always, Arktania managed to surprise me:
when I got down to twenty healing elixirs in my
inventory, the staircase came to an abrupt end. It
turns out I was right about its length being deter-
mined by my supply of healing elixirs, because as

soon as I finished my 21st bottle, the stone staircase in front of me literally dissolved into the air and reformed itself into a flat, open floor. I took my first careful step into the darkness, holding a Micro Chaos Shield in front of me as I prepared to use Shift to duck to the side at any moment. Almost immediately, however, a bright flash of light burst out from above and gave me the chance to look around. I found myself in a big cavern with a towering ceiling; it was shaped like an arena, except that instead of stands for the audience there were huge walls that soared all the way up to the ceiling, pockmarked with a huge number of black, yawning caves. It was hard to tell from a distance, but I'd say each of the caves was probably about as tall as a full-grown man.

"You've entered the Anaconda's cave.

Task: withstand as many waves of opponents as you can without dying.

Reward: experience for every wave (100,000 x number of last successfully-completed wave), random unique artifact with quality 10 x number of last successfully-completed wave. Reward will be calculated after the trial is complete.

No penalty for death."

The first thing that caught my attention, of course, was the experience reward. Holy shit, I thought — I'll level up four times if I can survive ten waves! From there, I'll be almost at fifty! And I might well make up that difference with the experience I get for killing individual opponents. Needless to say, this would solve my problem nicely — most importantly, I wouldn't have to find any more safe places to level up. That would be a huge load off my mind, because "Spirit of the Hunt" was still on my tail, and I could potentially cross paths with its enforcers in pretty much any part of Arktania. Thankfully, Pyrenth would be off-limits for teleportation during the event with the flying coffins, which meant that I would only have to deal with players who happened to be in the city already at the time the event started. Mind you, it would be a simple matter for us to unleash a wave of chaos that would be more than enough to distract anybody the Clan might send after us. We could just knock down a few coffins, and our pursuers would have their hands full immediately.

The next thing I noticed was the lack of any penalty for dying, which made me sigh with relief. I really didn't want to lose the levels that I had just acquired, especially by wandering into a trial that was a guarantee of certain death. Normally, minigames like this would entail waves of opponents coming at you from multiple sides and getting stronger with every successive wave. And my situation was shaping up to be pretty similar. I was standing in the center of a closed-off arena, surrounded by caves from which my opponents would obviously start appearing before too long.

Which, of course, is exactly what happened: without any warning messages or counters appearing on my interface, several enormous serpents suddenly poked their heads out of some of the caves, which were about ten or twelve feet above the ground. They looked a little bit different than the boss in the main instance had, although they were almost just as big. With their flat noses and thick bodies, they basically looked like normal anacondas (except, of course, for their size). There were only three of them, but even that seemed pretty intense for the first wave. I knew I would have a hell of a time fighting them off if they launched a simultaneous, coordinated attack, and this was only the beginning of the trial.

For some reason, though, the snakes didn't seem to be in any hurry to attack — in fact, they stopped slithering as soon as the bases of their heads were outside their caves. Then, all at once, they opened their mouths, and... Spat out a bunch of half-digested human corpses, which were covered in some sort of yellow bile or stomach acid. Their disgusting task complete, the snakes' heads ducked straight back into their caves, as if they had forgotten I was even there.

So, I thought... What the hell was that?

The long-awaited system communication popped up in answer to my question:

"Start first wave."

Naturally, I had already guessed that these poor half-eaten bastards hadn't appeared for no reason, but somehow they didn't look like powerful opponents at all. Figuring that it might be a good idea to take a closer look, I stepped carefully toward them until I was about ten feet away from the nearest one. I held my breath so as not to catch a noseful of the stench of acid-soaked rotting flesh as I examined the corroded corpse. Putting it mildly, it wasn't exactly a pretty sight: I could see glimpses of exposed muscle and tendon through the person's badly-dissolved clothing, but there was no skin left on their body at all. Its face reminded me more than anything of a freshly-made mummy, who had somehow managed to hang onto one of its eyes, as well as a tongue that was still hanging from its mouth (although it had been badly burned by the snake's stomach acid). Suddenly, that one remaining eye twitched and focused itself on my face. The corpse's mouth opened and began to speak in a hoarse gurgle:

"Help..."

Ugh, I thought... What the hell is this?! Without even meaning to, I began to back away from the revolting sight.

"Kill-ll me-ee..." The poor bastard kept gurgling as a dark-red info bar appeared above its head: "Victim, level 20."

I didn't need much persuading. Even knowing that this was an NPC, rather than a real person, I would have felt bad leaving them alive in such miserable condition, especially since I could actually see their body decomposing in front of my eyes — in fact, I saw their health bar drop from yellow to red as they staggered toward me. My impression was that the person would probably have died pretty quickly even without my help, but that would rob me of the experience I could probably get for killing them. So I took out my Shanbiao chain, in order to save mana, and swung a blow at the victim's head. Instead of meekly accepting the death they had asked for, though, the walking corpse (or rather, half-corpse? Demi-corpse, maybe?) reached up with surprisingly dexterity and snapped the chain's spearhead out of the air before it could land a killing blow.

"Help..." The victim repeated again, as if mocking me, before they turned and threw themselves at me.

"Ugh!" I blurted as the sudden movement finally made the poor bastard's tongue drop out of their head. I could see it all in excruciating detail, since the victim was running at me with arms spread wide when it happened. Apparently, they were about to wrap me up in a big, wet, revolting hug.

Dammit, I thought — absolutely not!

I used Shift, and suddenly I was right beside the half-eaten person and prepared to hit them with a serious attack. A blast of lightning literally blew their head apart like a ball of dryer lint and sent the body crumpling to the floor, where it disintegrated into several big chunks that kept crumbling into smaller and smaller pieces because of the acid. It all looked thoroughly disgusting, although I wasn't really paying attention by that point anyway — my attention was firmly focused on the other two half-digested corpses who were making their way toward me. They had already risen to their feet like the first victim had, and were actively decomposing as they raced toward me.

"Hell-llp..."

The only thing I could do to help them was to put an end to their suffering, and that's exactly what I did: two blasts of lightning blew their heads to pieces and left their bodies to crumble into piles of half-rotten flesh on the floor in front of me. Aiming at their heads, by the way, was pure instinct — the result of having watched a huge number of zombie movies. Thankfully, it worked perfectly against these opponents too. Although I have to admit, the fact that they had asked for help was a little bit off-putting...

After killing all my opponents, I found a small piece of low-quality armor lying on the floor where their bodies had been. Naturally, I picked it up; everything has its use, after all. Nothing at all happened for a few minutes after that; apparently, this time was for recovery between waves, but I hadn't really exerted myself too much, so I didn't bother taking out any elixirs.

"Start second wave."

I already knew that I would probably be fighting more people that the anacondas had eaten (but not fully digested). They certainly didn't seem like very serious opponents so far, but then again, I had only just started the trial. Who could say what else the snakes might have eaten? It was far too early to get complacent.

The second wave started with no fewer than six snakes, who emerged, spat out their human vomit, and then retreated again. I already knew that these people would soon be on their feet and lunging toward me, so I figured I would make the first move myself. I blew the first victim's head apart with lightning, but the second one suddenly leapt up and jumped to the side (with surprising agility for a hunk of flesh rotting in a bath of stomach acid).

"Help..." The second victim gurgled, before it suddenly whipped a dagger at me. I hadn't been expecting an attack like that, and I failed to dodge in time. I took a small amount of damage, but I fired back right away with some lightning. That was no longer enough, since this "victim" was at level 25, but thankfully Spin fired a killing blow right after me. To be honest, I had kind of forgotten about him in recent days, but thanks to his impressive level he was one of the pillars of my attack strategy. The wolf simply jumped, knocked my opponent off their feet, and hit them in the face with his clawed paw so violently that it tore the "victim's" head clean off.

"Good boy," I said. Almost imperceptibly, his little tail started wagging, and I could sense a little wave of pleasure emanating from him through our mental connection.

Meanwhile, the four remaining opponents were already running toward us; one of them let loose a small fireball, which I managed to block

The Sands of Eternity

with my Micro Chaos Shield. Spin and I took this second batch of enemies out without too much difficulty, but the third wave had me worried as soon as it arrived: this time, the snakes spat out twelve bodies, all at level 30, which made it pretty easy to deduce a very worrying general pattern. The next opponents would be five levels higher, and there would be twice as many of them. Most concerning, though, was the fact that all these "victims" had different abilities and a wide variety of weapons. I couldn't even begin to imagine how they had all ended up in the snakes' bellies together. It all seemed so illogical; after all, if they had weapons (like, for example, the guy whose two razor-sharp daggers I picked up after the third wave), why hadn't they simply cut their way out of the snakes' stomachs from the inside? Unless of course they were all somehow immobilized by poison while they were inside the snakes — possibly the very same slime that covered them all from head to toe.

All these thoughts were bouncing around somewhere in the background as I ran into the fray against another batch of "victims." This time, I spotted Elvish features among the half-digested unfortunates in the crowd: delicate bone structures, and even the occasional sharp-pointed ear that had somehow escaped the ravages of the acid. Somehow, they had managed to get swallowed along with their bows and arrows, which meant that they were soon raining down an incessant shower of arrows onto our heads as they groaned for help and begged us to give them a quick death.

I was able to blast some of the arrows aside with Improved Repulsion, and then I used Shift a couple times and managed to kill a few of the Elves, but the rest were still keeping up the same murderous rate of fire with the inhuman persistence of the undead.

"Why don't you help yourselves?" I grumbled as I jumped and ducked in my attempts to dodge as many of the arrows as I could. "Smash your heads against the walls or something!"

Spin barked and immobilized two of the victims, which allowed me to dispatch them immediately. As if to spite me, however, this wave of opponents had appeared from all different sides of the arena, and as Archers that gave them an enormous advantage. As a result, they hit me with a couple arrows that inflicted serious critical damage, and I very nearly died. Only by some miracle did I manage to chug some healing elixirs; by the time we finished off the wave of Elves, I only had sixteen bottles left. I decided to use the pause between waves to good effect, searching every one of the dead Elves for valuable trophies. But all I got for my efforts was a single bow, just as the system had promised. The idea of jumping out of the arena and into one of the caves occurred to me, but a whisper in my mind quickly put paid to that idea: "You must not. You would be eaten immediately." Okay, I thought... I guess I'll save that option for a last resort, then. If I'm going to die anyway, I may as well, and it'll be a good chance to check whether Whisper of Fate can ever be mistaken.

As I had feared, the next wave consisted of 24 opponents, all at level 35. These looked quite a bit bigger than the Elves, and they were actually much better preserved, as if they had partial immunity to poisons or something like that. Their health bars were almost in the middle of the yellow zone. Soon, I could see the characteristic flashes of green skin and minimal, makeshift clothing that gave them away as Orcs. The worst thing about the situation was that if we had been in a more confined space, I probably could have beaten even THIS group of enemies. Here in the arena, though, they would probably just stomp me into the ground. Thankfully, though, they weren't coming on in a coordinated wave. They all came rushing at me in berserker mode, rushing toward me headlong in a big, disorganized crowd (although a few of them still managed to hurl axes and spears at me as they came). At least there didn't seem to be any shamans in the crowd.

"Kill me!" The Orcs began to grunt. And when THEY said this, it didn't sound like a plea so much as a challenge.

With a quick jump to allow all the projectiles to crash into the stone beneath my feet, then another jump to take aim, I whipped a Concentrated Lightning Web at several Orcs simultaneously. Spin plunged into the crowd and started ripping away at their flesh with his teeth. The Orcs didn't even seem to notice him, though; it was like they had chosen me as their one and only target, to the total exclusion of all others. Chaosite... Well, Chaosite was just floating there in the air, although he was doing his best to look threatening by emitting sparks as well as his usual purple glow. True, this didn't do anything besides add some interesting visual effects to the scene, since he didn't have enough Chaos to activate his aura for any appreciable length of time. Besides, I was saving what energy he DID have for an emergency.

I landed, pushed the nearest Orcs away from me, grabbed one more and paralyzed it with my Paralyzing Electric Chain, then used Shift to dodge another flurry of blows and put some more distance between myself and my enemies. And basically, that was my plan: run circles around the Orcs and spray them with lightning until they died from the effects of the snakes' acid or Spin's attacks. Improved Repulsion allowed me to make the occasional magic-powered jump to get away from any pursuers who got too close.

"Kill me!" The Orcs kept snarling as they rushed along after me in a big crowd with Spin nipping at their heels (almost literally, in this case).

Despite all my cleverness and quick dodging, however, I was still taking damage. From time to time one or another of the Orcs would manage to hit me with some fast-moving ability like "Lunge" or plant an axe or spear somewhere in my body after picking it up from the floor. Even though the slime seemed to deprive these "victims" of their willpower, it left them with at least some of their reflexes intact. Which, by the way, was further evidenced by the way they used their abilities. I had already taken down seven Orcs when it suddenly occurred to me that they weren't the only ones who could pick up the spears on the ground. Why couldn't I try the same thing — especially given that their spears were made entirely of iron? Not that I had any intention of using the spears to fight, mind you; instead, I figured I could try to throw them into the walls and then use them as a support to hang or pivot. I already knew that the caves were off-limits, but I wasn't too proud to hang in the air next to them. And if I could slam several spears into the walls, my Magnetism would give me a lot more mobility and offer me a place to hide from any opponents who didn't have range attacks at their disposal. It took me a little while to snap up a couple spears, and a little while more before I finally threw one hard enough to make it stick into the wall. I finally managed it by using Repulsion and Magnetism together to give the spear an extra boost in velocity. I was worried that the stone might turn out to be too hard, but no — the spearpoint buried itself into the wall about eighteen feet above the ground.

Perfect!

A quick jump, and there I was, hanging in the air without expending any effort at all. My hands were simply magnetized onto the spear. Then I pushed off, jumped again, and slammed the next spear into the wall well above the first one. After three such jumps, I found myself about thirty feet above the ground, almost close enough to touch the ceiling. From there, I had no trouble slapping away the spears and axes of the Orcs below me. That said, I took a quick look around the arena and suddenly noticed that Spin wasn't attacking the Orcs anymore. Instead, he was lying off to the side, huffing and puffing and shaking his little head. I glanced at his icon on my interface and noticed the word "poisoned" next to it. He wasn't responding to my commands; in fact, I couldn't even get so much as an emotional reaction from him, no matter how hard I tried. I looked closer, and quickly figured out what the problem was. The slime. Not surprisingly, my little wolf had gotten thoroughly drenched in the stuff as he was biting the Orcs, and now its baleful effects were robbing him of his self-control. True, he didn't seem like he was going to start attacking me, but one of these big snakes was obviously trying to take control of the freedom-loving lightning wolf and break his will to resist.

As if that weren't enough, the Orcs had started stacking themselves into a living tower in order to reach me. They weren't doing it like a bunch of thinking, sentient beings would do it, either — instead, it was like a big pack of insects, pushing, grabbing, and climbing on top of each other in a mad dash to stack themselves as high as they could. They were actually damaging one another pretty frequently, sometimes even tearing off parts of each others' bodies. Not that any of this was much of a problem for me, of course; a little blast of Repulsion sent the tower tumbling right back down to the ground. As they made their next attempt to reach me, I decided this would be a good opportunity to start methodically killing my opponents, rather than simply knocking them down. I was just about to strike a blow as the first Orc came within range, but then suddenly — and with enormous difficulty — he began to snarl:

"Help... Slime... Get it off!"

I was so surprised to hear the Orc say something besides "kill me" or "help" that I didn't immediately register what he had said. To be fair to me, though, he was still swinging his axe in my face as he said it.

"The slime... Controls..."

I had already figured that out, of course. No surprises there. It was obvious that the stomach acid wasn't simply digesting its victims, but also forcing them to defend themselves, and even obey the snakes' commands. But that knowledge wasn't really very useful, since I had no way to get rid of the slime anyway. Had I been an Aquamage, I might have had some trick up my sleeve that could have done it, but what could an Electromage do in a situation like this?

"I don't have anything to clean it off with!" I shouted back as I fought off the Orc's attacks.

"Healing... Elixir!" He growled. "Pour it!"

Just at that moment, someone yanked the Orc's leg from below and sent him plummeting down, then took his place before he even hit the ground. I didn't feel bad firing a big blast of lightning into this new Orc's face. The critical damage literally blew the big bastard's head off and sent his body rolling down to the bottom of the living staircase below. I knocked the remaining Orcs down with another burst of Repulsion, just to give myself the chance to think about what I had heard. If the Orc was right, and a healing elixir could wash away the slime, then the best move would undoubtedly be to test the idea out on Spin. I really didn't want him to succumb to the snake's will and start attacking me. Then, if that worked, I could treat the talkative Orc who had given me the tip in the first place. He obviously wasn't just another run-of-the-mill character, given that he had somehow managed to resist the snakes' influence well enough to pass on such a valuable piece of information. Thankfully, I remembered his appearance very well: he was the only Orc who still had a long braid of hair attached to his head, which made him look kind of like a strange, rotten pineapple.

After replenishing my own health and mana, I pushed myself off the wall as hard as I could with Repulsion and jumped over the heads of the Orcs below. After dampening the force of my landing with Repulsion (as I was well used to doing by that point), I ran up to Spin and dumped some healing elixir over his head. He replied with a surge of joyful emotion, and his icon flashed back into life once again. Okay, I thought... The Orc wasn't lying.

Spin dashed forward immediately to put himself between me and the oncoming Orcs, then hit them with a Thunder Bark that stunned some of them for a few seconds. I took advantage of this to fire several blasts of lightning that killed a few more of my decomposing opponents. By the time the Stun debuff faded, there were only ten Orcs left, including the one with the braid. There was really no need to keep running from such a small crowd, so I just sicced Spin on them (after forbidding him from using his teeth to attack them) and ran forward into an attack of my own with the Shanbiao chain. Not to brag, but my sessions with Eidolon in the Tree of Fear had made me so good with the chain that I could take out more or less any "local" opponent in a close-quarters fight, as long as their level wasn't too much higher than my own. This was also thanks to Shift, and my ability to use Repulsion to bounce off any available surface — or to shove opponents away from me if they got too close. Taken together, these abilities made me highly mobile and maneuverable, as long as I had mana to use them.

I kept killing the Orcs one after the other, avoiding only the one with the braid. Once he was the only opponent left in play, I slapped him with a Paralyzing Electric Chain. While he was thus immobilized, I stepped closer and dumped some healing elixir onto his head. I was really worried that one bottle of elixir might not be enough, and that washing off such a huge body might require my entire supply, but it turned out I was wrong — the slime seemed to undergo some sort of chemical reaction when the elixir hit it. It basically just disappeared with a loud hiss.

My Paralyzing Chain's effect wore off just at the moment when the elixir finished washing the slime off. Instead of the gratitude I had expected, though, I heard a menacing growl:

"You killed my brothers!"

The furious Orc lunged at me, and was right next to me before I even realized what was going on, but using Shift had already become an instinct. Finding myself right next to him, I shot up off the ground using Repulsion, just to give myself a second to think. Already in midair, I watched as the Orc's level rose from 35 to 50, and the name next to his level changed from the nondescript "victim" to "One Noisy Jackal." A huge, two-handed axe appeared in the Orc's hands, and he started whirling it around as if it were no heavier than a pencil. Then he, too, jumped up off the ground and flew to catch up with me. I have no idea what kind of ability he was using, or how a half-digested Orc had so much goddamned energy, but he was flying hot on my heels in spite of all my attempts to lose him. Even Spin's Thunder Bark didn't have any effect on him at all. And as if that weren't enough, the system suddenly informed me that the fifth wave was starting.

Part 2

Jerboa Day

"I still can't believe this is actually happening," said Alexander as he slammed his fist down onto the table in front of him. "Why him, and not me?!"

"It's already been explained to you. The virtual Gods chose these Emissaries for themselves at some point," Sophia reminded him as she ran a soothing hand across his arm. "And we still don't know how it's all going to end. Who knows? Maybe he'll die of a hemorrhage in a few weeks or something. You never know what these capsules might be doing to their brains."

"Still, it's bullshit. I could do so much if I had my game powers in real life."

"Like what? All you have is combat skills anyway," the young woman reminded her husband-to-be.

"But this is MAGIC!" Alexander was genuinely upset now. "Actual magic! I mean, think what enhanced regeneration alone could do! Let alone strength! I could lift this table with two fingers if I had my character's strength!"

Almost unconsciously, he slipped his index and

middle fingers under the edge of the table... And easily ripped it off the bolts holding it to the ground.

"What the hell?!" Alexander shouted as his eyes widened.

It took the couple a minute to convince themselves that the guy's strength had actually increased, although he didn't get any divine quests even after the change.

"Wow... I guess there's still a lot we don't know," said Sophia. "But I DO know exactly who can answer our questions for us."

At "The Happy Vampire"

"Dressed in black from head to toe, a young woman flitted into the doorway of the morgue, then locked it as a happy smile spread across her face.

"Why, hello there, my lovelies," she crowed, looking out across the even rows of sterilized steel tables and the bodies lying on top of them. "I bet you're tired of lying around in here, aren't you? Any interest in taking a nice, long walk with a lovely young lady like me?"

One of the morgues at the Municipal Clinical Hospital in the city of Zhukovsky

"The candles in the basement were horribly smoky, to the point where the young man's eyes were so red and watery that he could barely see the pentagram in the center of the hall. But he knew that he couldn't allow anything to interrupt the process, since even the smallest mistake might cost him all the ingredients he had so painstakingly gathered together. The human heads laid out at the corners of the pentagram were whispering the text of his spell in unison with him, and a number of tiny, pig-like imps had already pressed themselves tightly against the room's walls. They could sense that a powerful demon was about to appear.

"Come on, already!" The gangly young man finally screamed as he raised his arms to the ceiling in frustration.

At that very moment, a portal began to open at the center of the pentagram. The leg of a lithe, athletic woman emerged from within it, with skin of such a deep shade of pinkish-red that you might have thought she had fallen asleep under a hot sun. Soon, however, the rest of the body appeared be-

hind it, and there was no longer any room for doubt: she was a Demoness. The Succubus was athletic, yet also strikingly curvy, with tight, black leather clothing that barely concealed those parts of the body that humans normally tried to keep covered. She straightened her back and glanced at her surroundings with evident disgust.

"What a hellhole," she purred. "How, you pitiful human, could you DARE to summon me into such a squalid place as this?" A long, black leather whip appeared in her hands. "I'll have to punish you for such a display of disrespect."

"You want to talk about respect?" The young man asked with a sardonic grin on his face; he waved a hand, and the Succubus fell to her knees and let out a shriek of pain. "I'm a Demonologist at the very highest rank." He held up a medallion hanging from his neck. "And you will carry out every one of my orders to the letter. You will be punished for any failures to comply or displays of disrespect. Have I made myself clear, Lamia?".

A basement somewhere in the suburbs of
Moscow

Chapter 1

I HAD TO KEEP RUNNING from the surprisingly-agile Orc behind me for quite a while; thankfully, though, every ability has its limits, and eventually he came to a sudden stop. At almost the same time, new snakes began to poke their heads out of the caves and spit out new batches of opponents; true to pattern, they were all at level 40. Judging by the tiny silhouettes, I was about to face a small army of Gnomes who had the misfortune of having turned into snake food.

"Enough running, you pathetic worm!" The Orc snarled in impotent fury.

Surprisingly, pouring the elixir over his head had not only halted the decomposition process, but simultaneously started regenerating him pretty quickly as well. I knew it probably had something to do with the increased regeneration rate that was typical of Orcs, or maybe with some sort of active ability. Whatever the case, he no longer looked like some leftover in a cannibal's fridge; with every passing minute, he was looking like a warrior who had come through a very difficult fight.

"Um, I SAVED you, in case you forgot!" I shouted as I ran ahead until there was enough distance between us for me to feel safe. "Ungrateful bastard!"

"Yeah — and you killed the rest of my brothers!" The Orc's furious roaring actually fit pretty well with his nickname, One Noisy Jackal, and the spraying saliva and double-headed axe rounded the whole image out pretty nicely. "Despicable worm! I'm going to tear your limbs from your body! I'll tear the heart from your chest and eat it in front of you!"

Okay, I thought... That nickname is perfect. This Orc looked just as muscular as the rest of his race, but his dimensions were noticeably smaller; he was more wiry than bulky, obviously oriented toward Dexterity as well as Strength. I also couldn't help but find it funny that the stomach acid had burned away all his clothing except for his loincloth. That particular item was invulnerable to damage.

"They were asking me to kill them," I reminded him from where I stood, still at a safe distance. "I just wanted to put an end to their suffering."

The Orc's glare didn't change in the least, but pretty soon he got distracted by the moans and groans coming from behind his back:

"Kill me!"

"Hell-llp..."

The Gnomes were on their feet and rushing to attack us, brandishing nasty-looking sickles. 48 opponents, all of them comparable to me in terms of level! I could only hope that they wouldn't end up having any explosives, mines, or firearms, because there wouldn't be a chance in hell of me making it through the wave if they did.

"I'll kill you as soon as I take care of these stinking midgets," the Orc growled as he brandished a fist at me; with that, he turned around and rushed toward the Gnomes with another furious roar: "Hey, pipsqueaks! I was just coming to shit all over your caves!"

Apparently, this shouting of his was actually some sort of ability: it aggroed all the Gnomes onto him almost instantly. Actually, it was almost a miracle that none of their aggro transferred to me, despite the fact that I was standing pretty close to the Orc when he shouted. Maybe it had to do with the fact that I wasn't a "pipsqueak." It finally gave me a chance to stop and let out a sigh of relief, mixed in with a healthy dose of happiness at the fact that the Orc had not only given me a break, but also drawn most of my other pursuers onto himself. No matter how many Gnomes he ended up killing before they eventually overwhelmed him, his presence would end up making my life at least a little bit easier. I would have preferred to play it safe and jump back up onto the wall of the cavern, so I could wait until the Orc actually died before putting myself in harm's way again. I mean, there didn't seem to be any possibility of reaching an agreement with him, although...

I double-checked my inventory to make sure that I still had the beads from that shaman who had been imprisoned in Kelevre. He had assured me that they could save my life if I showed them to other Orcs. Arktania always loves a sick joke, I thought; what if the shaman was joking or something? On the other hand, though... Well, what if he wasn't?

"Hey!" I shouted to the Orc as I slipped the beads onto my neck. "What say we join forces and try to get out of here alive?!"

The big beast swung his axe at full force, causing the thirty or so Gnomes who were hounding him to back away to avoid getting chopped clean in half. As he did so, however, he somehow still managed to catch sight of the Beads of the Great Shaman and recognize them. It was easy to forget it sometimes, but at the end of the day we were still living and fighting in a virtual world, which could certainly be forgiven for asking us to suspend disbelief once in a while.

"Only if I can kill you afterward!"

Okay, I thought... Not exactly the effect I was expecting these beads to have. But whatever. At least it's a start.

And it turned out to be not a moment too soon, either, because in the next instant a huge explosion erupted from beneath me and threw me off my improvised perch atop the spear I had thrust into the rock. Apparently, one of the Gnomes had managed to hang on to a supply of their beloved dynamite during their time in the snake's belly. I barely managed to use Shift in time to soften my fall, and when I regained my balance I found myself surrounded by Gnomes, who immediately sank so many blows into my body that my health plummeted straight into the red zone. I had to jump back off the ground like a grasshopper, and use a massive amount of mana to do so, just to put as much distance between me and them as possible.

"Kill me!" The Gnomes roared in unison as they hurled their huge axes through the air after me. They spun so methodically that for a second, I thought they almost looked like a big flurry of propellers. I turned on the axe that was headed straight for my face and responded immediately with a blast of Repulsion. Instead of knocking the flying weapon aside, however, it flipped it high up into the air and slammed it blade-first into the living rock of the ceiling. Sure, this wasn't a deliberate move on my part, but I was pretty pleased with it nonetheless — after all, it meant that there was something magnetic up on the ceiling. But I wasn't sure I had the mana to jump high enough to reach it.

After chugging a bottle each of healing and mana elixir, I took off running, ducking and dodging thrown axes as I tried to get away from the Gnomes. Several explosions shook the ground behind me, and a few axes ended up grazing me despite my best efforts, but as long as I could maintain the distance between us I knew I was relatively safe for the time being. I was really fortunate in that there were no archers or other shooters among the Gnomes, and that they were basically a bunch of melee fighters. Still, though, I knew that later waves would probably be full of archers, and that eventually I simply wouldn't be able to deal with such a huge number of opponents.

Strangely, Noisy Jackal was doing a pretty good job of fighting off the Gnomes. He actually thinned their number out by almost half, while I was spending all my energy simply trying to stay alive, unable to kill even a single one. If the Orc could have covered me somehow, I might have been able to cast lightning from behind his back, which would have helped the process go a whole lot smoother.

"Hey, get up on the wall!" I shouted to him. "Better for defense!"

"Orcs don't defend themselves!" Noisy Jackal barked back, swinging a vicious blow with his axe with each syllable he uttered. "Orcs aren't cowards! Orcs always attack!"

"Okay, you don't mince words, do you?" I muttered to myself.

I concluded that if I couldn't coordinate tactics with him, I'd just have to find somebody who was a little bit easier to persuade. I still had ten healing elixirs left, which meant that I could still free ten "victims" from the snakes' influence. This, by the way, made the purpose of the traps on the staircase abundantly clear: they were there to cut down the number of healing elixirs in your inventory to a reasonable number. If I had brought a hundred with me, for example, I could simply have assembled my own small army and let it do the work for me. As it was, though, I had to be very careful about how and when I used my elixirs. After all, the "victims" would only get more and more powerful with each successive wave, so using them all on the Gnomes in front of me would have been stupid. Choosing one of them who had explosives and bringing them over to my side, however... Well, that was a different story entirely.

The "victims" were all still ignoring my pet, so he just kept running along after the ones who were following me and doing them little bits of damage. At my command, he used Thunder Bark on a compact group of Gnomes, one of whom was wearing the remains of a black-and-red worksuit and holding a bundle of dynamite in his hands. Taking advantage of their stunned state, I rushed over to him and poured one of my precious elixirs onto his head. The Gnome's nickname changed to "Red the Blaster," and his level rose to 53 as his health slid slightly upward from the yellow zone into the green.

"Ugh, curse my beard..." The little bearded Gnome swore. Strange as it may sound, neither he nor the Orc seemed to have lost any hair to the snake's acid. "I'm free again, and I don't feel any of that horrible pain anymore! Thanks, man!"

Well, I thought... FINALLY! A reasonable reaction, and a little bit of gratitude.

"Now free the rest of my clansmen. They're the ones in black, with the red nugget sigils on their clothes. Screw the others."

As if to emphasize how serious he was, he clipped a stick of dynamite to each of the stunned Gnomes standing next to him, then ran away as fast as he could. I had no choice but to follow him, and a few seconds later the inevitable explosion crossed a few more "victims" off our list.

"Now let's go free my friends," the Gnome repeated in a businesslike tone of voice.

"Ah... I can't," I said, having decided not to explain that I was saving elixirs for myself and other, more powerful "victims" in the upcoming waves.

"What do you mean you can't?!" The Gnome snapped. "Listen, beanpole, you know where I'm gonna put my next stick of dynamite if you don't?!"

Yeah, I thought... That friendship didn't last long.

"The Orc already killed them all," I replied as quickly as I could. I was happy enough to blame everything on Noisy Jackal, given how ungrateful he was. "Look — he's already taken out almost all of them."

The Gnome's pupils contracted, and he stepped past me, walking slowly and methodically toward the Orc as he pulled a massive bundle of dynamite out of his inventory.

"Green-skinned son of a bitch..."

As I watched him trudge grimly into battle, I

realized that turning my only two allies in the instance against one another might not have been the best idea. That said, I was still thinking that I might be able to broker some kind of temporary alliance between the three of us. Using my Steel Handshake, for instance; so far, that had proven to be my most useless ability, but I figured that at some point or other it would end up proving its value. Trying to catch up to the Gnome and try to shake his hand was out of the question for the time being, however, partially because he was holding sparking, smoking bundles of dynamite in both hands.

"Die!" Red the Blaster screamed as he threw the huge pile of dynamite at the Orc and the other surviving Gnomes.

Apparently, I had guessed correctly when I said that Noisy Jackal had already killed all the Gnomes who were wearing black and red. Either that, or Red simply said "screw it" and blew his clansmen to bits along with the Orc. Whatever the case, the explosion was so powerful that all I could do was press myself against the ground and spare a thought for the Orc, who I knew had probably just been splattered all across the walls of the cave. If so, he certainly died a hero's death, because he wiped out almost the entire fifth wave for me before he went.

When the smoke cleared, however, I was amazed to see a still-living Orc lying amidst the rubble. Somehow, he had managed to jump out of the way of the dynamite and avoid being caught in the epicenter of the explosion. I can't even imagine what sort of abilities and/or attributes could have allowed him to take out so many opponents single-handedly AND react to a dynamite attack in time to survive. True, he was looking pretty worse for the wear: stunned, covered in wounds, with his health down to just a few points and no longer regenerating with the same unbelievable speed as before.

The Gnome pulled his pick out of his inventory and stepped toward the helpless Orc, obviously intending to finish the poor bastard off, but I stopped him before he could do it.

"No! We need him if we're going to get out of here alive!"

"Who's 'we'?" The Gnome asked. "And who are you anyway? Why should I listen to you?!"

"You and me — that's who "we" is. My name's Falk, nice to meet you," I said as I held out my hand.

The Gnome looked skeptical, but nevertheless he swung his pick up onto his shoulder and shook my hand. I activated my ability immediately. Sure, +100 standing with Gnomes wouldn't exactly move mountains for me, but it certainly wouldn't hurt my chances during negotiations either.

"You know our handshake?" The Gnome sounded surprised. "Hm... Some child of the mountains must have trusted you enough to disclose that secret to you. Reason enough not to kill you right after I kill this Orc, I suppose. Anyway, though — move aside."

The Sands of Eternity

Again, as with the beads, my handshake had turned out to have a pretty weak effect.

"The only way we're getting out of here alive is if we work together," I said hurriedly as I moved to block his path to the Orc once again. "In another minute, the snakes are going to come back and spit out a bunch more opponents. The two of us won't have a chance in hell."

The Gnome shot me a skeptical glance.

"But we'll cut them all down like grass if there's three of us, right?"

"Well, it certainly improves our chances," I replied firmly. "So I suggest you try to forget about your hatred of Orcs for the time being."

"Orcs?" Red the Blaster repeated. "I'm not some kind of racist. I don't have any problem with Orcs as a whole. I have a problem with THIS green-skinned bastard who just killed my clansmen."

Thankfully, the Orc was still stunned and basically at death's door, so he couldn't participate in our conversation. If he could have... Well, there wouldn't have been a conversation at all. Even lying inert on the floor, though, he somehow managed to shake the braid on his head and look reasonably menacing.

"They were under the Anacondas' control," I reminded him. "The Orc was just defending himself. If you need revenge, take it on the snakes."

The Gnome stared back at me in confusion.

"Snakes? There's only one snake here — the Anaconda."

"I've already seen dozens of heads. They come

"

and spit out — "

"There are dozens of heads, but only one snake," the irritated Gnome interrupted me. "And one enormous stomach, where the creatures that the snake devours," the Gnome's voice started to shake as he finished his sentence, "spend weeks in agony while being digested alive."

Meanwhile, the Orc's health finally rose out of the critical zone, and with immense difficulty he rose up off the ground.

"The Anaconda. The Devourer of Souls," he growled as he shook his head from side to side, trying to find his bearings again. "An ancient, terrifying creature. Ending up in its stomach is considered the worst possible punishment for criminals."

"Wow. So the fearless Orc is actually afraid of something?" The Gnome asked sarcastically. He seemed to have already reconsidered his plan to finish the Orc off.

"Orcs fear nothing," snapped Noisy Jackal. "That's why I'm here."

Maybe it was just me, but I could have sworn I heard a hint of sarcasm in his voice. Or maybe he was just stating the facts extremely bluntly, without implying any hidden meanings whatsoever.

"Stupid frogs," Red the Blaster scoffed.

"Stubby-legged weakling," the Orc snarled in response.

"Enough," I snapped. "Leave the insults for later. For now, we just need to do everything we

The Sands of Eternity

can to get out of here alive. Agreed?"

Both the Orc and the Gnome nodded reluctantly after a ve-eery long pause. Even then, though, nobody made any move to form a group. Apparently, my standing with both races was insufficient to get them to truly trust me, which meant that either of them would be at liberty to stick a knife in my back at any point.

"We should form a group and trust each other here," I reminded them, but they responded in nearly perfect unison:

"Dream on!"

"Yeah, right!"

And with that, the system sent me an announcement of its own:

"Start sixth wave."

Moving quickly, I handed the Orc a healing elixir so he could restore his health, then started glancing around frantically. The Anaconda's heads had already started spitting out new opponents. This time, it was humans, wearing both light and heavy armor. All of them were at level 45, just as I expected, but I was surprised (and beyond elated) to see that there were only 24 of them this time! Presumably, that meant that we would be seeing half as many opponents with every successive wave, rather than double!

"Quick!" I shouted at the Orc and the Gnome. "What are your strongest abilities?!"

I was worried that they would start squabbling

again, but apparently the Beads of the Great Shaman and my Steel Handshake were having the desired effect (belatedly, sure, but better late than never).

"I can shout to make any opponents within a thirty foot radius turn and attack me," the Orc replied as soon as he finished off his healing elixir. "And I can strengthen my armor in proportion to the amount of damage I take."

"I still have dynamite and mines left," the Gnome replied reluctantly. "I can amplify their power and attach them to my opponents. Unfortunately, I don't have any other weapons on me right now. Not counting the pick — that's not much use anyway."

I glanced around again. Thankfully, the bodies of all the "victims" we had killed were already completely dissolved, which allowed me to find and snap up the reward artifacts from the fourth and fifth waves: Orcish throwing axes and two-handed Gnomish sickles. After quickly darting out and picking them up, I handed them both to the Gnome.

"Choose."

Red the Blaster frowned.

"Nothing smaller?"

"I have an Elvish bow," I offered.

With a heavy sigh, and a look of unconcealed squeamishness, the Gnome reached out and picked up the Orcish axe. Meanwhile, the "victims" had already started rising to their feet and striking up the usual chorus:

The Sands of Eternity

"Kill me!"

"Save me!"

"End my sufferings!"

"Red — throw some mines around the Orc," I said. "Jackal — aggro them onto you as soon as the Gnome gets the mines in place. I'll distract the humans while you do."

I had eight healing elixirs left, but using one of them on these humans would have been rash, at least at the start of the wave. After all, there would be even more powerful opponents in the following waves. Besides, my own personal safety had to be top priority. I couldn't allow myself to die through a lack of caution.

24 opponents, all at one's own level, was not the kind of challenge that a run-of-the-mill player could reasonably expect to survive, especially in an empty arena. Not to mention the fact that the "victims" came in a wide variety of classes: they weren't all melee fighters. There were plenty of Archers, too, and even a number of Mages. Thankfully, the effects of the snake's stomach acid kept their movements chaotic and random. I ran through the cavern, drawing their attention with weak, inexpensive attacks in the hopes of aggroing them all onto me before I handed them off to the Orc. Several attack spells and arrows came flying at me as soon as I came within range, but Shift made it easy to dodge them. Next came a wave of melee fighters, who came running toward me at top speed and forced me to start jumping around the hall (because I knew I wouldn't stand a chance

against them in a close-quarters fight). I also ordered Spin to avoid getting entangled with the "victims" any more than absolutely necessary; I figured he would be most useful when it came to finishing off the wounded after they ran into the Gnome's mines.

"Ready!" The Gnome shouted. "Mines in place!"

I ran toward them, leading most of our enemies along behind me. As soon as I reached the spot where the Orc was standing, he let out a vicious roar that immediately attracted the "victims'" attention:

"Pitiful little humans! I was just coming to shit all over those shacks you call homes!"

Creativity obviously wasn't Noisy Jackal's strong suit, but the shout had its effect nonetheless. The "victims" turned and started rushing toward the Orc. Almost immediately, a series of explosions shook the cavern around us, and when the sound died down I heard the Gnome shouting with joy:

"Art — that's what that explosion was! A work of ART!"

Yeah, I thought... Like the Horror of Akatsuki.

Chapter 2

THERE WEREN'T VERY MANY "victims" left after the explosion, but somehow it also came very close to killing Noisy Jackal. His health was down in the red zone again, and I ordered Spin to help the poor Orc and save him from a couple of Mages who would otherwise have finished him off. After the wolf stunned them with Thunder Bark, I ran up and killed the first Mage with a pre-prepared Electric Shock, then wrapped the second one in an Electric Chain to make sure he didn't escape before I finished him off with lightning.

"Agh, just a little more would've done it..." The Gnome grumbled with genuine angst as he stared at the Orc through narrowed eyes. The look on his face alone was more than enough to betray his true feelings. The mines had clearly been placed a little too close to Noisy Jackal, and it was now equally clear that that was no accident.

"Come again?" I asked in a voice heavy with suspicion.

"I said just a little more would have done it," the Gnome said as his eyes disappeared beneath his bushy eyebrows. "Would have killed them all, I mean. Our enemies."

"I see..." I muttered skeptically as I poured a third bottle of my priceless healing elixir onto the Orc (including the one I had originally used to free him from the effects of the Anaconda's stomach acid). This Orc was costing me far too much considering the circumstances — especially since he was still refusing to form a group with me. On the other hand, of course, I had no idea how the next "victim" might react after I freed them from the snake's influence. At least the Orc was predictable.

After recovering, the Orc slapped his big green hand down onto my shoulder.

"Thanks for the healing, human. But I'm still going to kill you as soon as we get out of here."

"Of course," I agreed nonchalantly as I looked around the cavern. "I'm all in favor of you kicking ass and taking names. And you can kick mine, too, right after you kick the Anaconda's. Let's just focus on getting out of here before we start thinking about that."

We had finished off the sixth wave by that point, so I was looking for the trophy artifact. The bodies dissolved and disappeared pretty quickly, leaving a magical staff on the ground from one of the Mages. It turned out to be an artifact for a Fire

Mage. Something from a Water Mage would have been nice, but that would have made things far too simple. The Fire Mage's staff allowed me to cast fireballs with a pretty short cooldown period in between, which might have been nice except that they didn't really deal much damage at all — even less than my lightning was dealing after losing thirty levels. But it was still a lot better than the bow, which I didn't even know how to hold properly, let alone use.

"I'm out of mines," said the Gnome as he glanced demonstratively at my staff. "I still have some dynamite left, but not enough to take out all the opponents in these coming waves."

"That's not good," I replied as I quietly slid the artifact into my inventory. "We'll have to use the dynamite more efficiently than we used the mines. Although if we formed a group, we — "

"I'll be fine with my dynamite," the Gnome interrupted me.

He shot a sidelong glance at the Orc.

"Hey, greenskin — how about sacrificing yourself so a noble Gnome and a not-so-noble human can get through this one alive? It'd be a pretty heroic death if we strapped you with dynamite and let the Anaconda eat you."

The Orc spat contemptuously at his feet.

"The only thing an Orc sacrifices is someone like you, beneath a Blood Moon at the Altar of Gmorka. I'm not going to trade my life for yours. It wouldn't be a fair trade. Even together, you two aren't worth as much as me!"

Loner Book Eight

Ironclad logic — what can you say? The Gnome didn't seem to know how to respond.

I didn't manage to think of any feasible tactics for the three of us in the short time remaining before the start of the seventh wave (not that they would have listened to me even if I had). That said, I learned a little more from the Gnome about the Anaconda and the place where we were fighting. The many-headed snake used this cave as a nest to prepare food. It would vomit out the creatures it devoured into these caves so that it could feed them to its offspring later on. Naturally, I had wandered into the instance right as the Anaconda was about to hatch a bunch of tiny little snakes. As long as the "victims" were still alive, the stomach acid would devour them very slowly, which meant that the snake's offspring would have a chance to learn how to hunt. As soon as they killed a "victim" and started to devour the body, their mother's stomach acid would kick into action and turn the meat and bones into an easily-digestible porridge. With this in mind, it became pretty obvious that the mini-instance would involve meeting and defeating these children of the Anaconda, probably just before the giant snake itself. This realization calmed me down a little bit; after all, the "mother" snake was a legendary-grade monster, and it seemed unlikely that we could beat her even if we somehow managed to free every one of her "victims" and convince them to fight her alongside us. Simple math dictated that the baby snakes would comprise the eleventh wave, which would provide more than enough experience to get me to level 50. From there, I could get by without defeating the Anaconda.

"Start seventh wave."

I knew the next batch of enemies would be at level 50, but at least there would only be twelve of them.

When the snake spat them out, however, it took me a little while to figure out what exactly we were dealing with. I knew that the "victims" needed a little time to get their bearings before moving into an attack, so the Gnome, the Orc, and I each ran in a different direction, in order to attack as many of them as possible, just as soon as the game allowed us to do so. Nobody argued with me on that, and we managed to achieve some pretty cohesive teamwork even without having formed a group. As soon as the phrase "Summoner Mage, level 50" appeared above my opponent's head, I wrapped a Paralyzing Electric Chain around him, then took a moment to try to figure out what was going on. I killed my "victim" pretty quickly, as did the Orc and the Gnome, but the remaining nine Summoners had appeared in different parts of the arena, and by the time we finished off our respective opponents they had already surrounded themselves with protective magical barriers. These were the first "victims" who acted with any semblance of logical and tactical precision, and they were also the first to cast anything other than simple attack spells.

Each of them was wearing a robe decorated with the symbols of their element, along with depictions of various spirits and creatures. As soon as their barriers were up, lines of summoning runes began to glow across their surfaces, and some of these creatures started to appear in mid-air: fire elementals, gigantic wolves, black shadows, and even a huge Ogre made entirely of ice. Soon, we found ourselves facing a crowd of thirty beasts, each with its own unique array of powers!

Noisy Jackal rushed into battle with a savage roar, brandishing his heavy sickle at the Mage nearest to him, but an enormous ice giant suddenly appeared out of thin air in front of him and blocked his path. The sickle bit into the giant's icy shield with a loud crunch, but all that achieved was to force the giant to take a step back.

Meanwhile, almost all the other summoned creatures turned and started racing toward me. Only a few of them bothered to pay the Gnome any attention at all. The Orc was engrossed in his fight with the ice giant, and he obviously wasn't going to be available to help me any time soon. The crowd kept coming, and as I turned to look back at them I realized very clearly that I didn't want to take any unnecessary risks that might force me to use precious healing elixirs on myself. So I pumped about half of my available mana into Repulsion and jumped straight up, activating my Electric Chain as I did so in order to reach the axes embedded in the ceiling and pull myself up toward them. Thankfully, they were fixed firmly enough to hold my weight.

Armed only with the Fire Mage's staff I had so recently picked up, I started pouring fireballs down on the summoned creatures who were crowded together in the spot where I had just been standing. I was well outside their reach, but for some reason they still seemed to consider me their primary target. Although maybe it was my periodic attacks that kept them from redirecting their aggro to the Orc or the Gnome. The Orc was still hacking away at the Ogre, but the Gnome was in a relatively safe position that allowed him to start blowing up the creatures who were attacking him. That done, he was able to turn his attention to the Summoners themselves. It only took a little while and a couple more explosions to finish them all off, and every time a Mage died, the creatures they had summoned would disappear as well.

"Where are you going?!" The Orc roared in impotent fury as he watched the Ice Ogre disappear in front of his eyes. "I haven't beaten you yet!"

I thought about staying up on the ceiling until the next wave started, but I soon remembered that I had to drop down and pick up the artifact while it was safe to do so. More importantly, there would only be six "victims" in the next batch, and if we could attack them right as they appeared, we might be able to get rid of half of them before we even had to do any serious fighting. From there, we could pour elixir onto the remaining three and lure them onto our side, and do the same with all the "victims" in the two remaining waves. All that, and we'd still have a few elixirs left in store for our fight against the baby snakes.

"Well, you can go find that Ogre's cave and shit in it to your heart's content once we get out of here," said the Gnome acidly to the still-fuming Orc.

The seventh wave rewarded me with a decent piece of armor for a level-50 player. True, I was still only at 45, which meant I couldn't actually use it, but it was still a pretty good find.

"What a superb piece of armor," the Orc crowed as he caught sight of it. His eyes were almost literally shining with a desire to possess the artifact himself.

And really, I didn't have much use for the armor anyway, so I held it out to the Orc and watched as — oh, happy day! — his attitude toward me improved!

"Awesome!" The Orc shouted. "Orcs value gifts very highly when they're sincerely given. I know I can trust you now!"

An instant later, an offer to form a group with him suddenly popped up on my interface. Wow, I thought... Could it really have been that easy all along?

"Hey, Gnome — I saw you looking at this staff, right?" I called to Red. "Want it?"

The little pyromaniac didn't take much convincing, and sure enough, as soon as the artifact was in his hands, he added himself to our group. This meant I would no longer need to worry about catching a knife in the back, and it would also give me more ability to coordinate our actions.

I wondered, though — would the same thing work with higher-level "victims," too? If so, I could just give them some sort of artifact and avoid all the endless squabbling.

"Start eighth wave."

Well, I thought... I guess I'm about to find out.

Just as I expected, the eighth wave consisted of a mere six opponents, all at level 55. We could have split up and killed half of them before they recovered their senses, but my intuition was telling me that was probably too good to be true in this case. So I ordered the Orc and the Gnome to stay with me, and I turned out to be right. These "victims" recovered almost instantly, and before we knew it they were hurtling toward us at top speed. They were all Killers this time; this was one of the most inconvenient opponents for a player like me to fight, mainly because they could turn invisible — which all six of them did after only a few seconds. I also noticed that these "victims" dispensed with the usual cries for help. The second problem when fighting Killers was dealing with their amazing Dexterity. This usually made it impossible for me to hit them with my abilities, at least when using them the way I normally did. Worst of all, though, was the fact that these "victims" seemed far more intelligent than anything in the previous waves. Before they slipped into invisibility, I also noticed that the corrosion from the stomach acid was essentially superficial: just some burns on the skin. Their identical clothings and masks (which completely concealed their faces) suggested that they were not only from the same game class, but from the same clan as well. Mind you, that was the case with almost all the "victims" we had faced so far. It seemed like the snake had devoured the characters unit-by-unit as they came to hunt her down.

I ordered Spin to stand next to me, since his passive ability could detect invisible players within a radius of fifteen feet. Even with that, though, I was still a little worried, because if these "victims" were as intelligent as they seemed, they might well be able to attack from farther away than fifteen feet.

"Are you sure you're out of mines?" I asked the Gnome.

"Mines and dynamite both, actually. Almost all gone. Only a few left," replied Red. "I'll start whipping fireballs around. Maybe we can hit one of them by chance."

"Nonsense," snorted the Orc. He grabbed Spin by the scruff of his neck and ran forward. "Hey! Invisible weaklings! I was just coming to empty my bowels in those shacks you call homes!"

He managed to get about ten steps in front of him before all six "victims" suddenly appeared around him and started attacking. I ordered Spin to use Thunder Bark, but it didn't do anything. The Gnome tried shooting them with fireballs from his staff, but the artifact was pretty weak against opponents like these. Since the Orc had managed to lure our invisible enemies in, however, I decided to take advantage of the situation and try to free one of them. So I jumped forward, using Shift mid-jump so as not to catch a dagger in the face or something, and immediately doused the nearest opponent in healing elixir. This time, however, the "victim's" status didn't change; instead, a poison bar appeared above his head, which was only a third of the way full. Again, the math was pretty simple: it would take three more elixirs to free this opponent, and since I was already started, I figured there was no point giving up.

Unfortunately, the "victim" seemed to regard the healing elixir as an attack, and his aggro transferred from the Orc to me. I had to use Shift again, although it didn't really help this time — the invisible bastard threw a whole fan of daggers at me, and a few of them inevitably hit me and took off about a third of my health. Worst of all, though, was that the Orc had taken Spin from me, which meant that I couldn't see my invisible opponent as he lined up his next attack. I could only wait until he reappeared on his own.

"I'll get him!" The Gnome shouted as he let loose a flurry of fireballs into the space around me. But all his attacks simply roared past and dissipated into the darkness.

Chaosite had been floating uselessly above me the entire time, with a small reserve of Chaos in his reservoir which I had been saving "for an emergency." That emergency, it seemed, had finally arrived, so I ordered him to activate his aura. This turned out to be a good move, because the Killer appeared from behind me at just that moment and hit me with a savage blow. Had the damage been purely physical, I would definitely have died from a mass of critical damage, but the Killer had used some sort of ability instead, which Chaosite's aura successfully blocked. I whirled around and splashed two healing elixirs into the Killer's face, but somehow the son of a bitch managed to dodge one of them.

So I used Shift, which barely succeeded in saving me from another blow, then used my Electric Chain to make sure the next elixir would hit him before I dumped the bottle over the Killer's head. Finally, the poison bar next to his name was full.

The Killer's nickname changed to "Shang Longknife, level 62," and suddenly I could see the spark of free will in his eyes as he stared at me from beneath the mask that covered his entire face.

"Thank you," he said with a slight accent and a polite bow. "I'll take care of the others."

With that, he flitted over to help the Orc, who was doing a fairly good job holding off two opponents single-handedly. Actually, "holding off" may be a bit of a stretch — he was simply very good at staying on his feet and keeping up the fight while he took damage. His strength wasn't infinite, though, so the Killer's help would definitely come in handy. Sure enough, the five remaining "victims" were dead in a matter of seconds; formidable though they might have been, they were still mere puppets of the Anaconda, and they couldn't hold their own against an analogous character who also had his own free will.

This time, our acquaintance with the newest member of our unit got off to a nice, smooth start. Shang had none of the delusional mental baggage that the Orc and the Gnome had brought with them, and he joined the group immediately. If I had known things would be that easy, I might have used more elixirs on some of the opponents from previous waves. Unfortunately, though, we still had two waves to go before the baby snakes would appear, and I only had three elixirs left to work with. It was by no means certain that these would be enough to free the stronger "victims" coming in the next waves, and plus, I knew that the elixirs would definitely come in handy for me personally, especially in the tenth wave. On the other hand, though, three level-60 opponents wasn't the worst challenge in the world, especially now that there were four of us in the group.

The artifact from the eighth wave was no use for me personally, but it was perfect for the Killer: a belt full of throwing knives. I didn't even have to think twice about it this time — I just handed the belt to Shang, even though he had already joined the group by that point. The Killer turned out to be a man of very few words, but he was obedient and strong. In many ways, he was the polar opposite of the Orc and the Gnome. The latter, by the way, could no longer do much more than shoot fireballs from his staff, although I was still hoping that we could use the little bit of dynamite he had to good effect at the end of the instance.

The ninth wave was surprisingly easy to defeat. Sure, they were warriors at level 60, but again — there were only three of them. Our quartet operated like a well-oiled machine, and we took all three of them down pretty quickly. The Orc took two of them while the Gnome provided covering fire, and I held the third one at bay while the Killer struck him with blow after blow. Once our enemy was down, we moved in to help the Orc and the Gnome with theirs. When it was all over, I picked up an artifact sword that didn't really suit any of us as a fighting weapon.

And with that, it was time for the tenth wave. As expected, it consisted of just a single opponent, but this time he jumped up out of the snake's mouth on his own! And instead of the usual "victim," the man in flowing red robes was shown as "Urban, Master of Blood Magic, level 90," from the very start.

Dammit, I thought — level 90?! What the hell?!

I was immediately worried by this deviation from the norm, so I didn't rush into battle against this new character; instead, I decided to hang back and wait to see what he would do. At my command, Shang slipped into invisibility and started moving slowly over toward our opponent. Just to be safe, he approached along a wide arc (I could see him the whole time, since we were part of the same group).

After looking around, the man smiled with satisfaction and gleefully rubbed his hands together. Apparently, and very much unlike the other "victims," ending up in the cavern was all part of his plan. And the look in his eyes as he turned to us made it clear that we were most definitely NOT part of those plans at all.

"Hey! Peasants!" The man shouted. "Get out of here."

The Orc, the Gnome, and I all glanced at one another. We certainly hadn't been expecting an opponent like this in the tenth wave.

"I've come to slay the Anaconda myself, and I have no intention of sharing either the spoils or the glory with anybody else!" The Mage shouted.

I wanted to say that that was fine with me — he could have all the glory and spoils he wanted, because all I wanted was to get out of there alive and get as much experience as I could. Plus, the Anaconda was way, way out of my league as an opponent anyway. Alas, the Orc stepped forward before I could reply.

"The snake is MINE, you pallid worm!" He roared.

The Gnome and I both looked over at the Orc with expressions normally reserved for total idiots. What, I wondered, could he possibly be expecting to achieve? We had just discussed the question, and agreed that the boss was way beyond our ability to kill.

"If he gets to the part about relieving himself

in this guy's house, we're screwed," the Gnome whispered.

"I was just — " The Orc started to shout, but I kicked him behind the knee and interrupted his ability.

"Shh."

Only then did it occur to me that I still hadn't seen any message about the tenth wave starting. The red Mage had appeared on his own.

"Start tenth wave."

The system communication confirmed the thought that was taking shape in my head as a bunch of enormous eggs started rolling out of the caves in the cavern wall around us. For some reason, I felt like I was trapped in that really old video game, where the wolf with the basket tries to catch eggs that fall from all over the place. Except that nobody made any effort to catch these eggs as they fell to the cavern floor, where they cracked and released the little snakes who had reached maturity inside them. Well, maybe "little" is a stretch. They were about fifteen feet long...

Chapter 3

ANY INTEREST THE MAGE might have had in us disappeared in an instant, as he started destroying the newborn snakes with an insane, cackling laugh. Blood-red spears were flying out of his hands in all directions, and most of them hit their targets, punching straight through the heads of the Anaconda's baby snakes and leaving their motionless corpses pinned to the floor of the cave. The Blood Mage not only possessed an extremely well-developed ability to deal critical damage; it was also quite clear that he was thoroughly enjoying the slaughter. An NPC with some serious mental illnesses, I guess.

The Orc glared at the Mage and roared:

"He's trying to take the spoils from us!"

Personally, I was content simply to survive the wave and get the experience I needed so badly. Obviously, we might get some points for any kills we managed to make, but I would have preferred to minimize risk and let the Blood Mage take care of the baby snakes himself.

"Wait." I grabbed Noisy Jackal by the shoulder. "Don't even think about shouting at him."

A few of the snakes were attacking us, naturally enough, but it wasn't much trouble to take them out. The problem, though, was that there were more and more of them all the time. I could have jumped up to the ceiling and hung onto the axes that were still embedded in the rock, but that would have made me a tempting target for the Blood Mage. Besides, I didn't really like the idea of leaving the Orc and the Gnome to fend for themselves. The Killer, on the other hand, was perfectly calm throughout the whole experience; only once in a while would he drop his invisibility to finish off a wounded snake.

The slithering beasts were only level 40, but there were a hell of a lot of them. I killed a few dozen of them myself over the course of about five minutes, but somehow there seemed to be just as many as before. The Orc was whirling around once again, chopping through everything in his path, while the Gnome and I tried our best to stay behind him and use the path he was clearing for us.

"This staff of yours is totally useless," grumbled Red the Blaster as we walked. "You couldn't find me anything better?"

"You couldn't have stocked up on mines and dynamites a little better?" I snapped back with frustration. "Or save some of the ones you had, instead of trying to kill the Orc?"

My little comrade just scoffed derisively in response. Or maybe what I took to be a scoff was actually the sound of him panting; after all, he was probably getting a lot more tired than I was in the process of hopping over the dismembered bodies of the dead snakes. Spin was running along next to us, letting out the occasional bark to stun the closest snakes. Whenever he succeeded, he would start slapping away at them with his paws.

I tried as hard as I could to save my three remaining elixirs: I barely attacked anything at all, and swung into action only occasionally, when I used Shift, jumps, or my Micro Chaos Shield to avoid the snakes and their attacks. The shield was pretty small, to be sure, but it actually did a pretty good job protecting me from the little snakes' teeth, since their attacks were always head-on and very predictable.

Time passed, but the number of snakes didn't seem to be dropping at all. It gave me the impression that the Anaconda probably had a side business exporting high-quality material for fashionable boots. I say this because every baby snake that disappeared would always leave a small piece of snakeskin lying on the floor behind it, which was obviously intended for use in crafting. At a certain point, even the Blood Mage got frustrated and started going nuclear, sending huge mass-damage spells surging out around him. Drops of blood flew like bullets within a radius of twenty or thirty feet, dealing horrific damage to any slithering beast unlucky enough to find itself within range, and even dealing a little bit of damage to our invisible Killer.

"What do we have here?" The Blood Mage asked with a dissatisfied frown. "Well, well, well..."

He waved his hands through the air and summoned a blood-red cage that snapped the Killer up inside itself, then quickly started to shrink. Shang tried attacking the bars with his daggers, but all that did was send red sparks spraying out into the cavern; the bars themselves were completely undamaged.

"We need to save him," I said quickly.

"I'm on it!" The Orc shouted happily, as though this were the exact scenario he had been hoping for. "Hey! I was just coming to relieve myself in your house!"

The Mage stopped and glanced at the Orc with derisive arrogance.

"I only stay in hotels."

The aggro effect seemed to have failed; most likely, the Mage was simply too high-level for it to work.

Realizing he wasn't going to be able to break the bars of the cage, the Killer decided on a different strategy. He started hurling daggers at the Blood Mage himself, but the latter had several spheres of blood flying around him that smacked the projectiles aside with ease. I hadn't noticed them up to that point, and I felt really envious. I wished my Micro Chaos Shield could have worked the same way... I could probably level the shield up later, of course, but the prospect of having time to work on it seemed very, very distant indeed.

The Gnome wasn't much use with his lackluster little fire staff, and the Orc had plenty of aggro on his plate already, so I was the only one who could do anything to help the Killer. To be honest, I really didn't feel like getting involved in a battle with such a high-level Mage, but I simply couldn't abandon a character who had joined my group and agreed to fight alongside me.

So... Screw it!

"Attack him!"

I jumped up off the ground into a long horizontal jump and hit the Mage with lightning from above, using Shift in mid-jump to avoid getting hit. This turned out to be a good move, because a cluster of blood spears slammed into a very specific spot on the stone floor less than a second after I passed it. Before I even touched down, I used Repulsion again to change the direction of my flight. Acting on my command, Spin tried to stun the Mage with a bark, but the latter didn't even seem to notice.

"Little bugs," laughed the Master of Blood. "I'm starting to tire of you."

"I relieved myself all over every hotel you've ever stayed at!" The Orc snarled somewhere behind me as he lunged into an attack.

Suddenly, a big red sphere appeared in midair in front of me and exploded like a grenade. The shockwave hurled me violently back, and a spray of little blood droplets stung my face like little bits of red glass. The pain was intense, but even worse, this single attack took away almost all my health. I'm sure the Mage would have finished me off just a second later if it hadn't been for the Gnome, who used all his remaining dynamite. The Blood Mage disappeared in a huge explosion, bigger even than the one that had almost killed the Orc back in a previous wave.

I bent down to the ground and rolled to the side, just to make sure I wasn't right where the Mage would expect me to be, then leapt up onto my feet.

To my horror, I saw that the trap around our Killer had finally closed. Shang's nickname dimmed and lost its color, and his nickname disappeared from our group.

"Son of a bitch," I swore as I quickly knocked back a healing elixir.

I only had two more left.

As the smoke from the explosion faded away, it became clear that all our attacks together had only cost the Blood Mage about a tenth of his health. The Orc threw himself into a furious headlong attack, whipping his axe around with terrifying speed, but every blow he struck ran straight into one of the Mage's flying spheres of blood.

The Gnome was still spraying his fireballs, but they were so ineffective that the Mage didn't even seem to notice them. Just then, however, I suddenly got an unexpected system communication:

"Start eleventh wave."

The Sands of Eternity

Whoa, I thought... I didn't even notice that the snakes were all dead! That means I've survived ten waves, and I'll get enough experience to rack up four levels, maybe even five! I'm almost there!

The earth began to tremble beneath our feet. Or more accurately, a vibration rippled out through the entire cavern, sending sheets of dust and small rocks sprinkling down onto our heads. All the cave mouths and underground passages that the snakes' heads had been emerging from were soon sealed with fallen rock. There would be no escape for any of us. A huge, horizontal crack exploded into being across one of the walls, and quickly started spreading wider and wider like a sadistic smile. Before long, the Anaconda's several dozen heads appeared from inside it.

"Finally!" The Blood Mage exclaimed. "She's here!"

The Orc, the Gnome, and I were all frozen in place, spellbound by the spectacle that was about to unfold in front of us. More and more heads kept appearing, and soon the Anaconda's whole body was in the cavern with us. Up to that point, I had been wondering why they weren't referring to this beast as a Hydra, but when I saw the rest of its body I realized that this was an entirely different creature. In most games and books, Hydras resembled big, fat dragons with tons of heads, but this beast looked like a strange sort of reverse cuttlefish with no identifiable body. The serpentine heads literally emerged straight out of the middle of a big mass of flesh, and the beast used them to move around as if they were limbs.

"Young Anaconda, level 120," read the information above her. An involuntary shudder passed across my body as I realized that there must be an adult somewhere, and maybe even some sort of elder or ancient Anaconda. The latter would have to be somewhere around level 200. Needless to say, the three of us fighting together couldn't even begin to dream of defeating this beast.

"What's the matter?! You're annoyed that I killed all your little kids?!" The Master of Blood roared; he seemed to have forgotten about us entirely. "Come on, then! Take revenge on me!"

"Yeah, do it," the Gnome muttered as he stepped back (in unison with me, I might add). "We'll see."

"This is MY prey!" The Orc roared. Every muscle in his body was tensed to the breaking point.

"Which one are you talking about?" The Gnome asked sarcastically.

"Both! I'm going to kill them both!"

The Gnome and I both rolled our eyes. Noisy Jackal seemed to make a habit of overestimating himself.

"He STILL hasn't had enough killing," Red snorted.

In spite of all his bravado, I couldn't help noticing that the Orc was backing away from the Anaconda just as quickly as we were; he didn't seem in any hurry to claim his "prey."

To be honest, I had never really faced such a powerful boss before, but I already knew that players never, ever fought bosses like this on their own. As for how the Blood Mage was planning to defeat a beast thirty levels more powerful than himself... Well, I had absolutely no idea. I would have preferred to simply flee the cavern as quickly as possible (especially since I was already on track to get enough experience), but where could we possibly go? The caves were all blocked by rubble, and the only passage into or out of the main cavern was the big crack in the wall — the crack that was completely blocked by the Anaconda's enormous body.

As I frantically weighed our options, the Master of Blood used some sort of buff on himself that shrouded his whole body in a film of blood and turned him into a blood golem about twice as tall as a normal human. Admittedly, it didn't look like much with the Anaconda looming in the background, but it was still a pretty considerable boost in power. It certainly seemed that way, at any rate, since the yard-long blades at the ends of both his arms started lopping off snake heads like they were made of Play-doh. He reminded me more than anything of Carnage, from the Marvel Universe — brother of the more-famous Venom. He even moved the same way, covering a dozen yards in a single leap and shooting razor-sharp red tendrils out of his body.

"Got any explosives left?" I asked the Gnome. "Maybe we could blast one of the passages open and get the hell out of here?"

"I used them all," replied Red in a defeated

tone of voice.

"Well, I guess we'll just have to wait for an opportunity and attack whichever one of them starts to lose," I concluded. "No point getting involved in this one."

"Very reasonable," the Gnome agreed.

"I can't just stand on the sidelines!" The Orc roared as he clenched his fists tightly around his sickle.

"Calm down, already! These opponents are way, way out of our league!" The Gnome finally snapped at him. "I'd be willing to risk it if we had respawn tattoos. But why would we throw away the only life we've got for no reason at all?"

I turned to them with a look of surprise on my face.

"You don't have respawn tattoos?!"

For some reason, the Gnome sounded sheepish when he responded.

"They don't give those out to just anybody, you know. We're just rank-and-file grunts."

Hearing this made me look at them in a whole new light. I knew, of course, that a large percentage of NPCs had no ability to respawn after dying, but for some reason, I had always thought that the ones who took an active role in rare quests like this were exceptions to the rule.

"So our Killer didn't have a respawn tattoo either?" I asked, feeling tense.

"Of course not," snorted Red.

I turned to look at the Master of Blood, and again, it was in a whole new light. That son of a bitch had killed — I mean, KILLED — a member of my group! Sure, Shang and I hadn't really exchanged more than a few words, and I never even saw his face, but that wasn't what mattered. What mattered was the fact that I had saved him, then brought him into my group, and thereby taken responsibility for him. More than that, the news made me reconsider my attitude toward my allies as well. After all, unlike me, they wouldn't have the chance to respawn if they ended up dying.

"Okay, we need to find a way out of here right now," I concluded, as I started looking around even more frantically than before (while simultaneously using Magnetic Sensitivity to look for iron in the walls). "Let's leave these two to kill each other in peace."

"But my prey..." The Orc tried to object.

"Ugh, give it up!" The Gnome and I shouted at him in unison.

The Blood Mage had no time to spare for us; all his attention was focused on the Anaconda. I'll admit that for just a second, I thought about trying my luck and whipping a blast of Ball Lightning right at his back. Maybe it would work out for me. If it didn't, though, I would probably draw the Mage's attention, and with the buff coursing through his system he'd probably blow us all to smithereens in a matter of moments.

That left only one option: summon Lady Aishorth and have her knock both our opponents off the field at once. My hands were itching, longing to pick up the Heart of the Blizzard, but I knew it would probably be a bad idea to use my weapon of last resort (even though it also happened to be the only weapon in my inventory that could actually make a difference in such dire circumstances). After all, I knew we might end up needing Aishorth's help the following day when we tried to resurrect Artyom.

Unfortunately, every single passage — including the ones at the very top of the cave — ended up being completely blocked. It became obvious that the only escape route still open to us lay directly across the Anaconda's dead body. On the other hand, though, the chances of that happening seemed pretty good: the Blood Mage was actually doing quite well. Severed snake heads were flying all over the place, and no new ones were growing to take their places, which was yet another indication that there was no logical connection between the Anaconda and a hydra. The heads that still remained, however, were still more than enough to rip the blood monster into tiny little scraps of flesh the moment let his guard down. With every bite they took, the blood golem was getting smaller and smaller. The battle took its twists and turns, but all we could do was wait on the sidelines and watch events unfold; perhaps we might also get a chance to attack, if the right opportunity presented itself. Whether that opportunity came or not, though, the difference in levels was so huge that our damage would barely do anything to either combatant, so all our hopes were pinned on the possibility that they would beat each other to within an inch of death before either of them actually died.

And before too long, things actually seemed to be going in that direction: the Master of Blood had only 30% of his health left, while the Anaconda had a mere 15%. But even then, our potential to do damage was so insignificant that we had no choice but to keep waiting.

"I swear by the name of Radegast, if I had just ONE chest of dynamite right now, I could take them both out without leaving so much as a wet spot on the rock," the Gnome sighed wistfully.

"We don't need dynamite. We need strength and self-sacrifice!" The Orc snarled. "In the name of Gmorka!"

With that, Noisy Jackal started to hum some sort of dolorous melody.

I was about to object, but to my surprise the Gnome suddenly kicked me in the leg and hissed at me not to distract the Orc.

"Never interrupt someone who's turning to their God with their last request."

"What do you mean by 'last'?!" I hissed back, feeling every bit as outraged as the Gnome.

"Shh!" The Gnome hissed again.

The Orc's song grew louder and louder until a faint glow started to spread out around him. It slowly grew brighter and brighter, and gradually spread over to me and the Gnome as well.

"Youv'e received a level-3 blessing from the God Gmorka.

+50 to all attributes;

+500 to health and mana;

every 10% that is taken from your health will result in +10% damage from any of your attacks;

this blessing will last for as long as the Noisy Jackal is alive."

Whoa, I thought... Seriously?! Why didn't he do this earlier?!

"Well, I guess now we just have to wait for the right moment," I said with a satisfied smirk as I read through the blessing description again. "And we actually have a pretty good chance of being able to kill whoever's..."

I trailed off as I realized that the Orc was no longer standing next to me. Instead, he was rushing straight toward the Blood Mage and the Anaconda, sprinting as fast as he possibly could.

"I'm coming to shit in your caves, and YOUR hotels!" The Orc's roar sent an echo booming through the cavern: "Hotels! Hotels!"

At the exact same moment, the Blood Mage and the Anaconda both turned around, caught sight of the green-skinned psychopath, and proceeded to attack him. The Gnome elbowed me in the shoulder and shouted:

"Come on! This is our chance!"

Basically, my attributes were comparable to what they had been at level 73. This meant a significant increase in our odds, because a level-90 Mage really wouldn't have posed too much of a problem for me before I lost my levels. As a result,

The Sands of Eternity

I caught a little bit of the Orc's psychotic enthusiasm and rushed into battle with a shout of joy.

Taking advantage of the fact that the Anaconda and the Blood Mage were busy attacking Noisy Jackal, I bounced closer to them in a few big jumps and threw an Electric Chain onto the Master of Blood. The Gnome raced straight over to the paralyzed Mage and started laying into him with his pick (apparently having decided that the fire staff wasn't dependable enough in the circumstances), inflicting astronomical amounts of damage with every swing. That said, I realized when I glanced at his info that the Gnome was also somehow doing damage to himself in the process; in fact, he had already cut his own health down to 80%, although of course that only made his blows with the pick even more powerful. The sheath of blood around the Mage's body was absorbing a lot of the damage, but every time the pick hit the Mage's body it would take off something like a hundred points of health.

The Orc was whirling around as if possessed, smacking back the snake heads. There were only fifteen or twenty of them left in total (the biggest and strongest ones), but just to be safe I sent Spin to the Orc's assistance. The blessing affected my little wolf as well, which meant that my pet's attributes were truly impressive. Most importantly, his Thunder Bark had no trouble affecting the Anaconda; it stunned every one of the beast's remaining heads as soon as Spin used it.

Meanwhile, the Blood Mage's health was

plummeting at a furious rate. When the chain's effect wore off, I started hitting him with lightning. As I did so, I realized to my immense satisfaction that we were going to win, without even having to summon Lady Aishorth or use Ball Lightning.

"Ah, you filthy bugs!" The Master of Blood screamed, his voice breaking into a shrill falsetto as his health plummeted to the very bottom of the red zone. "I should have slaughtered you all right away!"

The Gnome just snickered in reply and buried his pick in the Mage's flesh, thereby inflicting yet another devastating blast of critical damage.

"Coulda, shoulda, woulda — it's too late, my friend!"

A few more blasts of lightning finished the Mage off, and his body crumpled to the cavern floor with a loud splash. Looking closer, I realized he had turned into a big pool of thick, viscous blood as soon as he died. The Gnome and I both rushed over to help the Orc, but to my great surprise he had actually killed the Anaconda on his own by the time we got there.

"This prey is MINE!" The badly-wounded Orc screamed with joy as he leapt up on top of the mound of flesh that had once been his opponent. He raised his sickle above his head and let out a furious roar: "In the name of Gmorka!"

Noisy Jackal certainly had every right to be proud of himself, because we could never have done it without him. Once he stopped yelling, however, he did something strange: he stepped down from the dead snake's body, fell to his knees, leaned forward to rest his weight on his sickle, and froze. The Orc's icon went dark and disappeared from our group.

"What?! What the hell is going on?! We WON!"

I ran over to Noisy Jackal, and found that he was actually every bit as dead as he seemed to be. I had to check, of course, because just a second before he had quite a bit of health left.

"He would have died no matter what the result," said the Gnome as he walked over to stand next to me and bent his head somberly toward the ground. "That was his death prayer. The Orc gave his life for this victory."

I guess that explained why his buff was so incredibly powerful. I had never heard of such a powerful effect before. Still, though... Voluntarily sacrificing your life just to defeat some beast, when you weren't even protecting somebody or anything, solely in order to claim something you regarded as your prey? It sounded kind of stupid to me. Or maybe it was just heroic? I mean, Noisy Jackal's aggro-attracting shouts had definitely sounded stupid as well, but there was a very real spirit of self-sacrifice inherent in the ability.

A system communication popped up in front of my eyes:

"You have withstood every wave of opponents without dying.
Reward: +6,600,000 experience, random unique artifact with quality of 110."

Loner Book Eight

"You have completed an additional task by defeating the Anaconda.

Reward: ability improvement scroll, +300,000 experience, Heart of the Anaconda."

227

"You've leveled up!"
"You've leveled up!"
"You've..."

Chapter 4

IN THE END, I LEVELED UP five times and made it to level 50 before I even left the instance! I had exceeded my own expectations by quite a bit, and I suppose I should have been happy. Strangely, though, I was in a terrible mood. I felt bad about losing the Orc. Perhaps I had just gotten used to his hilarious battle cries and his insatiable urge to fight. Most importantly, I felt directly responsible for all three of the people I had saved from the Anaconda's slime, and two of those people were now dead, with no hope of ever respawning. I still had two healing elixirs in my inventory, and I couldn't shake the thought that maybe, if I had given them to the Orc and the Killer in time, they could have survived. Dammit! I guess I had just gotten too carried away with trying to save my supplies and worrying about my own physical safety. And let's be honest: planning has never really been a strong suit of mine at all.

The bodies of the Blood Mage and the Anaconda disappeared, leaving two artifacts behind — one each for the tenth and eleventh waves. As with the previous opponents we had faced, the Master of Blood gave us neither experience nor loot. That said, the third artifact (for the ninth wave) was lying pretty close by. In the end, I acquired an amulet, a shield, some boots, and an additional artifact for killing the Anaconda: a Shanbiao chain at an eye-watering level 110. I guess you could say I had hit the jackpot, finding such a rare weapon that would suit me perfectly as I continued to develop. On the other hand, it raised the pretty serious question of whether I would actually live long enough to use it at all. For the time being, I was losing (and set to continue losing) levels much more quickly than I was gaining them back.

The general anxiety I was feeling led me to walk the battlefield and pick up every last piece of snakeskin that the Anaconda's children had dropped. You never know — what if it turned out to be some kind of incredibly-rare craft material? You also never know when something that seems insignificant might come in handy — a skill you've always considered useless, for example.

"Well? Have you finally picked everything up?" The Gnome asked with a derisive look on his face.

I felt a little bit embarrassed to be pinching pennies and picking up trinkets right after the Orc and the Killer died fighting alongside us, but what else was I supposed to do? It was a very strange feeling, knowing that I was inside a virtual game that was much more than just a game, but which still required me to engage in typical RPG-player behavior. Nevertheless, that's just the way it was, and I had absolutely no intention of leaving loot behind on the field. The very thought of it almost caused me physical pain.

"Yep," I said sheepishly.

"Then let's get the hell out of here. This place is about to collapse." The Gnome nudged me toward the horizontal crack the Anaconda had made in the cavern wall. "This place will be a fitting tomb for all those who died inside this disgusting snake."

Spin and Chaosite had been bobbing around next to me the entire time, but I decided to recall them at that point and give them a chance to replenish their health and mana. Although actually, that was something only Spin could do, because Chaosite's supply of Chaos wasn't self-replenishing. He had to be fed with all sorts of ridiculous crap, like bungled metalwork from apprentice Smiths or failed attempts at potion-brewing.

We passed through the massive crack and found ourselves inside a narrow underground tunnel that led upward at a thirty- or forty-degree angle. After about ten minutes of unhurried walking, we saw sunlight filtering through the rock up ahead of us. When we finally left the instance, we found that for some reason we weren't in Katar anymore — instead, we walked out onto a rocky plateau high in the mountains, which was obviously well outside city limits. But I soon realized that was actually for the best, since it meant that there would be very little chance of running into anybody from "Spirit of the Hunt."

"Well, I suppose this is where we say goodbye," said the Gnome as he held a huge, callused hand out to me. "Thanks for getting me out of the snake. Find me if you ever need anything. Every Gnome in Katar knows Red the Blaster."

As I shook his hand, a system communication popped up in front of me:

Ability "Steel Handshake" has advanced to level 3.

This is a secret handshake which will allow you to increase the level of trust you instill when you speak to any Gnome (temporary +500 to standing). The strength of your grip has also permanently increased by 10%.

I didn't really know what the strength of one's grip was good for, but it certainly couldn't hurt. I'd say the same about pretty much any bonus, especially when it came with the word "permanent" in the description. Plus, experience had already shown that making friends with Gnomes was a good idea. Of all the game's races, they were the ones I tended to have the smallest amount of conflicts with.

The Gnome was already walking away when he suddenly turned around.

"One other piece of advice for you as well. We've been touched by a blessing from an Orcish God. Sure, it didn't last long, but powerful death prayers like that leave traces on you forever. If you ever meet a Shaman at any point, make sure you express some homage to Gmorka. Otherwise you might piss him off. Personally, I'm planning to stop in at an Orcish temple as soon as I can."

"Thanks," I said (very genuinely, I might add).

Alas, his advice didn't lead to any quest popping up on my interface. Intuition, however, was telling me that the Gnome had given me that advice for a very good reason, and that it would be a very bad idea to disregard it. Especially since my next sword just so happened to be waiting for me in the lands of the Orcs...

Thinking of that made me realize something: if I had saved Noisy Jackal, he could have been my guide in the Kingdom of Gromga! I was so focused on racking up levels and resurrecting Artyom that I had neglected my own divine quest.

"Don't be a stranger," the Gnome shouted over his shoulder as he wandered off, whistling a happy melody.

After a little more hand-wringing about my shortsighted behavior, I took out my tablet and turned to matters more pressing than my usual self-flagellation. Once I checked the map and realized where I was, I opened my messages, most of which (naturally enough) were from Mark.

"Okay, I'm finally back in my capsule. Where are you?"

"Just don't tell me you went to meet with your uncle and he did something horrible to you."

"Come on, man, this isn't funny anymore. I can see you're online."

"Fine. Just message me as soon as you get a chance to use your tablet again."

"I hope you're okay."

"I have a teleport ready for you if you need it."

Mark seemed to be acting kind of like a needy girlfriend for some reason. But I decided not to mention that. Really, the guy was probably just worried about me. I also had a message from Boris, reminding me about my ancestral lands, but that didn't require an immediate response.

"I was in an instance, didn't have time to respond. I'll send you a pin for my location in a second," I replied to Mark.

"On my way!" He responded almost immediately, as if he had been waiting with his tablet in his hands for me to message him back.

A few seconds after I sent him the pin, a portal opened up about fifteen feet in front of me and disgorged a sweaty, red-faced Illusionist. I had never realized it was even POSSIBLE to sweat so much in-game. The big guy looked like he had just finished a difficult gym routine that had tested his physical capacities to the limit.

"What's going on?" I asked suspiciously.

"Ugh, don't get me started. My sister's been hounding me with questions, trying to find out why her little buddies are hunting you down. That goddamned Charisma stat of hers messes my character up pretty bad. It's really hard to resist her influence."

"But you didn't say anything, did you?" I asked anxiously.

"No, of course not," said the Illusionist dismissively, although his voice betrayed him by trembling a little bit. "I have to tell you, though, it was pretty difficult. I have to level this character up as soon as I can, to give him some better defense against sweet talk. Trish isn't even the most charismatic player in the game, but she can make you dance like a marionette if your Intelligence or your resistance to mental effects isn't leveled up high enough."

"I know," I nodded. "I met her myself, not too long ago."

Mark's eyes bulged.

"WHAT?! And you didn't think to mention that?!"

I had to wonder — when did he imagine I would have had the time to tell him about it?

"Although given that Trish was asking about YOU, I'm assuming you didn't tell her anything either?" Mark asked a little bit more calmly after thinking for a moment.

"Of course not. She wasn't even that insistent, actually; even her threat was a little bit weak, to be honest."

"Really?" Mark's eyes narrowed as he glanced at the space above my head. "I seem to remember you being at level 53, but now you're down to 50. My sister really didn't have anything to do with that?"

"Actually, I lost ten levels, but it was my uncle who did it," I corrected him. "But I actually recouped seven levels pretty quickly."

"What?!" Mark didn't seem to believe me. "You've been in the game for five hours, absolute max. And you leveled up seven times? That's impossible!"

"Well, after the meeting with my uncle, I played an instance and found a secret level," I explained.

Condensing things as much as possible, I proceeded to tell Mark all about what I had found, which left him almost literally green with envy. He actually seemed like he might rush off to complete the sewer instance himself, in the hope that he could find the same secret passage in the stone; if so, however, he soon remembered that it would have to wait. First and foremost, we had to head down to the Inventory Directory and complete the quest related to my ancestral lands. I could have just teleported right to the building, run inside, and taken care of business on my own, but having a layer of illusions to protect me as well certainly couldn't hurt.

"Let's run into the city real quick so I can do the instance too!" Mark urged me. "You have some portals, right?"

"Tons of them," I confirmed. "Boris is keeping me pretty well stocked. I don't even have to actually go and buy them."

"Man, sounds like you've got it made..." Mark sounded slightly amazed.

"Exactly. Which is why I have to get my hands on these lands as soon as I can, so I can pay him back at least a little bit for all his help."

"Well, let's get teleporting, then. I'll throw an illusion on you and — "

Suddenly, a portal began to spread out into the air right in front of our faces, and a red-headed woman in an armored bra stepped out. This time, she was wearing very short shorts made of chainmail and resting a huge sword against her shoulder.

"Trish?!" Mark said with breathless indignation. "What the hell?! How did you find us?"

The warrior ruffled Mark's hair with her free hand.

"Come on, Marky Mark. I'm one of the Clan's generals. I can pinpoint any member of "Spirit of the Hunt" at any moment."

Mark let out a long, measured breath. He was obviously trying to restrain his emotions.

"Trish, I'm sick of you calling me that. Also, I don't know how you have the free time to be following me around like this."

"I'm not following you," said Trish, before predictably pointing a finger at me. "I'm following him. I was just at the Guildhall and I heard some news that might be of interest to you both."

Mark obviously intended to keep arguing with his sister, but I stopped him.

"Hold on." I turned to the red-haired woman; she had piqued my curiosity. "What is it?"

"Answer me one question first: are you planning something in Pyrenth tomorrow?"

Mark and I just looked at each other.

"Why do you ask?"

"No need to answer," she scoffed. "Way to keep it a secret, boys. Basically, after meeting you in that store, I found out that the Clan's assembling most of its forces in Pyrenth tomorrow. Preparing for something important. So I decided to find out whether it had anything to do with you. But I have my answer now."

Shit, I thought... What did they find out?! There's no way we'll be able to resurrect Artyom with "Spirit of the Hunt" getting in our way at every turn. There would have been some players from the Clan in the city anyway, of course, but I had been hoping that the "Unnameables" might have enough people on the scene to help take the pressure off while we were working. If the most powerful Clan in Arktania sent its most powerful players to interfere, though, we wouldn't have a snowball's chance in hell.

Mark let out an exhausted sigh.

"Fine. So you somehow learned that we're headed for Pyrenth. So what now? What do you want from us?"

"I still don't know why Zach's looking for you. I want that question answered."

To be perfectly frank, I didn't see any real reason to keep hiding things from Trish. She was Mark's sister, after all. It didn't seem likely that she would subject him to any serious danger or go running to her Clanleader with the information we gave her. That said, the Illusionist obviously felt quite justified in not telling her what was going on, so I figured it might be best for him to decide what to do.

"You decide. I won't object either way," I said to Mark with a wave. In my mind, I was already thinking frantically about what to do next. Postpone our search until the next event with the flying coffins? That would mean asking Boris to drop everything and find out when the next event would be taking place.

I took out my tablet and sent the merchant a message immediately. Meanwhile, the Illusionist was silent for a minute as he thought about what to do.

"Listen, Trishy. I'll tell you what's going on if you promise to help us." He sounded very reluctant.

I could tell that the young woman didn't appreciate being addressed as "Trishy," although she kept her emotions in check very well. Still, though, I could tell it would come back to haunt Mark at some point.

"NOW we're talking! I'll warn you right now, though: I'm not going to fight against my Clan for you."

"You won't need to," Mark assured her. "But some information about the number of players, their classes, and the abilities of the strongest ones would be really useful."

Trish just scoffed; her eyes narrowed.

"How will that help you? There's going to be an

entire army. Hundreds of players. They'll wipe you off the map in a second."

"That's for us to worry about," said the Illusionist. "Whatever we decide to do, though, the information will be useful."

"Suicidal," said Trish as she shook her head. "But whatever — I'll give you a list of everybody who's going to be in Pyrenth. Especially since I don't think it'll do the Clan any harm anyway. There's certainly nothing YOU can do to harm the Clan."

As she spoke, I thought frantically about how the hell we could possibly face down an entire clan. Even if the "Unnameables" agreed to help us, it wouldn't be enough to swing the balance. I mean, they had already lost the war to "Spirit of the Hunt" by that point anyway. If the curse from the God of the Dead was still in effect in Pyrenth, though, then maybe I could suborn the undead copies of any characters who got killed and sic them on our enemies. I still had Eidolon's blessing, which meant that they might actually listen to me. In theory, acquiring my ancestral lands would give me the ability to summon my own feudal levy (as Boris had mentioned), but I still had no idea how any of that actually worked. Whatever the case, I had three options in mind already. I would simply have to talk to the appropriate people... And maybe, if there was time, a certain appropriate God, living in a cemetery in suburban Moscow...

"I'll give you half an hour," Mark said to his sister. "Come see me. I'll tell you everything."

The Sands of Eternity

"Sounds iffy," said Trish skeptically. "Why can't you just tell me here and now? Am I going to show up and find you gone, with a new phone number and nothing but an empty apartment left behind you?"

In response, Mark just spun a finger around by the side of his head.

"Don't be an idiot. You think I'd leave Rita and Mila? Come on. Believe me, you won't regret it. Once I tell you what's going on, you'll practically be begging me to let you help."

"Keep this in mind, though," said the red-haired woman in a menacingly deep voice. "If it turns out you're lying to me, you won't make it out of the respawn zone for a week."

With that, Trish Merisilver left the game, leaving Mark and me on our own. We discussed the developing situation, and I quickly learned that the Illusionist had come to the same set of conclusions as me. The upshot was that unless we could find the flying coffins in a different spot, our only option would be to assemble all the forces at our disposal. We would throw everything we had at "Spirit of the Hunt" to keep them occupied while we resurrected Artyom.

After I finished sending messages to Daddy Rothschild, Pinky, Ne-Tarok, and Sergei to keep them all up to speed, we teleported straight to the Inventory Directory in Katar. Mark threw an illusion over us even before we teleported, so I was able to walk into the building like a normal person, without rushing or worrying about catching a crossbow bolt in the leg as I entered.

Once again, I was the only visitor in the place. The woman at the desk was even friendlier this time around, as though she already knew that I had completed all the necessary task requirements this time.

"How can I help you?" She asked with a smile.

"Hello, I'm Falk Fudre. I've come to get the title to my ancestral lands."

"Alright, let's see..." The woman dove into a pile of papers on the table in front of her and pulled out a small folder.

"City of Kelevre. I see your standing in the city is more than sufficient, and you've obtained permission from the head of the family. All that's left is a payment of 300,000 gold."

I opened the payment window and forked over the necessary sum. I immediately felt like I had been robbed, since that sum represented three-fourths of the money in my account.

"You've completed the task "Ancestral Lands."
The City of Kelevre has officially been designated a part of your ancestral lands.
You must present yourself at City Hall within seven days to affirm possession."

So, I thought... another trip to Kelevre? Makes sense. I guess I'll get the details on all my new opportunities once I get there. To be honest, I was already itching to go see what sort of army I might be able to raise, and how much money I could expect to earn from the various income streams in the city. I made a mental note to warn Thram I was coming this time, though; experience had already shown that you could never predict what might be happening in that city at any given time.

"Here are your documents," the woman announced as she handed me a scroll with a big waxen seal on the front. "They're indestructible, and they'll serve as total confirmation of your rights to the City of Kelevre. Congratulations, Count de Fudre."

After thanking the woman for her help, I rushed out of the building and hurried back to where Mark was waiting for me.

"Hey, sexy," said a Gnome who happened to be passing by. Needless to say, this was so utterly unexpected that I actually tripped over my own two feet.

"Mark," I hissed as I marched over to the Illusionist, who was obviously suppressing a smile. "What illusion did you just put on me?"

"Sexy she-Gnome by the name of Thylka," he said with a wink. "With a seductive beard and nice, feminine sideburns. Just so nobody would suspect a thing."

"Dumbass. Anyway, let's get out of here before some high-level player comes looking for us."

But Mark didn't seem to be in any hurry to reach for a teleport.

"Uh... Where are you headed now?" He asked impatiently.

"Kelevre. I have to find out what conditions I

need to meet to raise some fighting forces. And I also have to officially accept the job, so to speak."

"Ahh... How about you do that on your own? I think I could run through the instance once before Trish comes," Mark quickly explained. "If you're cool with that, of course."

I would have preferred him to come with me; I always felt calmer knowing the Illusionist was nearby. But my conscience simply wouldn't allow it; I felt bad forcing him to follow me around like a shadow all the time. So we said goodbye right there outside the Inventory Directory — I teleported into a forest near Kelevre, while Mark ran off to the sewer on foot.

I stepped out of the portal right near the stone wall that surrounded the city (and yes — it was very much a city, in every sense of the word). Almost immediately, I heard a shout from the walls:

"Stop! Don't move!"

"Stopped. Not moving," I shouted back. I looked up and saw three archers with their bows drawn and their arrows pointed straight at me.

"Per Captain Blaze's orders, you've been declared a dangerous spy, to be arrested for further interrogation!" One of them shouted down to me. "Wait here for the patrol to come back."

Hm, I thought... This is basically what I was expecting. Given that my standing in both the Empire as a whole and Kelevre in particular were still positive, they didn't actually have anything to charge me with. These orders were obviously the product of the Captain's personal feelings toward me, so I was pretty eager to get inside and rub his nose in the documents confirming my ownership of the city. And then kick him out on his ass, along with anybody else who had anything to do with hounding and harassing the residents of my dear old start location.

Chapter 5

I HAD INITIALLY BEEN PLANNING to teleport into a nearby forest, rather than right to the base of the city walls, but apparently Kelevre had grown again in my absence. Actually, the spot I had chosen to teleport to was still within the city limits, but since I was technically banned from the city the teleport had simply thrown me outside the limits and left me right at the base of the wall. The formerly-tiny village had expanded quickly and relatively quietly, since stone walls didn't actually need to be completely rebuilt in the game: they could simply move themselves to correspond to city limits.

"Don't move!"

Several Imperial soldiers came running toward me at top speed. They were clad in plate armor that gleamed in the sun, and led by a Mage with a long beard (who nevertheless didn't really look that old). Their levels were only in the seventies, but of course that made them pretty dangerous opponents for me in my leveled-down state, especially considering the archers who were watching from the walls and who were prepared at any moment to turn me into an arrow-filled pincushion.

"I'm not moving." I even raised my hands as I repeated this to signal that I meant no harm.

"Follow us, and don't even think about trying to run," the Mage snapped.

Strangely, they didn't put any shackles on me, or even anything to block my inventory or abilities. They just led me to Kelevre's main gate and brought me past the guards (which, of course, dovetailed quite nicely with my own plans). The guards were openly sneering at me as I passed, but the players who flitted past in the streets seemed more interested than aggressive. Players never really got arrested like this; when they did, it was almost invariably part of some sort of quest, or at least indicative of some special circumstances. Normally, a player with insufficient standing would simply be turned away at the gate. Or, if their standing was really bad, the guards would just shoot them to pieces from the walls. Seeing me being led into the city by a convoy, therefore, was more than a little bit suspicious.

"Hey, you need help?" A player in armor (not unlike what the guards were wearing) shouted to me from the crowd.

"I'm fine," I replied with a wave.

"No talking!" The Mage shouted.

Loner Book Eight

I just shrugged and kept looking around. The city was teeming with life: players were scurrying around all over the place, and there were guards on every corner (in addition to those who were stationed along the walls). We walked past a training arena, which was full of players practicing new skills, and then past a row of artisans' shops that were also designed to train players in their chosen professions. My thoughts turned immediately to the possibility of buying up some of the defective by-products from these shops to feed Chaosite. I made a mental note to do this as soon as I had a chance, but for the time being I was more interested in checking out the city and trying to spot any familiar places that still remained. I couldn't even begin to tell where my old friends' houses used to be: Korn's smithy, the houses of the Priestess and the Archer, Rathmir and his wife's place... There was clearly no room for Thram's garden anymore either. Every single building had been rebuilt, and the city's whole layout had changed along with them.

I wondered, as I looked around, whether all the Imperial guards surrounding me would remain at their posts and start reporting to me once I became the owner of the place. It didn't seem likely that they would all flee the city at the same time and leave it defenseless, especially since it was so close to the Orcish border. If they stayed, would I be able to bring them to Pyrenth with me? On second thought, I realized that no portal in the world could possibly transport such a huge contingent of soldiers.

The convoy led me into an impressive stone building right in the middle of the city with a huge stone clocktower soaring up out of its roof. Barely-visible waves of light energy were pulsating slowly out of the top of the clocktower, presumably from the Glass Rose. Where else would the artifact be, I wondered, if not here? The soldiers guarding the entrance all had levels above 100 — they were the strongest I had seen in the city up to that point, and their impressive levels spoke volumes about how important the place had become.

Once inside, they led me up a staircase and into the Captain's office. The soldier had a huge scar running across his face, and as I walked into the hall I saw him sitting at a huge table, sorting through a stack of papers. In addition to the documents, though, his gaze would occasionally freeze on something in the space in front of him; if I didn't know better, I'd have thought he was looking at an interface. But he couldn't be, right? NPCs — a.k.a. "locals" — couldn't see menus or attribute windows. Insofar as they dealt in such terminology at all, it was essentially a matter of intuition.

As he raised his eyes to meet mine, Captain Blaze — officially an Imperial Army Captain at level 80 — grimaced as though he had just chewed up and swallowed a whole lemon. His lips were so thin that his mouth looked like it had been incised into his face with a scalpel, and his cheekbones completed the overall impression of triangularity. Every single feature of his face seemed to be radiating intense displeasure.

"And why have you brought him here?"

"You added him to the wanted list yourself," the Mage responded in a puzzled tone of voice.

"Well, yes. But why did you bring him to City Hall? Send him to jail."

The Mage exchanged a glance with the guards, who just shrugged.

"We don't have the authority. Falk de Fudre has good standing in the Empire and in the city. You're the only one who can judge him and pass sentence."

Huh, I wondered... How will this commandant react when I show him my deed to the city? I watched him with mild interest as he sat behind his desk. To be honest, he didn't really look like the total villain Thram had described; really, he just looked like a very tired, very irritated administrator.

A folder with my name on it suddenly appeared in the Captain's hands.

"So," he said pensively as he glanced first at the folder, then at me. "Trespassing into forbidden territory, attacking an Imperial Guard, and conspiracy with a Gnomish terrorist. More than enough to lower your standing in the Empire to "hostile," I should think."

Gnomish terrorist, I thought? Did he really just call Thram that?!

Captain Blaze picked up his Imperial Seal and lifted it into the air above my folder.

"In my position as Commandant of..."

The Sands of Eternity

I could just feel it: intuitively, I just knew that something irreversible might be about to happen. If he actually brought that seal down onto my folder and ruined my standing, it would complicate my entire life in a big way.

"Hold on!" I said in a hurried stammer. "I have — "

Just at that moment, a massive explosion shook the ground below us. The wall next to me started to collapse.

"What in the name of Dharna?!" The Captain shouted. "What's going on?! Get to the bottom of this, NOW! Sound the alarm!"

The guards and the Mage tore off down the stairs. For some time, all I could hear were shouts and the clanging of weapons, echoing up the stairs from somewhere down on the first floor. Soon, however, the noise died down, and after the brief thunder of footsteps on stone a group of very familiar faces suddenly burst into the office. First came Korn, who was literally wearing shining armor, followed by Thram in his characteristic goggles. Next came thin, elegant Amina in a dark blue dress, and finally gray-haired Rathmir, the village's former headman.

"Hey there, Falk," they greeted me almost in unison.

"Okay, Blaze, enough's enough," Thram growled as he entered, brandishing a fist menacingly at the Captain. "It's one thing to put restrictions on us, make us work as servants for your new recruits and all that. Arresting our friend for nothing is a whole different matter. We're taking the Glass Rose and getting the hell out of here."

"This is treason against the Empire!" The Captain roared indignantly.

"The Empire betrayed us first," said Amina, calm as always. "First they turned their backs on us and forced us to become outcasts, and now they've even intruded into our quiet little backwater and started hemming us in with their rules. They've taken enough from us!"

Thram rubbed his hands in gleeful anticipation.

"I say we tie a stick of dynamite to his unmentionables and hang him upside-down from the tower. Imagine the fireworks!"

The commandant stood up from his desk and drew his sword.

"You're very welcome to try, pipsqueak."

Naturally, I knew the four of them working together could easily have taken down an opponent like Blaze, even if he was thirty levels higher than any of them; after all, the level-100 guards outside the door hadn't given them too much difficulty. Even without Whisper of Fate, though, I knew that everybody in the room would be worse off if I let things get out of hand.

"Everybody stop!" I shouted. "Nobody needs to leave. This city officially belongs to me!"

I took out my deed and showed it to the Captain.

He took it, studied it for a long time, then handed it back to me and... Smirked with joy. The scar on his face grew a little bit whiter and spread a little bit until it seemed to be dividing his face into two halves.

"Finally!"

His reaction came as a complete surprise.

"What?"

"Thanks be to all the Gods of Light, I won't have to answer for what happens in this city anymore," Captain Blaze explained as he sheathed his sword. "I'm so tired of all these shenanigans!"

He turned to the quartet standing near the door.

"And the four of you can all go straight to hell! You'll have somebody else to babysit you from now on. I can finally get back to "Freedom" and my actual military career! I'd rather be surrounded by Orcs than stuck here in this accursed city, having to bear responsibility for all the crap that happens here!"

As the four members of the Union of the Damned looked on in surprised silence, the Captain strode quickly past them, then practically started skipping with joy as he ran down the stairs. The guards who had been running to meet him suddenly froze at attention. They clearly had no idea what was going on, still less any idea of what they were supposed to do.

"I've been relieved of my duties," Captain Blaze informed them with a joyful shout. "This city belongs to Falk de Fudre now."

For some reason, the system chose that particular moment to send me the long-awaited communication:

"You have assumed the role of Overlord of the City of Kelevre.

The city management interface will only be available to you when you are inside City Hall.

You may administer the city yourself, or appoint a commandant to do so in your place.

All further details and hints are available on the interface."

The guards watched their former commandant leave, then turned to me.

"You're free to go," I said, feeling just a little bit sorry for them. "I'll call everyone back together in a little while."

"But they're criminals," one of the guards objected rather half-heartedly. "These four attacked the City Guard and ruined the City Hall building!"

"Ahem... It was all a test, carried out at my orders." This was the best excuse I could think of on such short notice. "Very good work, all of you. Your response was exceptionally punctual. For now, though, you're free to return to your homes."

Strange as it may sound, they actually listened to me and walked away.

"Well, well," said Rathmir, who still sounded surprised.

"So does this mean you're the new commandant, then?" Korn asked. He sounded preemptively overjoyed.

"Not quite. I'm the owner of the city and the

lands it sits on, and I'm authorized to appoint a commandant."

Thram jumped up into the air excitedly.

"That's amazing! Now you can appoint Rathmir to the post, and everything will be back to normal again!"

The old man actually went pale as the Gnome spoke.

"No, no, no. No way. I'm officially retired. Margia will kill me if I go back to work."

"Everybody calm down," I said. "I have somebody who'll be perfect for the role. He'll be able to sort out all these problems and help the city prosper at the same time."

"As long as he doesn't hound us like Blaze did," Amina responded for the group. "We can figure everything else out when the time comes."

I took out my tablet and checked my messages. To my relief, Boris had finally reappeared, although he came bearing some rather unpleasant news. The location of the next Dead Immortals event would only become known once the event in Pyrenth was over. Until then, there was no way anybody could know whether it would be the next day, the next week, or the next month, which meant that we absolutely couldn't afford to risk rescheduling our attempt at resurrecting Artyom. We would have to meet "Spirit of the Hunt" face to face after all.

"Boris — I got control of the city, but I don't really know how to run the management interface yet. Any interest in joining me here?"

"Of course!" The Merchant replied immediately. *"Let me walk you through how to add me to the list of people who can open portals in the city and the City Hall building."*

It's not that I couldn't have handled it myself, of course, but why wade through a whole mountain of menus and tutorials when I could get clear, concise instructions from a guy who actually knew what he was doing? As a result, a portal opened right next to me about a minute later, and my gangly red-haired friend stepped out of it. He looked around, eyes wide with wonder, then nodded to Korn and the others before heading over to me and squeezing my hand in his own.

"Appoint me commandant of the city, so I can get access to the management interface."

I opened the menu and figured things out pretty quickly, so within a few seconds Boris was officially appointed to the role. I didn't have any doubts about the wisdom of my actions at all; sure, I was a pretty cynical person most of the time, but I trusted Boris completely.

"Okay, I'm going to need some time to study all this," the kid announced, enthusiasm still burning brightly in his eyes. "Give me half an hour."

Before leaving Boris to figure out the city management interface, I sent a meeting invite out to everybody who was planning to participate in "Operation Resurrection" the next day and added their names into the approved teleportation list. Daddy Rothschild responded almost immediately; he promised to get in touch with Pinky, Darya, and

Sergei in the real world and bring them to the meeting with him. I figured that meeting in Kelevre, in complete safety, would allow us to discuss our plans for as long as we needed to. I sent a message to Ne-Tarok as well, even though I had a strong suspicion that Pinky would pass my message on to him even without my involvement. Mark hadn't been in the game for some time; presumably, he was meeting with his sister in the real world, but I sent him a message just in case and made sure to add him to the list so he could teleport in as soon as he finished his real-world business.

I left City Hall with the rest of the "Damned" and headed off to Rathmir's house, where we found Margia waiting for us at the door. The heavy-set peasant woman was so happy to see me that she almost broke all my bones in a huge bear hug that took off a full 25% of my health. With that, she sat me down at the table and fed me in style — so much so, in fact, that I actually caught a light "overeating" debuff that temporarily reduced my Dexterity by 10. Later, Lerth the Archer came to join us as well. He was slightly drunk, as always, and was having some trouble staying on his feet. Young, gangly Varth came to join us as well. The young man was strutting around in clothing that seemed to have been made in imitation of Thram's, complete with big, bulbous goggles. He even brought some sort of disassembled mechanism with him to the table, which he continued to work on, taking only the occasional break for food.

Basically, we just had a really nice meal and chatted about everything that had happened in my absence — things that explained a lot about the new rhythm of life in Kelevre. In particular, I learned that the city's main function was as a supply depot for the "Freedom" fortress, which it helped to keep stocked with food, weapons, armor, and elixirs. Some of these things came from other cities, and some of them were manufactured right there in Kelevre. Given that the city had only just begun to expand, there was a severe shortage of craftspeople, which led Captain Blaze to force my friends into working as much as they possibly could, in order to meet all the various quotas for deliveries (and training of new recruits) for which he had to answer. The city itself was on a permanent war footing, but it came under attack only very rarely. Also, to my considerably surprise, Amina told me that they had somehow managed to get their hands on a Mellorn Acorn and a Phoenix Feather for creating the Lesser Blood Essence of a God. The Acorn wasn't a huge surprise, though; I figured Gethaniel had probably helped them get it. Whatever the case, it meant that the only things left to find were the heart of a Royal Wyvern and the tooth of a Black Dragon. And also, somebody who would be willing to create a Great Blood Essence, because I certainly wouldn't be able to help them with that. Hearing this news also reminded me that I still had to ask Boris whether he had found any of the ingredients, and tell him not to waste any further time or resources on the stuff the "Damned" had already managed to collect for themselves.

"Listen, Falk — you're the owner of these lands now, and Imperial laws give you the power to officiate at my wedding to Amina," Korn suddenly announced, right after taking a single massive gulp that drained a goblet the size of my head.

"What?!" I was extremely surprised to hear this.

"That's a great idea," the Priestess agreed as she took an elegant sip from a narrow crystal wine glass. "Other than you, the only person who has the power to marry people is me, and it would be pretty weird to officiate at your own wedding."

"Sure, but..." I paused, not really knowing how to respond. "I mean, I'm..."

"The ceremony's in a week and a half. We'd love you to be the one to conduct it," said Korn with a big smile.

Dammit, I thought... How could I refuse?

"Okay," I agreed, feeling like I didn't really have any other choice. "It'd be an honor."

It really would be, I thought, if I could somehow live to see it.

"I can tell you're going through some problems," noted Amina. "If there's anything we can do to help, just say the word."

All of the "Damned" — or maybe more accurately, the "Twice Damned" — were stopped right at the edge of level 50, and Korn and Amina didn't even have respawn tattoos. So I didn't even think about asking them to help me with my upcoming fight. In fact, if I'd had my way, I'd have simply kept them all in Kelevre, where it was safe.

"I'm always going through some sort of problem or other," I replied with a pained smile. "But I'll figure it out."

Pretty soon, I got a message from Boris letting me know that he had finally figured out how to work the interface, so I hurried back to City Hall.

"Gods help me. Whoever put all this in place was a complete idiot. How could you take such a promising start and end up operating at such an enormous loss?!" The red-haired kid groaned as soon as I walked back into the office on the second floor.

"The former commandant didn't exactly seem full of passion for the job," I agreed. "This post was basically a huge burden for him."

"Idiot," snapped Boris.

"That's for sure," I agreed. "Anyway — what did you find out about hiring soldiers? How many can I get, and how do I use them?"

"The maximum allowable number has already been hired. Apparently, the former commandant must have been a soldier himself, given that he spent every last resource on outfitting the soldiers despite the fact that the place hasn't even seen an attack yet."

Ah, I thought... So THAT explains why I saw so many guards on the way here. I thought it was just because of how close the Orcish border is to the city.

The Sands of Eternity

"But I have to disappoint you here," Boris continued. "They can't travel very far from Kelevre. It actually makes a lot of sense in principle."

"Yeah, it does," I admitted. "Still sucks though."

"For now, though, while we have a little bit of time, I'll explain to you how we're going to make our money." Boris pulled up the interface and started explaining at high speed: "Look. We have a limited amount of experience that we can dole out to players for completing quests on behalf of the city. This means we can give out quests that involve finding certain ingredients — we can pay the players in experience, and then fork over just a little bit of cash when we actually buy the ingredients off the players at the end of the quests. The players will be happy to work for us, and we'll make a fortune! And if we plan our coefficients and product timetables correctly, orienting ourselves to whatever's in demand at a given time, we can eventually sign a contract with the Empire and have a guaranteed buyer for optimum-quality shipments at awesome prices..."

The kid was on a roll, chattering away almost without stopping to breathe, but nevertheless I felt like I basically understood what he had in mind. Sure, I yawned, but that was just because I hadn't slept. For the same reason, I actually started to doze off at a certain point, and I think I even managed to fall asleep just before the first portal opened in the former commandant's office.

"Hello, everybody!" Ne-Tarok shouted happily.

"I hear there's something serious going on? Some sort of problem with tomorrow's little outing?"

As always, the Gremlin was dressed in badly worn, multicolored rags, stitched together in the most haphazard and strange-looking manner. Somehow, though, his clothes looked just a little bit nicer than they usually did. And I felt pretty sure that I knew who he had decided to dress up for.

"Exactly," I said. "Somehow, "Spirit of the Hunt" found out that we're going to be in Pyrenth tomorrow, and they decided to gather all their forces there to meet us."

The Gremlin's huge eyes bulged even more than normal.

"What?! Why do they care?!"

"Who knows?" I shrugged.

As we spoke, several more portals opened in the room, bringing Daddy Rothschild, Antibiotic, Sergio, and Pinky to join us. Hot on their heels came Poison Ivy, otherwise known as Darya. Her level-129 character looked pretty strange: she was wearing form-fitting, bright-red coveralls, and her face was concealed by a clown mask. She actually reminded me more than anything of Harley Quinn from the DC universe, although that didn't really fit with her nickname.

It took me a moment to introduce everybody to one another, and when that was done, Boris used his powers as commandant to create a huge table for our meeting.

"First off, I'll quickly remind everybody why

we're here," I began. "In Pyrenth, tomorrow at sunrise, there's going to be an event featuring flying coffins, one of which contains Artyom. Artyom's girlfriend will help us find the coffin we need, because according to the God of the Dead, it can only be done by a loving heart. We're presuming that means somebody who genuinely loves the deceased person, but we still don't know exactly when or how this ability will actually kick in."

Poison Ivy nodded in silence.

"I have an artifact from the God of the Dead, which we'll need to slip onto Artyom's arm once his health drops into the red zone. As soon as that happens, I'll create a Great Blood Essence and bring him back to life." I sighed as I came to the most important part of the story. "But we recently learned that we have a big problem on our hands: according to Mark's sister, who's one of the "Spirit of the Hunt's" generals, they somehow found out about our plans and decided to disrupt them. And before you ask, no — I have no idea what's motivating them to do this. Although I'm pretty sure they're not doing it just to be jerks."

"Maybe they want to blackmail you and make you tell them your real name?" Antibiotic suggested. "Assuming, of course, that their Clanleader is one of the Emissaries."

I didn't immediately realize who was talking, because the Dark Inquisitor suddenly had a human voice again. Apparently, the healing had restored his vocal chords, too, and his brain had fixed the growling sound on its own.

"Even if so, we still don't know how "Spirit of the Hunt" found out about our plans," noted Daddy Rothschild. "After all, nobody but the people in this room knew that we needed to find the flying coffins. I can only assume that one of us is a traitor who's leaking information."

I looked around carefully at everybody in the room. Nonsense, I thought — impossible! I mean, which of them would have done that, and why? None of them really had anything to gain by betraying us. Even Sergio, with his abrasive personality, had been happy to help, albeit only because he was interested in seeing whether you could actually resurrect somebody in the game.

The Healer noticed my eyes lingering on him and frowned.

"What? Don't you dare look at me."

His lively, delicate Elvish face stood in stark contrast to both his mannerisms and the tone of his voice. I still had no idea how he had managed to attract Princess Ariella, who was such a classically arrogant and chauvinistic Elf.

A portal flashed, and Mark flew into the room.

"Hey, everybody! Hope I'm not late? My sister was pretty bowled over. Actually, I'm pretty surprised she let me go at all."

"Did she believe you, though?"

"Would've been hard not to, after the show I put on for her. All of Hollywood's top celebrities doing a striptease right in front of her. Didn't leave her much choice but to believe."

"Ahem..." Boris raised his hand. "I've been

thinking about it. I actually don't believe in magic anymore, either."

"You're a merchant," replied Mark with a sarcastic smirk. "You just need to believe in the law of supply and demand."

"Does anybody think that maybe Mark told his sister what we're planning?" Ne-Tarok asked with feigned nonchalance from his seat right next to Pinky. "That would explain everything."

"You're just gonna come right out and accuse me, huh?" Mark asked with a grin that belied the anger in his voice.

Yeah, I thought... These two aren't off to a good start, and I'm pretty sure I know why.

"Actually, my sister promised to send us all the info she has on the number and positions of the "Spirit of the Hunt's" players right before the event," the irritated Illusionist snapped. "According to the preliminary info she already passed on, there are already about 5,000 players in Pyrenth right now, and there probably won't be too many more by tomorrow morning. Everybody who's available is basically already there. Also, she's going to try to talk to the Clanleader and learn more about what he's hoping to achieve here."

"She couldn't be one of the beta-testers, could she?" The Healer asked, turning to Darya. The young woman had been sitting there listening intently the entire time, but she still hadn't said a word.

"All beta-testers are under Skolas' control. The company already had all their personal information, so it wasn't hard at all for him to convince everybody to keep working for him. Money for some, threats for others. I didn't know them all personally, so I can't really say who's a beta-tester and who isn't, but what I do know is that they all work for RussVirtTech."

"Okay, but that's not important at all right now," noted Antibiotic, whose voice sounded harsher than before. "Unless we're dropping our plans, we've got a direct confrontation with "Spirit of the Hunt" on our hands. Teleports won't be working during the event, so they won't be able to call for any reinforcements."

"They've got a third of the Clan there. Why would they need reinforcements?" Ne-Tarok chuckled.

"5,000 players isn't a third of that Clan," Daddy Rothschild shook his head. "It might be a quarter, at most. And that means…"

"We can get revenge for everything they've done to our Clan over the last few months," said Antibiotic as he slammed his fist down onto the table with excitement. "They think they're setting a trap for you, but when the event starts they're actually going to find themselves bottled up in Pyrenth by the "Unnameables." We're already a step ahead of them, and tomorrow morning we're going to wipe them out!"

Chapter 6

"DO YOU REALLY HAVE THE MUSCLE for that?" Mark asked in a slightly derogatory tone.

As a member of the "Spirit of the Hunt," I would have thought he might prefer to keep silent and let sleeping dogs lie, but apparently he just couldn't help himself.

"You've already lost your position in the ratings to 'Spirit of the Hunt'," Sergio reminded them, just in time to prevent a certain green-skinned, long-eared player from saying something nasty to Mark. "And as far as I've heard, a lot of players have left your Clan."

Antibiotic's reply was completely calm:

"Only the dead weight. The entire professional core is still there, and they've all been leveling up like crazy ever since we went dark. We can put 5,000 or 6,000 players into the field too, and their average level will be a hell of a lot higher.”

“I can confirm that,” nodded Daddy Rothschild. “I put out the call as soon as I heard what was going on. Everybody’s stocking up on teleports. Just to make sure we don’t scare away “Spirit of the Hunt” before the event, they’ve all temporarily left the Clan.”

“Seriously?!” Pinky sounded shocked. “What about Clan bonuses?”

“We’ll get by without them,” replied Antibiotic with total confidence. “We’re totally oriented on the element of surprise here. Which is also why we can’t use mercenaries. They’d spill the beans for sure.”

“And these players won’t?” Mark asked, sounding very dubious indeed. “You really think EVERY member of your Clan will keep their mouth shut about this?”

Yep, I concluded... Mark simply can’t help himself, can he?

“Nobody knows where we’re actually going, or who we’re going to be fighting. They’ll get that information at the last possible moment.”

“Well, then... Sounds like you’ve thought it through pretty well,” Mark was finally forced to admit.

“We’re really glad you approve — it means a lot,” replied Daddy Rothschild, his voice dripping with sarcasm. “Maybe you could give us some tactical advice while we’re at it?”

Surprisingly, the Illusionist finally seemed to realize that he was trying to punch above his weight, and he finally stopped prodding the Naumovs.

"As for tactics, I could bring a hundred Elvish Archers with me as a personal guard," said Sergio. "They'd only be at my level. But they definitely wouldn't tell anybody anything either. They could help protect Andrey... I mean, Falk."

"We've assigned a number of players with suitable classes to protect Falk," explained Daddy Rothschild. "Tanks, and Mages who specialize in shields. It won't be a problem."

"Actually, yeah, I can't die during this," I belatedly remembered. "I don't know exactly how to do it, but I'm at level 50 right now, and resurrecting Artyom's going to require a Great Blood Essence. That'll cost me twenty levels, so if I drop down to 49, I won't be able to create it."

"How about I create it instead?" Darya suggested immediately. "You've already lost a lot of ground in your development, which is going to make it hard to complete your quest from the Goddess. Plus, it'll make you weaker in real life and make you a much easier target."

"I'd love to say yes," I sighed. "But my Essence is the only one that'll work. It's a precondition of the resurrection."

Suddenly, Ne-Tarok burst out laughing.

"So we need to protect you from "Spirit of the Hunt," who have their strongest players all gathered to find you, knock your friend down to about 10% health while making sure we don't kill him, prevent any other players from killing him, and give you enough time to slip that amulet on his neck and feed him a Great Blood Essence. All that, provided that Poison Ivy can even find the coffin in the first place."

"Yeah, that's basically the situation," I nodded. "And don't forget that the whole city is under a curse from the God of the Dead, and anybody who gets killed will come back after a few seconds. But there's an upside to that, too: I have a blessing from the God of the Dead which means that the undead players won't touch me."

Mark snorted.

"I wouldn't get too cocky about that, but if we accidentally hit one of the flying coffins — "

"Which somebody definitely will," Ne-Tarok interrupted him. "And then all hell will break loose."

"I still have one more summons for Aishorth Bludstein. She was at level 225 last time I saw her. Although even she won't be able to take out ALL our enemies this time."

"Who?" Darya asked, whereupon Pinky (who was sitting next to her) leaned over and started to explain who Aishorth was.

"Summon her right away, then, and have her protect you and Artyom as soon as we find him," suggested Ne-Tarok. "Why wait?"

This idea had already occurred to me as well.

"Hang on," Mark objected. "We have a few aces up our sleeves here, including the Ice Lady, but we can't lay them all on the table right away. I'm sure the most powerful clan in Arktania has something that can somehow take her out of the equation."

The Sands of Eternity

We had already spent quite a bit of time discussing the situation, but we still hadn't thought of anything new — and besides, the confrontation between the two Clans was bound to be a bloodbath no matter what we ended up doing. I was still thinking that it would be good to go talk to Eidolon, but that would require me to go back to the scene of my battle with the dark faction, and I still couldn't decide whether that would be worth the risk. For the time being, therefore, I didn't mention that possibility to anyone.

After agreeing to meet an hour before the start of the event the next morning, everybody started to go their separate ways: Mark rushed off to run through the instance again in the hope of finding the secret level with the Anaconda, Antibiotic and his dad went off to prepare their Clan for battle, and I suddenly realized that Sergio had actually left before we even finished our discussion. We lost Boris as soon as he opened the city management interface, while Pinky and Ne-Tarok headed out to walk around the city. They seemed to have become even closer after our group meeting in the real world. A lot closer.

In the end, it was just Darya and I left in the room. Obviously, there was some pressing reason she had stayed behind and waited for everybody else to leave.

"Look, I didn't want to say this in front of everybody, but I have an ability that will really come in handy for you tomorrow. I can switch two characters' physical appearances and nicknames, as long as both parties agree to it."

"Why didn't you say that when we were all talking just now?"

"YOU may have known these people for a long time, but this is the first time I've ever met most of them," the Acrobat explained. "And somehow, "Spirit of the Hunt" has already found out about our plans in Pyrenth, so I'd rather not take any unnecessary risks. My advice would be to summon this Ice Lady of yours and switch appearances with her."

The suggestion was very unexpected, but it struck me as a very good idea. The main question was simply whether Aishorth would agree to help me. Although actually... If I looked like a level-225 character, any opponents who decided to attack me would probably hit me with every ounce of power at their disposal. Wouldn't I just be exchanging the target on my back for another, much bigger target?

"Let's not rush into anything," I decided. "Let's keep thinking about how and when to use your ability. In any case, though, you're right — it might be really helpful."

We were still talking as we left City Hall, and at the entrance we suddenly ran into everybody from the "Union of the Damned." Korn, Amina, Thram, Lerth, Rathmir, and even little Varth had all come to meet me, and they all looked deeply dissatisfied.

"So you have all these problems, and you never even mentioned them to us," Thram shook his head in dismay. "Agh, it's such a disappointment."

Darya jumped, obviously preparing for a fight, but I laid a hand on her shoulder and shook my head.

"It's like you don't trust us," said the Priestess, seconding the Gnome.

"It's insulting, actually," Korn agreed as he brandished a huge fist in front of my face. "You could catch a beating for something like this."

Dammit, I thought... What a mess. But how did they find everything out so fast?

"We heard every word," said Vath as he held up the little machine he had been working on during our lunch. "My little spider crawled into City Hall and passed on your whole conversation."

"Eavesdropping, then?" I frowned.

"You seemed a little too nervous. So we had to apply our curiosity, along with a little bit of insolence," admitted Thram. "But it's your own fault, really. You shouldn't hide your problems from your friends."

"Just tell us what's really going on, unless you want to insult us some more," said Amina, in a softer voice than before. "I'm sure we can help you out."

I hadn't been expecting this at all, of course, and I was thoroughly at a loss. Mind you, they had come to me on their own initiative, so there really didn't seem to be any point in trying to keep my plans concealed from them any more. I led them back into City Hall, to get away from the prying ears of the players who were passing by, and then told them all about what we were going to attempt the next morning.

"We're going with you," Thram announced as soon as I finished. "I'm not going to miss a party like that!"

"Me either!" Korn agreed.

Thram turned to the Smith with a skeptical look.

"Actually, by "we," I meant me and Lerth. You and Amina don't have respawn tattoos, and you can't leave the Glass Rose's active radius."

"Yeah, but — "

"No 'buts'," said Lerth as he laid a hand on Korn's shoulder and breathed a big, boozy breath right into the Smith's face. Darya and I could smell it even from where we were standing, about ten feet away. "You've got a *hic* wedding coming up. It'd be completely stupid to die right now."

"I'm leaving for Pyrenth right this minute," said Thram. "I have connections there. I'll get my friends together and prepare a nice explosive surprise for your enemies. Honestly, they've been working on updating the city infrastructure for a while now, so if a few buildings disappear it'll actually be good for Pyrenth."

Lerth immediately announced that he was going with the Gnome, but everybody else had to stay behind. Rathmir would respawn in the Dead City if he died again, and nobody needed that (not that Margia would have let him go in any case). Having to sit the fun out hit Korn harder than anyone, but he couldn't say no to Amina, so he just promised that he would help me put together a nice set of equipment for my newly-lowered level. The Priestess told me to come visit her the next morning before we left, so she could give me and my friends the most powerful of her blessings from the Goddess of Fate. Everybody wanted to help in whatever way they could, and even Varth brought me the little spider he had used to listen in on our conversation. And it turned out that with my Power over Machines skill, the little spider would obey the commands I gave it, even at a pretty considerable distance. Sure, I couldn't quite imagine how it might come in handy for me, but it seemed virtually certain that I could find some application for it at some point.

As long as we were all gathered together anyway, I turned to Boris and asked him how the hunt for ingredients for our Lesser Blood Essence of a God was coming along. It turned out that he was already negotiating with someone who owned a Phoenix Feather, but so far he hadn't had much success other than that. After telling him that we only needed two of the ingredients, I headed off to the artisans' shops to get Chaosite some food before finally exiting the game — just like Darya, who had decided not to show her face in Kelevre any more than necessary. In real life, she had Naumov to help her hide from the other beta-testers, but finding her in the game would have been quite a bit easier: all it would have taken was for any player, from any clan that was led by Skolas' underlings, to catch sight of her once, and she'd be screwed.

After climbing out of the capsule, I collapsed exhausted onto my bed. I knew I still needed to gather my strength in order to go see Eidolon and try to convince him to help us in the battle with "Spirit of the Hunt," but I barely had the energy to make myself a cup of coffee. I didn't even notice myself falling asleep; I simply woke up and found that I had been asleep for about ten hours. Thankfully, I didn't oversleep till lunch this time and miss the Dead Immortals event. That would have been the epic fail of the century. Even so, though, it meant I didn't have any time to go meet with Eidolon, so I tried frantically to think of some other way to get my request to him. I remembered him saying that he could transmit his will to the dead via his temples, which meant that there was at least a chance I could get in touch with him that way.

It was 10:00 AM. There was still an hour to go before our scheduled rendezvous in Kelevre, which meant that I had plenty of time to find a Temple of the Dead. If only I knew where to look for one...

I jumped into the capsule, flew down the rainbow tunnel, and found myself in the City Hall building once again. Boris was still sitting in exactly the same spot as before: right at the table, digging around in the city management interface in front of him.

"Did you sleep at all?" I asked with a yawn.

"Huh?" He asked; it took him a second to refocus his eyes. "No — why would I? It's only..." He glanced back into the space in front of him. "Oh. 10:00 AM. Damn, I guess I went down a rabbit hole."

"I'll say," I agreed. "Listen, though — any idea where I can find a Temple of the Dead? I want to visit one to get in touch with Eidolon."

"Yeah, sure — keep dreaming. Nobody knows where they are, except for one very specific one I know about in the zombies' city that people call the Accursed Temple. But there's no way a living person could get in there."

Thankfully, I had Eidolon's blessing, so the dead wouldn't hurt me.

"And where is the zombie city?"

"They occupied some ruins not far from Ditmar and Pyrenth. But you won't be able to teleport there, it's considered hostile territory."

Shit, shit, shit, I thought! I just HAD to fall asleep for ten hours last night, didn't I?! How the hell am I going to talk to Eidolon now?! Unless I can somehow use one of the zombies to get in touch with him? They're all friendly toward me, at least as long as I have his blessing.

"Listen — does the God of the Dead's curse affect Kelevre, too?"

"Check the interface yourself," Boris grumbled. "Look to the right of your status icon — no curses. The God of the Dead only cursed the very biggest cities, and it wasn't so long ago that Kelevre was nothing but a little frontier outpost."

Dammit... Time for a new idea.

"What's the nearest city where the God of the

Dead's curse is still in effect?"

"Katar or Pyrenth."

Neither option sounded good to me at all. If I ended up running into anybody from "Spirit of the Hunt," dying, and losing a level, it would make the whole scheme completely pointless. But how else could I find a zombie to get the word to Eidolon — and hopefully bring his answer back to me — in time before the event started?

On second thought, though... What does it matter how close a city is, if you're going to teleport anyway?

"Veritha?"

"Also cursed," the red-haired kid nodded.

Perfect, I thought — that's where I'll teleport, then. All that remained was to find someone to go with me. Mark would be ideal, with his illusions, although Darya would do the trick as well. A quick glance at my tablet revealed that Artyom's girl-friend was the only one online anyway, so that's who I called.

"It'll be five minutes," I explained as soon as she appeared through the teleport. "In and out. We teleport into Veritha, negotiate with a player to let us pay him to kill him, then I talk to his undead body for a second and we're out of there."

"I have no idea what you're talking about, but it sounds interesting enough," the Acrobat replied, sounding thoroughly puzzled. "Why do you need to talk to a zombie, though? More importantly, why would you pay this player before killing them?"

"I need them to pass on a message to the God of the Dead. I'm hoping for some divine help in Pyrenth," I explained without going into too much detail.

"But why PAY them, though?"

"So I don't get labeled a PK."

"I think you worry about this kind of thing way too much," she snickered. "Just kill somebody — it's not that big a deal. You're actually going to ask their permission?"

I don't know whether it was the Harley Quinn makeup, or just the way she was smiling, but for some reason the look on her face made me feel a little uncomfortable.

I had already been to Veritha, and I knew the "Unnameables" had a residence there. Actually, it was where I had met Daddy Rothschild for the very first time. I could only assume they had lost the place after being defeated in the war with "Spirit of the Hunt;" it was far too convenient a location. The city itself was located on the sea, and it had a very Italian flair to it: small houses, cute little gardens, and a ton of other charming little details that made me think in a sort of cutesy voice when I thought about the place.

"Okay, now we just have to find our victim," I said as I looked around.

"Why do we need to do that?" Darya giggled as she pointed a finger at me. "They're right here."

"I don't get it," I said with a frown.

"Here's what we'll do: we'll exchange appearances, and then I'll head down some of the more dangerous streets where the guards don't usually patrol. I'll definitely run into somebody before too long. And we won't have to pay anybody a dime."

"Makes sense," I admitted.

"Also, it'll give you a chance to see how my ability works. It's a pretty weird feeling. It'd be good for you to get used to it."

And that's exactly what we did. I had no idea what sort of feeling Darya was talking about, though, until she used her ability on me. The system sent me a request, asking if I was okay with "Swapping Persons," and only when I confirmed it did I start to feel a slight tingling sensation all across my body. After a few deep breaths, my body had completely transformed. It was more athletic, more flexible, and... Well, bigger in certain places. Everything inside it felt more or less the same as before, but I found that I could physically feel all the changes too — they weren't like Mark's illusions.

"Holy crap!" I gasped, and heard Darya's voice instead of my own.

"Just keep your hands to yourself," she cautioned me. Or rather, Falk cautioned me. "Don't touch my boobs or take off your clothes."

"I hadn't even considered the idea," I lied. "Wow. I thought this was going to be something like Mark's illusions, but we've almost literally exchanged bodies here."

"More like exchanged skins," she corrected me. "Now you keep away from me while I head down the streets that don't have guards on them and find us a victim."

The plan seemed pretty good, and in the end we found our victim — or should I say "victims" — really quickly. A pair of players took the bait offered by a relatively-weak, level-50 player, and decided to beat him down for all he (or rather, I) was worth. Poison Ivy killed them both with two quick swings of her saber. By the way, I was pretty surprised to see her wielding this specific type of weapon; I felt like Harley Quinn's enormous sledgehammer would have suited her better.

I ran over to join her (or rather, myself — it's hard not to forget that we had switched bodies) and arrived just as the two zombies started rising to their feet. They were already preparing to attack Darya, but I moved to put myself in front of her.

"Stop."

As usual, the zombies were still moving shakily and hesitantly, as if they were still trying to remember how to move their bodies. They couldn't speak yet, either, but I didn't need them to.

"I want to send a message to Eidolon," I explained, so slowly it almost felt like individual syllables were falling out of my mouth rather than words. "There's going to be a battle with the "Spirit of the Hunt" Clan in Pyrenth today. They're trying to stop me from resurrecting the Emissary of the God of the Dead. I think it's in his interests to help us. Ask him to make the dead refrain from attacking any players except the ones from 'Spirit of the Hunt'."

The zombies listened to me in silence, and I

thought they were about to turn around and leave, but suddenly the dead players started to speak in perfect unison:

"Whoa. You're aging well," they said sarcastically. "How could I refuse a request from such a beauty?"

"Eidolon?" I asked.

"The very same," came the zombies' synchronized reply. "I heard what you said, and I'll be happy to join in the fun on your side. If this all ends well, though, I want you to come see me. We have something to discuss."

"Zombies!" A shout rang out from behind us. "Take 'em down!"

Darya and I jumped aside and allowed a crowd of players to take out the zombies with their long spears. Nobody messed with us at all, since there was a guard standing nearby — and even if there hadn't been, messing with a player at level 132 was generally a pretty dubious prospect.

Darya shot me a suspicious look.

"He wants to you visit him?"

"He's speaking figuratively."

With our message to the God of Death already sent, and an affirmative reply already in hand, I immediately felt a whole lot better. I couldn't even begin to imagine how many zombies would rise once the fight between the "Unnameables" and "Spirit of the Hunt" kicked off. If the zombies focused all their attacks on our enemies, the latter wouldn't last for very long at all. I could only hope that the "Steel Rats" would make an appearance, too, and get at least a little bit of what they had coming to them.

To avoid tempting fate, we exchanged appearances right after our little chat with the zombies and headed straight back to Kelevre. Our little dream team was already starting to gather when we arrived: Daddy Rothschild, Ne-Tarok and Pinky, Mark, and a couple dozen high-level players from the "Unnameables." Sergio was supposed to teleport to Pyrenth with his Elves in advance and scout the area a little bit, while Antibiotic and most of the "Unnameables" army were planning to teleport in at the last possible moment — maybe ten minutes before the event was supposed to start. Boris wasn't planning to come with us, but he helped everybody sort out their equipment and gave us all a good supply of elixirs and teleportation scrolls. Amina gathered us all together in the town square and gave us a pretty powerful blessing, which would increase our chances of dealing critical damage and help block any damage inflicted on us. Once preparations were complete, we gathered around a big map of the city.

"Here's what I suggest," Daddy Rothschild took the floor as soon as everything was ready. "You and your bodyguards teleport here, right into the center of the city, about twenty minutes before the event is supposed to start. I doubt that "Spirit of the Hunt" will attack you right away. They obviously have something else in mind with all this; they're not just aiming to send you back to the respawn point. They'll want to talk and give you their terms first, and it'd be good if we knew what they're hoping to achieve before the battle starts. The rest of our fighters will teleport into the city after that."

"Makes sense," I agreed. "As long as we aren't overestimating their common sense, of course."

"Actually, my sister's already in Pyrenth, trying to get the Clanleader to tell her why he's hunting you so obsessively," Mark warned us as he looked around at everybody in the room. "If possible, try not to hurt Trish Merisilver. She's kind of on our side here."

"Kind of?" Ne-Tarok repeated. "I guess we'll 'kind of' try not to attack her, then."

"Well, YOU can attack all you want," snickered the Illusionist. "Not that there'd be any point to it, of course."

The look on the Gremlin's face said that he was about to lay into Mark once again, so I hurried to intervene:

"I'm not 100% sure about all the details, but I have an agreement with the God of the Dead. He's going to make sure any zombies who pop up because of his curse will only attack people from 'Spirit of the Hunt'."

"Sweet!"

"Seriously?!"

"That's awesome!"

I found it interesting that the first reaction came from Daddy Rothschild; it certainly didn't fit with either his age or his overall vibe.

I told them about how Darya and I had passed

on a message to the God of the Dead, and how he had promised to help. Plus, I knew that I had his amulet in my inventory — the amulet that was supposed to turn Artyom into Eidolon's Emissary within Arktania. So he obviously had some pretty clear incentive to help us in any way he could.

After checking the map one more time to find and memorize the drop zone for every member of our group, I teleported to Pyrenth with Darya, Pinky, Ne-Tarok, and my bodyguards from the "Unnameables." Mark decided to keep his distance from me this time, choosing instead to appear in another part of the city and link up with Sergio from there.

Operation "Resurrect Artyom" had begun.

Chapter 7

PYRENTH MET US with an atmosphere of deceptive calm. The calm before the storm, as it were. The air was practically sparking from the tension, as if a huge peal of thunder and lightning might erupt at any moment. The streets were almost empty, which was very unusual for such a big city. Here and there, groups of twenty or thirty players were huddled together on street corners. From time to time, a lone player would come running through the area, but they soon realized that whatever was coming was going to be bad, at which point they would either duck into the nearest tavern or teleport out of the city entirely. None of the locals even ventured out of their houses; in fact, for all I knew, they might have evacuated the city en masse.

"Feels dangerous," said Darya. "It feels like one wrong move will bring the sky crashing down on us."

I winced a little bit as I thought about this, then summoned Chaosite and Spin (the latter in his base form as a little ball of light). They were both ready to release their auras at my command, in order to protect me from attacks as well as they possibly could.

"Yeah," I agreed. "What worries me more than anything is that this is all happening because of me. Back at school, they used to tell us that "the world doesn't revolve around you..." Ah, I miss those days, back when it really DIDN'T revolve around me."

Darya shot me sidelong glance.

"What the hell are you talking about?"

"I'm just nervous," I explained. Saying that, however, I suddenly remembered that the Heart of the Blizzard was still lying in my inventory. After pulling the artifact out, I grabbed it in my hand and calmed down instantly. Once I did, I was able to pay a lot closer attention to what was going on around me, and I noticed some interesting little details: the place we were standing afforded us an excellent view of the port and the multitude of ships moored there, all of which were teeming with players. Guards seemed to have disappeared from the streets completely, even though they should technically have been there to maintain public order. And high up in the sky, way above the clouds, I could see several dozen flying mounts soaring through the air together with their riders. These warriors were exceptionally valuable, because only pets of the very highest rank could even attain a flying form at all. Even the most powerful Clan in Arktania couldn't afford all that many of them.

"The world keeps on turning. Let's just hope it doesn't spin out of control and crush you to death," said Ne-Tarok with a nervous chuckle, which earned him a slap in the back of the head from Pinky. "Ow! Hey, look — there's our welcoming committee."

Sure enough, several players with "Spirit of the Hunt" badges next to their names came strutting toward us. The most powerful of them was a certain Zacherial, at an eye-popping level 139. The mysterious Clanleader and Universal Mage was a young man with close-cropped chestnut hair, and he was wearing some kind of cloak that completely concealed his body. He didn't look all that impressive, actually, other than his astronomical level. Another ten or so high-level players were clustered around him; they were just a little bit lower in level than he was, but they looked much more imposing with their shiny armor and special weapons. It seemed like the Clan's entire upper management team was there, with the sole exception of Trish Merisilver.

"Well, hello there," the Clanleader/Mage greeted me with a friendly smile. "I've been looking for you for a long time now."

"Hi." My voice was completely calm, thanks to the Heart of the Blizzard in my hand. "I've been avoiding this meeting for a long time now. Although I don't even know what you want from me."

"It's quite simple. You're a Man of Fate, like me," Zacherial announced with a look that suggested this meant something important. "And therefore you should be working with us, ready to stand beside me at the critical moment and determine the fate of this world."

I quickly glanced around at the other "Spirit of the Hunt" players next to him, but I saw that they were just as confused as I was.

"I don't know what you're talking about," I admitted.

The Clanleader wasn't put off by my response at all.

"Nobody ever understands until it's too late. Although understanding everything too early is no better."

Gods, I thought... This guy's insane. What if all these problems are coming up because he's having some sort of schizophrenic episode?!

"I think he's sick in the head," Ne-Tarok whispered from behind me.

I checked the time and saw that we still had fifteen minutes to go until the start of the event. Just a little bit more, and the city would start flooding with hundreds of players from the "Unnameables." And I still didn't know what the leader of "Spirit of the Hunt" wanted from me.

"Can you explain that in a human language, please?" I couldn't restrain my annoyance, even despite the artifact's calming effect.

"All Emissaries must either join my team or die," Zacherial explained with the same friendly smile on his face as before. "And I don't give a shit what faction they belong to — dark, light, neutral. There's only going to be one faction, and it's going to be mine."

See, I thought? Things can actually be pretty clear when you use human language to explain them. All that crap about too early, too late, Man of Fate... Well, that's exactly what it was: crap.

"I'd be interested to hear how you're planning to do that," I said.

"You come to our base, and you live and play there until the Hour arrives."

"What's 'the Hour'?"

"Ooh..." The "Spirit of the Hunt" Clanleader said with a predatory grin. "So you don't know? Well, I can — "

My usual bad luck kicked in: just as he was about to get to the interesting part, the "Unnameables" started arriving in advance of the event, and the whole city started to glow with teleportation flashes. After a very brief delay, combat spells started exploding out all over the city as well, soon accompanied by screams and the clanging of steel on steel.

"I suppose that's your backup?" Zacherial didn't seem surprised at all. "Interesting. What exactly are you hoping to achieve, coming out in arms against the strongest Clan in Arktania? This whole city is under our control. I have thousands of people here."

Suddenly, he glanced carefully at the body-guards surrounding me, then exchanged a few words with a female Elf in aggressive-looking war-paint who was standing right next to him.

"Ah. I recognize a few of these faces, they're from the "Unnameables." You thought nobody would recognize you once you left your Clan? And I suppose all these people teleporting into the city right now are your friends, out to get their revenge? This is actually great — we won't have to run all over Arktania looking for you."

I knew it might be a good idea to flee at that point, but I just couldn't resist asking a few more questions:

"And you brought all these players here just to catch me?"

"It wasn't difficult. I just had to give a few quick orders. I hear you consider it really important to participate in this event with the Dead Immortals." The Clanleader winked at me. "Well, I'll let you do that, but only if you give me your real-world address. We'll stand here until my people can confirm that they've found you, and then you can do whatever you want."

So, I thought... Whoever told him what we were planning, they didn't tell him what our actual goal was. That made me feel a little bit better, although I still didn't have any idea who could have sold us out so treacherously.

"So if I give you my address, you'll let us go?" I asked.

"Of course," the Mage assured me.

After thinking for a moment, I gave him the address for the previous apartment that Hotei had provided me.

"He's lying," said one of the players standing next to Zacherial.

"I can tell that much without your ability," the Clanleader scoffed derisively. "Well, then you're going to have to stand here and watch the coffins fly over you, and you won't be able to do anything about it. It'll be funny for us to watch, if nothing else."

With that, all the high-level players lunged at us, and a vicious battle broke out between them and my bodyguards. The people Daddy Rothschild had provided were lower in terms of level than our assailants, but they were all specialists in defense. After covering themselves with magical shields, the bodyguards extended their reach to cover us as well, then transitioned over to a static defense. Before long, however, their enemies simply mowed them down, without any apparent concern for their own losses.

"Weak stuff," noted Zacherial drily as he strode toward us. Before he could cast anything, though, the first slain bodyguards were back on their feet, along with a couple players from "Spirit of the Hunt" who had been killed. As I had hoped, they turned and attacked our assailants as soon as they were up.

Pinky, Ne-Tarok, Darya and I took off running, trying to make it to the next street, where (according to our plan, at least) we were supposed to find Sergio and his Elves waiting for us. Somebody obviously tried to throw something lethal at us as we fled, but Chaosite's aura kicked in and threw the spell off — in fact, this happened several times as we were fleeing. Wow, I thought... Could my luck finally be changing?

"Credit Obligations!" Ne-Tarok shouted as he cast one of his abilities.

A ripple passed across the space around us, and then some golden chains suddenly burst out of the ground and wrapped themselves around the arms and legs of a few invisible players who had been following us. Before it was over, Antibiotic and his team of the "Unnameables'" most powerful generals had come charging on the scene.

"We'll take care of this from here," the Dark Inquisitor shouted as he sank his blade into one of our invisible pursuers. "Sergio and Mark are waiting for you right where they said they'd be."

I managed to catch a glimpse of Antibiotic and the other players who had arrived with him as they tore their way into "Spirit of the Hunt's" ranks, just before we turned and ducked behind the corner of one of the nearby houses. Battle was unfolding rapidly in the spacious, stone-built city. Stone sidewalks started bursting apart as nature spells sent rapidly-growing roots right through them; we could hear the screams of humans and the roars of summoned beasts; and the sound of steel on steel soon slid together into one long, synchronized shriek. Thankfully, Pyrenth was actually a pretty big city, and the buildings were close enough to one another that the players usually tended to split up into small groups. At one point, we saw a unit of Ice Mages lift their staves to the sky and send a flurry of ice spears whistling toward their opponents, only for the latter to block them with their magical shields. Fiery flashes reflected off the stone walls all around us, filling the streets with the smell of burning and a strange, spark-filled light. A pair of soldiers from "Spirit of the Hunt" jumped out to attack us; one of them was holding a little ball of purple energy in his hand which he threw at us as soon as he saw us. Darya, however, reacted quickly by throwing out her own yellow ball (this one more reminiscent of a child's toy), which the purple ball turned and began to pursue immediately. By that point, I was ready for battle, and I slapped one of my opponents with a Paralyzing Electric Chain. It didn't work, though — the difference in level between us was simply too great.

"You should stay out of this, with your level. You'll only get in our way," said Ne-Tarok (with just a hint of mockery in his voice) as he threw up a handful of coins that started biting the enemy player like a cloud of mosquitoes. Within a second, though, Darya's saber finished the player off.

"Just try to stay alive," said Pinky with a reassuring slap on the shoulder. "We're all here to protect you."

Yeah, I thought... She's right. It sucks, but this is obviously one of those times when the only abilities that might come in handy are Shift and Micro Chaos Shield. Even jumping was out, because I didn't want to attract any more attention than I absolutely had to.

Suddenly, an earsplitting, slightly-nauseating shriek split the air somewhere at the edges of my perception. The Dead Immortals event was about to start. Soon, the air would be swarming with coffins, which meant that we would need to link up with Mark as soon as possible in order to make use of his illusions. They would up our chances of finding the coffin we needed; then, once Darya had found Artyom, Pinky and I would exchange skins, and she would go off to draw our opponents' fire. I was a little worried about using this ability right away, because it would stop working after taking a certain amount of damage, and according to Darya it took twenty minutes to recharge.

"Watch out!" Darya shouted, and we all moved out of the way. Right in the spot where we had been standing not a second before, a huge Griffon suddenly slammed down onto the ground from above, together with its rider who threw a big fan of bombs at us.

The one that fell at my feet ended up being a dud, thanks to Chaosite's aura, but Pinky just barely managed to throw up an electric shield in time, and she still ended up taking a significant amount of damage. Ne-Tarok teleported over to a coin he had thrown to the side a moment before, while Darya did an impressive backflip that took her out of harm's way. As she flew, she whipped a handful of throwing knives at the Griffon, but the beast simply slapped them aside with its wings.

"Son of a bitch," the Gremlin growled. "Credit

Obligations!"

Golden chains burst out of the ground again, but they dissolved the moment they touched the Griffon. In response, however, the beast began to cackle, and I suddenly sensed that my body wasn't listening to my brain anymore. Presumably, it was some kind of powerful stun effect. I could still use Shift even despite being stunned, though, which saved me from being disemboweled by the Griffon's claw-studded paw.

"We're screwed!" Ne-Tarok shouted from where he stood, unable to move a muscle, let alone throw a coin to teleport. But before the Griffon had time to hit anybody else, it was suddenly slammed to the ground by a torrential downpour of arrows. The damage was so colossal that both beast and rider both died almost instantly.

"Ha ha! Half griffon, half hedgehog!" I heard Mark's overjoyed voice echo down the street. A second later, we caught sight of a group of Elf Archers wearing their classic green-leather armor.

"Come here, I'll heal you guys!" Sergio shouted from his position right in the center of the Elvish unit. "We'll travel together from here on!"

Unfortunately, such a huge group of players was virtually guaranteed to attract unwanted attention, and we soon came under a hail of bombs thrown from the backs of the flying mounts above us. A chain of explosions burst through the air and threw the Elves around like bowling pins. True, very few of them actually died; they just took a huge amount of damage. Sergio and several other

The Sands of Eternity

Healers activated a powerful combined aura, and before long everybody's health was climbing back toward the green zone.

Meanwhile, the dead Griffon stood up from the ground and began to cackle as it soared up into the air to attack its former comrades-in-arms. Its rider came back as a zombie, too; he turned to look at us with his half-blind eyes, then slowly turned around and strolled off down the street in search of other opponents. Apparently, Eidolon was as good as his word: the zombies only seemed to be attacking people from "Spirit of the Hunt."

"How about you guys take care of these flying enemies, while we keep moving in a tight circle?" Mark suggested. "That'll make it easier for me to keep everybody covered with my illusions. We have to get moving here — look, the coffins are already flying in!"

Sure enough, a group of flying coffins started to drift toward us across the sky. They were coming beneath the area where the flying mounts from "Spirit of the Hunt" were throwing their bombs. Made of wood, steel, stone, in all shapes and sizes, colorations, and even dimensions, the coffins were floating in at a leisurely pace, almost low enough to scrape the tops of the city's buildings. Man, I thought... I'd hate to be the player who accidentally drops a bomb on one of these. I can't even imagine the kind of pain that'll come roaring out of it.

"I'll throw an illusion over us to make us look like normal players, so they'll still be attacking us," warned Mark. "But at least they won't be focusing all their energy on you."

After passing by a few more cross streets, we found ourselves right underneath the first coffins in the "flock" that was drifting over us.

"Now for the interesting part," I said nervously. "I have no idea how this works, Darya, but this part's all you. Find him."

Ne-Tarok scoffed.

"Shouldn't we give her a piece of his clothing so she can get the scent?"

Pinky slapped him in the back of the head (something that seemed to have become a habit for her by that point).

"Quiet."

With her Acrobat's Dexterity, Darya had no trouble climbing up onto the roof of the nearest building. I followed her, using Repulsion to jump up off the ground and bringing Mark with me when I did, so he could keep the illusion running. Ne-Tarok threw a coin up and teleported, but Pinky had to climb the stairs like an ordinary mortal.

"I'll try to make us invisible, but I'm not sure it's going to work against such high-level players," Mark warned us all.

There were a huge number of coffins — they filled almost the entire sky, and for the first time it occurred to me that we might not even find Artyom at all. Even if Darya DID love him, after such a short time knowing him, would she actually be able to find the coffin we needed when there were so many of them up there?

"Feel anything?" I asked; I was whispering, for some reason.

"No," Darya whispered back; then, a little louder, she added: "I knew this was a stupid idea. I mean, what the hell does that even mean — 'love'?!"

"Well, maybe it's kind of like a power that you can feel inside you," said Ne-Tarok as he scratched the back of his head. "The power of love, right? Maybe the game will mark the coffin for you somehow. A pink heart, for example…"

We stood there on the rooftop, seemingly unnoticed by anyone around us. Darya was studying the coffins carefully as they flew by above us, but to no avail. The rest of us kept looking around, prepared to react to an attack at any moment. The rooftop gave us an excellent view of the spells and explosions flashing throughout the city, along with big columns of light that marked players with blessings and a whole sea of various auras that decked the city out in all the colors of the rainbow.

"So pretty," said Pinky.

I was far too worried about the fact that Darya wasn't finding the coffin we needed to enjoy the beauty of the battle all around us.

"Maybe we should approach this logically?" Mark suggested. "What if we try to look for a coffin with some external mark that would tie it to Artyom?"

"There are too many coffins. We'll never find him if we do that," I replied anxiously. "We need something like a pin on the map, or at least a specific direction."

Darya clapped her hands.

"Of course! A compass! It's worth a try!"

She pulled out a throwing knife and laid it in the palm of her hand.

"Artyom gave me this knife. Remember — he thought I was a low-level player. Maybe this'll work."

Sure enough, the knife started to turn on her hand, stopping when it was pointed toward the port.

"That wasn't you moving it, was it?" I decided to clarify.

"No, of course not! Let's go!"

With that, the Acrobat started jumping from house to house, still holding the knife on the palm of her hand. Even in the game, that required some pretty amazing skills. I can't even imagine what her Dexterity was, given that she was at level 135. Unfortunately, Pinky didn't have any abilities that would have let her jump across the rooftops as quickly as the rest of us, and Ne-Tarok's coins could only teleport the Gremlin himself.

"Go on. I'll catch up," said Pinky with a wave of her hand. "Don't waste any time."

Mark immediately jumped up, wrapped his arms and legs around me from behind, and exclaimed in an overjoyed voice:

"Now ride like the wind, Seabiscuit!"

That's right: I had to jump along with the Illusionist on my back, making stupid jokes the whole time. Darya stopped after about ten jumps. The dagger on her palm had risen up onto its hilt and was pointing straight up toward the sky.

"Somewhere in this group here," she said confidently as we all turned to look at the stately coffins that were flying past above us.

"Which of them..." Mark began to wonder aloud, but Darya pointed to a coffin before he could finish. "That one!"

Amidst all the wooden and steel coffins, there was a noticeably shorter stone box that was decked out with yellow gemstones.

"Ah, that's right — you said he played as a Gnome," Mark snapped his fingers. "We could have guessed that his coffin would be shorter than the others."

"Well? Should we smash it?" I asked impatiently.

"Come on, man! Get to work!" Ne-Tarok and Mark shouted almost in unison.

I held my arm out and sent a blast of lightning cracking into the side of the coffin, but it didn't leave so much as a scratch. Darya jumped up and smacked it with her saber, but all that achieved was a big shower of sparks that came cascading down onto our heads.

"Ugh, you people can't do ANYTHING right, can you?" The Gremlin snorted sarcastically as he raised a hand to the sky and shouted: "Expired Insurance!"

Cracks immediately rippled out across the surface of the stone, and within a few seconds it actually split in half. It didn't fall to the ground, though; it just kept floating along in the air. A Gnome suddenly appeared on one half of the coffin; he was wearing gleaming armor and carrying a huge scythe that was almost as tall as he was. An inscription soon appeared in the air above his head:

"Artamon the Terrible, level 150."

No way, I thought — we actually found him! This is amazing! But how did his level get so high?!

Chapter 8

"YEP, HE'S REALLY A GNOME," noted Ne-Tarok. "Listen, Poison Ivy — we'll resurrect him, but he's still going to be a tiny, bearded little wiener. Will you still love him? I mean, you must love him NOW, since you managed to find the coffin."

Pinky wasn't nearby to give him a slap in the head, and I was too far away. But Mark suddenly seemed to discover quite a sensitive conscience; it was like he had been waiting for a chance to give the Gremlin a good kick.

"Too much, man," the Illusionist hissed.

"Artyom!" Darya shouted at the Gnome. To my surprise, he answered:

"Who dares disturb the slumber of the Great Warrior Artamon the Terrible?!"

We all looked around at one another, suddenly feeling hesitant. We had been expecting that finding the right coffin would be the hardest part of the task, but now we had a whole other problem on our hands — how the hell were we going to get this guy down into the critical zone?! I had no idea that Artyom had managed to rack up such an impressive level.

"He," Mark said as he pointed at Ne-Tarok. "Just smashed your coffin in the most thoughtless way. He's really a terrible guy — ah, I mean Gremlin."

With a furious roar, the Gnome jumped down from the coffin and whipped his sickle through the air. Ne-Tarok screamed as he teleported to the side (fortunately for him, he had scattered some coins around before the battle). A huge crack was soon yawning in the spot where the Gnome's sickle sank into the roof.

"Hey, why ME?!" The Gremlin shouted as he pointed at Mark. "This guy was in on it too!"

The Gnome turned around, lunged into a lightning-fast dash, and appeared next to the Illusionist before the latter had time to react. The sickle slammed into his head and inflicted enough critical damage to take the poor guy's health down to zero with a single blow.

"Oops," the Gremlin sighed. "Didn't mean to do that."

Mark fell, and almost immediately came back as a zombie. He turned and glanced at us with his glassy eyes, then jumped down to the ground and ran off, presumably in search of someone from "Spirit of the Hunt."

The Sands of Eternity

Artamon the Terrible swung his next blow at me, but I used Shift to duck to the side. Just as he swung his sickle, Darya tried to attack him from behind with her saber, but he reacted with almost mind-boggling speed and parried her thrust. He tried to hit her next, but she ducked into a graceful roll and escaped. The Gnome didn't seem upset by this at all, though — he just changed tactics and brought the pommel of his sickle slamming down onto the roof, causing us all to lose our balance and fall. A second later, the roof itself collapsed as well. It obviously hadn't been designed to absorb attacks from a level-150 character. All four of us crashed down in a pile of rubble onto the floor below. Amidst the cloud of dust kicked up by the collapsing roof, Darya grabbed me by the hand, kicked out a window, and jumped out of the building.

"We need help," she said. "I can't take him on my own."

"Captain Obvious," I said in a nervous chuckle. "We should try to find Antibiotic, or at least somebody from the "Unnameables" who we can trust."

The wall next to the window we had just jumped from suddenly shook under the weight of a fearsome blow, and a huge crack burst out all along its surface. Another equally-fearsome blow, and suddenly the house had a brand-new doorway to nowhere on the second floor.

"Embargo!" Ne-Tarok shouted, and his spell covered the huge new hole with a layer of gold foil.

Loner Book Eight

I couldn't even begin to imagine how much money he must have been burning through. I could only hope Daddy Rothschild would compensate him for it; otherwise it would be up to Boris and me.

"Let's get the hell out of here!" The Gremlin shouted. "Some people from "Spirit of the Hunt" are headed this way! I saw them from the roof!"

Makes sense, I thought. Mark's illusion disappeared when he died, so of course somebody was bound to spot us. On the other hand, though, we couldn't just leave Artamon the Terrible to his own devices. He might run off — or, worse, somebody might end up killing him.

"Antibiotic's dead," said Darya after glancing at her interface. Unlike me, the other members of our team had combined to form a single unit, so they could check in on each other at any time.

"Well, we need to keep Artyom's aggro focused on us anyways," I said as I checked my map. "Let's lead him toward the Elves."

"Let me take care of that," replied Darya decisively.

By that point, Ne-Tarok's gold foil had succumbed to repeated blows from Artyom's sickle. The Gnome was already outside, although I couldn't help but notice a moment straight out of "The Shining" when the hole was just big enough for us to see his face.

"Hey! It was me who disturbed your slumber!" Darya screamed. "Good luck catching me!"

And with that, we ran. To my intense delight, we ran into more risen dead than anybody else on the streets of Pyrenth. As usual, they just watched us pass with blank, emotionless stares. Whenever they caught sight of anybody from "Spirit of the Hunt," however, the zombies seemed to lose their minds immediately. They would attack with everything they had — weapons, abilities, even their teeth and fingernails.

"Who's even alive from our group at this point?" I asked Ne-Tarok as we ran.

"Everybody is. Most of them just haven't gotten back from the respawn point yet. Pinky's nearby, but she probably won't be able to help very much."

From somewhere off to the side, a magical arrow suddenly slammed into the Gremlin and took off a third of his health in the blink of an eye, but we kept running; we had no idea who had fired it anyway. The next stray shot ended up hitting me; not even Chaosite's aura could stop it. And given that I was only at level 50, the hit very nearly killed me. I stopped for a few seconds, just long enough to chug a healing elixir, then kept running, turning around from time to time to make sure that Darya and Artamon the Terrible were still within sight. Thankfully, the Acrobat was dodging the Gnome's attacks without too much difficulty and leading him along after us, just like we had planned.

When we finally ran out into the square where the Elves had planned to dig themselves in, we found nothing but a much-reduced crowd of zombies. Somebody had apparently managed to kill them all, most of them twice.

"Shoot him!" I shouted to the zombies (on the off-chance that this would work), but they didn't listen. Apparently, their brains were hardwired to attack only people from "Spirit of the Hunt," a category into which the undead Artyom most certainly didn't fall.

Without warning, an Assassin appeared from invisibility right next to me, swung a knife across my neck, and disappeared back into invisibility before I could even comprehend what had happened. A system communication informed me that I had not only lost a lot of health, but also been badly poisoned. It was all too much for my brain to handle, I guess, because my motor skills suddenly gave out; I tripped, fell, and slid across the cobblestones. Ne-Tarok tried immediately to summon his golden chains, but the invisible bastard was already gone.

I could only resent the fact that I couldn't change Spin's form mid-battle, because his ability to sense invisible characters would really have come in handy just then.

"Bastard," I muttered as I slammed a healing elixir and an antidote. I was spinning and turning where I stood in an effort to dodge any further attacks, and I was prepared to use Shift at any moment.

"Take a step back," I suddenly heard Whisper of Fate inside my head.

I quickly used Shift to move back, and as soon as I looked back, I saw a ten-foot-tall icicle crash into the ground on the spot where I had been standing a second before.

"Oh man. Just barely missed," said a familiar voice from somewhere nearby. Almost immediately, Zacherial and four of his generals stepped out from behind a corner. "You're a lucky one. Definitely a Man of Fate."

Ne-Tarok started slinking to the side, clearly preparing to flee. Darya was still parrying the Gnome's attacks with her saber, sometimes coming within just a few steps of me. The undead Archers immediately found themselves a target, and started pelting Zacherial with arrows, but the Clanleader blocked them easily with a shield of fire. The arrows literally burned up in midair before they even came close to him. And meanwhile, several other high-level players from "Spirit of the Hunt" appeared and quickly took out the remaining Archers.

"Don't move," I suddenly heard a soft female voice command from behind my back. I felt a dagger pressing against my back, right between the shoulderblades. "It'll be so much critical damage, you'll be dead after a single jab."

My Shift was literally created for this exact sort of situation, but I decided not to rush anything. Every minute that passed increased the odds that somebody from the "Unnameables" would show up to help us, so I was only too happy to stand around and chat for a minute.

The invisible player who had just attacked me suddenly appeared next to Darya and scattered a bunch of tiny bombs at her feet; a moment later, the little spheres turned into some sort of thick, black tar that wrapped itself around her legs and prevented her from moving. The Gnome took advantage of this immediately — with redoubled energy, he raced forward and slammed his sickle into her, taking away about a third of her health in the process.

"So it was all for this?" Zacherial asked, sounding slightly puzzled as he stared at Artamon the Terrible. "Just to kill this Gnome? What's the catch? Is it part of a quest, or is he supposed to drop something valuable?"

"It's part of a quest!" I quickly replied, and almost immediately regretted it.

"You're lying, obviously," smirked the head of "Spirit of the Hunt." "But what the hell — let's see what all the fuss is about."

I was already thinking about summoning Aishorth Bludstein; in fact, I would have done so long before, if I hadn't been worried that she might accidentally kill Artyom. Actually, forget "accidentally" — she might well kill him on purpose, given the way she always tended to interpret orders in her own idiosyncratic way.

With a wave of his hand, Zacherial created three enormous, fiery butterflies, which spread their wings and dove toward Artamon the Terrible and Darya. Noticing this new attack, the Gnome chopped the first one clean in half with his sickle, but it exploded all over him nonetheless, burning him pretty badly and knocking off a full 10% of his health. For a single blow, against a player like him, that represented a LOT of damage. For some reason, the second and third butterflies seemed oriented specifically against Darya. Just when it looked like she might be done for, however, the Acrobat split into two identical copies, one of which turned and took the brunt of the attack onto itself and disappeared instantly in the resulting explosion, while the other turned and tried to hit the Gnome in an effort to draw his aggro back onto her. But Artamon the Terrible only had eyes for Zacherial at that point; the Mage had dealt him far too much damage for him to ignore, and he turned and rushed immediately into an attack.

After a lightning-quick lunge, the Gnome's sickle started hammering the Clanleader's magical shield with a hailstorm of vicious blows; and yet somehow, amazingly, the shield held, at least for the time being.

"Attack," the Mage said to his generals with a yawn. A cold shiver ran down my spine. If they unleashed everything they had on the Gnome, I knew he'd be dead in a matter of seconds.

"Merciless Inflation!" Ne-Tarok suddenly screamed. In the blink of an eye, the health of every character in the square — including that of Artamon the Terrible — was twice as full as it had been a second before.

Even taken together, all the attacks that hit the Gnome were barely enough to take off 5% of his health. He threw himself at the players who were attacking him with a furious roar; since their health stats had also just doubled, though, the

Gnome's attack didn't actually produce much of a tangible result.

The worst part about it was that we couldn't even run away, since we had to stay with Artyom. The situation was developing into a sort of tragic farce, and yet somehow I had a very distinct feeling that I was on the losing side.

One of the generals from "Spirit of the Hunt" (apparently an Air Mage) turned to focus on the Gremlin, and attacked him with something that was barely visible in the surrounding air. A battle erupted between the two of them, just as another separate battle was developing between Darya and two of the other generals. So I was the only one who had to stand there like an idiot, pretending I had no way to escape from the Assassin while I thought frantically about what the hell we were going to do. As soon as Ne-Tarok's spells ran out, the Gnome was done for, and there would be nothing at all that I could do about it. The Ice Lady was starting to look like our only possible solution — I would just have to hope that she wouldn't hit Artyom too hard and kill him.

I was about to use Shift and activate the Heart of the Blizzard when Antibiotic suddenly rushed into the square. Or rather, "Antibiotics" — one living, one dead. He came with a small unit from the "Unnameables," which numbered about fifteen players.

"Zacherial!" Shouted the Antibiotic who had just come running back alive from the respawn point. "You're a dead man!"

The Sands of Eternity

"I'm starting to wish I was," snapped the "Spirit of the Hunt's" Clanleader. "This kid just never learns. He keeps dying and dying."

Both Antibiotics came running at Zacherial, along with the rest of the players from the "Unnameables." With near-perfect timing, Ne-Tarok's spell chose that precise moment to stop functioning and return everybody's health to normal. Admittedly, a closer look made me realize that the Gremlin's spell had stopped functioning because he had been killed — the general from "Spirit of the Hunt" was fighting a newly-risen zombie.

Just then, Pinky joined the fray as well (having finally caught up with us) and came in swinging to help Darya take out her opponents, whereupon the Acrobat landed a blow on the Gnome and finally drew his aggro back onto herself. Thankfully, Zacherial had his hands full, and he didn't have any time to spare for us. Not only that, but the Acrobat also managed to lead Artamon the Terrible away from the battle between the two Clans pretty quickly.

Unfortunately, it wasn't long before "Spirit of the Hunt" started hemming Antibiotic in from all sides. He had lost a level and gotten slapped with a debuff after his first death, and even having an undead copy fighting alongside him wasn't enough to turn the tide in his favor. The rest of the "Unnameables" were getting wiped out by the "Spirit of the Hunt's" generals one after the other. And then suddenly, the cobblestones beneath their feet flew up into the air in an explosion so intense that

I caught some serious damage, despite being at least thirty or forty feet away.

"What the hell?!" The Assassin snarled from behind my back.

I knew the time had come: I used Shift to escape her clutches, then took off running behind Darya and Pinky. Within a few seconds, I heard another explosion behind me, which apparently must have killed the invisible Assassin.

"Double jackpot!" A joyful shout rang through the air, as a very familiar Gnome stuck his little goggled face out through a nearby window.

"Thram?" I was overjoyed. "How did you do that?!"

"I've been waiting for a good opportunity," the Gnome explained. "Me and some friends went on a little stroll through the city. Set a couple mines. A couple hundred, to be exact. There's no way any of them survived."

"Thank you!" I shouted with joy before turning and running off to catch up with Darya and Pinky, who were still locked in battle with Artyom.

Thanks to "Spirit of the Hunt," Artamon the Terrible's health was quite a bit lower than it had been before; a little bit more damage, and I'd be able to slip the God of the Dead's amulet onto him. Darya and Pinky were darting and jumping all around the Gnome, slowly whittling away his health, when I finally arrived on the scene to join them. Just a little more, I thought — one last push, and we can do this!

"Invisible nearby," said Whisper of Fate inside

my mind.

"Ivy!" I shouted to Darya. "Switch!"

Realizing immediately what I had in mind, the Acrobat threw a smoke bomb to the ground at our feet, and a request to exchange appearances popped up in my interface. I felt my body take on female features, but I didn't let the strange sensation distract me from blasting the Gnome with lightning; I could only hope that my invisible assailant wouldn't notice any discrepancy between our appearances and our abilities. Once she assumed my appearance, Darya switched from swinging her saber to throwing knives, and as a result she was standing a little off to the side when my invisible assailant suddenly appeared. It was the same girl who had held the knife to my throat during the battle between the Clans back in the square; she had taken some serious damage from the explosion, but she was still alive and still dangerous. Her knife sank into Darya's back and took off almost three quarters of her health — it must have been a colossal amount of damage, given that Darya was at level 135. It wasn't quite enough to kill her, though, and Darya didn't miss a beat; she whirled around, and in one swift motion separated the Assassin's head from her body.

Almost at the same time, Pinky and I finally managed to get the Gnome's health down to 10%, and I rushed toward him, pulling the amulet out of my inventory as I ran. The Gnome's aggro was focused on Darya, so he had been preparing to attack me, but the Acrobat switched our appearances back at just the right moment; the Gnome was utterly bewildered, and for just a second he froze, trying to figure out where his original target had gone. That second was all the time I needed to slip the amulet around his neck.

"You've received a request to create a Blood Essence for Artamon the Terrible. Confirm?"

Yes, I thought!

I felt a surge of weakness wash over my body as I lost twenty more levels. It felt something like giving a little too much blood at a blood drive, although of course the only thing I was actually losing were points from my base attributes.

Artamon the Terrible's level started to drop, stopping only when it reached 125. Apparently, the levels I lost got added to his character's original level, just as had happened with Aishorth Bludstein.

"Artyom?" I asked; I could hardly believe what I was seeing. "How are you?"

"Good, man," he replied in his normal voice as he looked back at me with a perplexed expression on his face. "How did we end up here, though? Last thing I remember, I was meeting with that guy about the ESGUMI block, then — "

"Doesn't matter right now," I quickly interrupted him. "We just have to get out of here, now!"

My friend glanced around the street; not surprisingly, he was still utterly bewildered.

"Where ARE we, though?" Suddenly, he spotted Darya, which only made him more confused. "Poison Ivy? I see you've finally met each other, then?" His eyes flitted up to the Acrobat's level. "Whoa! Since when are you at level 135?!"

"Ooh, it's a long story," she replied evasively as she glanced warily back at the Gnome. "Is that really you?"

"Who else?" Artyom's confusion was getting worse by the second. "Guys — what the hell is going on?"

Darya threw her arms around his neck (not an easy feat, considering the height difference between them) and started telling him breathlessly about everything that had happened over the past few days. The four of us ducked into a nearby building to take shelter until the event was over; my plan was for us all to teleport back to Kelevre. While we waited, we had a chance to explain everything to Artyom from start to finish; needless to say, he was shocked.

"So you started a war with the biggest Clan in Arktania for me?" Artyom let out a long, low whistle of surprised admiration. Somehow, the war seemed to surprise him even more than the fact that he had just been brought back to life, after being dead for quite a while. To be fair, though, I knew that the full intensity of that information would probably take some time to settle in.

"That's what friends are for," I shrugged, feeling just a little bit proud of myself. Okay, okay — maybe more than just a little bit.

"Dude. That's pretty intense, even for a friend,"

the Gnome laughed. "But thank you — I don't know what I'd have done without you."

"Well, you'd be dead." THAT gap in his knowledge, at least, was easy enough for me to fill in. "So, yeah... You're welcome." I checked the time and made sure that the event was definitely over. "Anyway — I suggest we get the hell out of here ASAP. I don't know if you have a respawn tattoo, as the Emissary of the God of the Dead, but there's no need to tempt fate."

I handed my friend a teleportation scroll and told him to teleport to Kelevre (thankfully, he had already been there and knew exactly where it was). After waiting for him to disappear, followed by Darya and Pinky, I activated my own scroll, but I didn't actually have a chance to hop into the portal.

"So you did it anyway," an irritated Hotei growled after appearing in midair right in front of me. "So ungrateful."

" I'm very grateful," I objected, feeling tired but also very pleased. "But that doesn't have anything to do with resurrecting Artyom."

"You're down to level 30. You've pissed away all my hard work." The little God's voice was gradually getting louder and louder; I don't think I had ever seen him so angry before. "The Goddess of Fate will be disappointed in you. And more importantly, the Goddess will be disappointed in ME!"

This time, instead of his usual black-and-white abacus, Hotei pulled an enormous hourglass from behind his belt. Well, maybe it wasn't exactly enormous, but it certainly looked pretty big compared to the tiny little God. More interesting than its size, though, were the grains of sand inside it — they seemed to be glowing from within a soft, golden light.

I could sense that something very bad was about to happen, and I started backing away from the little God. Perhaps I should have simply turned and run away as fast as I could, but that would definitely have provoked him even further. And I still hadn't given up hope of finding a peaceful solution.

"Look, the levels won't be a problem. I'll recoup everything I've lost as quick as I can, I just need a little time — "

"Time. One person's eternity is another person's second. One person's second is another person's eternity..."

He turned the hourglass upside down, and the sand began to flow.

"Moments flow by like grains of sand. And you tell me you want a little time, for your own personal use?"

"Well, that's not exactly what I said."

The movement of the sand in the hourglass suddenly became unnatural: some grains floated up into the air, while others started to fall more rapidly than before, as if they were moving to the beat of some imperceptible rhythm.

"Okay, then. I'll give you some time." I looked at Hotei's face and saw that he was smirking at me. "Lots of time."

With that, he threw the hourglass onto the floor, where it shattered and sent the sand billowing up into the air.

"Let the Sands of Eternity take you away!"

There must have been a whole desert compressed inside the hourglass, because the cloud of sand just kept growing and growing. It turned into a whirlwind and lifted me into the air before I could run. I tried to use Shift, then Improved Repulsion, but sand seemed to be holding me firmly in place. Then came a sudden feeling of falling, which for some reason reminded me of the rainbow corridor I went through whenever I entered the game (except that here, everything was the same soft golden color as the sand).

And then suddenly, everything stopped. My back slammed painfully to the ground, and I lost a hundred points of health.

Chapter 9

I BLINKED A FEW TIMES and looked around. A stretch of forest rustled peacefully in the breeze above me. Some distance away, I could see the outline of a village; there were only a few dozen houses, but somehow it looked vaguely familiar. If I'd been in a movie, I probably would have rubbed my eyes at that point, but of course that doesn't actually do anything to get rid of hallucinations. Besides, it was already quite obvious that I was looking at Kelevre, in the same primordial state I had found it in on my very first day in Arktania. If memory serves, I thought, it's about time to look down and discover something lying in the grass...

Sure enough, I noticed a gleam amidst the blades of grass, so I reached down and picked up a very familiar artifact: Varr's Ring of Wisdom.

"What the hell..." I muttered to myself when I

saw that the artifact's parameters were exactly the same as before. This added a whole new layer of confusion, because I had already found this artifact once before — and I was still wearing it on one of my fingers. "Please don't tell me this is — "

"Hey, who are you?!" Rathmir's hoarse voice boomed through the air.

The gray-haired old man looked exactly the way I always pictured him. Tall, with a long staff in his hands, and bearing more than a passing resemblance to Sean Connery.

"Hey... Uh, Hello." I spoke slowly, trying to choose my words very carefully. "I think I'm a little lost."

"My name is Rathmir, I'm the local headman. And don't try to lie to me, it's two days to the nearest village from here," he scowled threateningly. "And what happened to your clothes?"

I wasn't totally certain, but it seemed like he had said the exact same thing the first time we met. More than that, though, he was speaking with a noticeably mechanical tone, and his body language didn't seem to be changing at all as he spoke.

"My airship crashed," I quickly replied. "And I don't really remember who I am. I think I'm suffering from amnesia."

"Well, you're right about the airship, at least. It crashed in Hellscream Gorge two days ago," the old man nodded. Listen, you were walking through here, you didn't see a ring by any chance, did you? It's gold, I lost it here yesterday and still haven't managed to find it."

"Yes, actually." I held the ring out to him, feeling an intense sensation of deja vu as I did so. "I just found it right here."

"Thank you, my good man." The old man's face brightened immediately.

Reward: +1000 to your standing in the village of Kelevre-2 (current status — "friendly," to "admiration": 1000).

Shit, I thought... What the hell is going on?!

I checked my character window, just to make sure that I was still at level 30, and that the game hadn't literally started over. It hadn't, and my standing in Kelevre was the same as it had been before, but suddenly there was an additional line labeled "Kelevre-2." What could that possibly mean?

"I can see you're a good man," said Rathmir. His eyes narrowed somewhat unnaturally as he spoke, almost as if he were parodying his normal mannerisms. "I'll have to bring you to our healer, she'll be able to tell you right away if you're healthy or your mind is afflicted."

I was about to say that I'd be very grateful if he would, but I stopped myself at the last moment. Why should I say that if I already knew where Amina lived anyways?

"Alas, I'm very busy," said the old man, for all the world as though I had actually asked him for help rather than staying completely silent. "I think you'll be able to find her on your own. The healer's name is Amina, her house is on the opposite edge of the village from the side nearest us."

You've received the quest "Speak with the Healer."

Task requirements: the healer must be the first character in the village to whom you speak.

Reward: +30 experience points.

Thirty whole points for a quest, I thought... Hilarious. I'll have to complete a couple THOUSAND of these to level up to 31.

"In the evening, when I get back from making the rounds, come to us for dinner, my wife makes a wonderful roast. Then we'll decide the question of where you'll stay for the time being, we're not going to leave you to sleep on the street."

Having said that, the old man set off toward the forest at a quick pace, leaving me more confused than ever about what was going on. Naturally enough, the very first thing I did was open my tablet; instead of providing answers, however, this merely left me even more confused than before. For the first time ever, I saw the words "No connection" displayed across the entire width of the screen, and I also found that I couldn't activate chats, apps, or even the encyclopedia.

"What the hell?" I muttered indignantly.

I took out a teleportation scroll and tried to use it, but this gave me another bewildering surprise:

The Sands of Eternity

"Teleportation is prohibited."

This was definitely strange — after all, the game normally sent a system communication with a warning and explanation whenever it imposed a ban on teleportation. This time, though, it was a bald statement of fact, with no indication as to why teleportation was banned, or how long it would be banned for.

After thinking for a moment, I summoned Chaosite and ordered him to search the area for Chaos emanations. If this was some sort of strange instance, there would have to be an exit somewhere. True, he had burned through a lot of Chaos in Pyrenth, which meant that his search radius would have to be pretty small. But that, at least, was one thing I didn't really have to worry about. If this place was actually Kelevre, then there were bound to be forges and sand in the area, which meant that I could make some of my trademark low-quality condenser worms and feed them to Chaosite if need be. With that in mind, I decided to walk through the village and try to determine whether it really was just a copy of the old Kelevre, and whether the rest of the characters living there would behave the same way as they had the first time I met them.

As I walked into the village and looked around, a feeling of melancholy nostalgia began to rise in my chest. The warm, well-lit log houses with their little gardens, the businesslike townsfolk (most of whom, admittedly, I had never even spoken to)...

Loner Book Eight

The whole place seemed infused with a spirit of calm and kindness. Looking at it, you'd never have guessed that it would soon turn into a battlefield in the war against the Orcs, then into a fort, and finally into a full-blown city. The wooden structures would soon give way to monumental stone buildings designed for defense, and the whole place would soon be enclosed by towering stone walls.

The dull clang of hammer on anvil could be heard throughout the village. I could see a big, powerfully-built man standing behind the smithy's heavy leather "door" as he pounded out a bar of steel, flexing his enormous muscles rhythmically as he worked. Korn was a Smith, after all, in addition to being a former Paladin.

I was about to go over and introduce myself to him, but instead I decided to conduct a little experiment — I just walked right past his shop and attempted to catch his eye to see how he would react. Would he recognize me or not? In the event, the Smith just kept hammering his anvil, staring blankly down at the steel in front of him as if he were a background NPC in some older-generation game, rather than a complex character in the most realistic virtual-reality universe on the planet.

This didn't really bother me, though. I felt like I had already started to understand what was happening. Sure, I still had to answer the questions "how?", "why?", and "what the hell is the point of all this?"

I had obviously ended up in some location that

had been torn out of the main world of Arktania. Yet another secret zone like the Tree of Fear or the Anaconda's Cave. The characters all seemed almost deliberately stiff and unimaginative — in fact, they could almost have been copied and pasted from other, older NPC templates. Nothing too surprising. But what was I supposed to do?

I found Amina's house without any trouble and knocked on the door. The Priestess of the Goddess of Fate opened the door, wearing a white robe and lab-grade safety goggles.

"Oh, a new face!"

From there, the dialogue went more or less exactly as it had the first time. Amina told me about the harvest festival, examined me using her abilities, and confirmed that I hadn't suffered any brain damage. When it came time for her to look into my past, however, she remained frozen with her hand on my forehead for quite some time. Then her eyes rolled back into her head, and she collapsed to the ground.

Now THIS was something new!

The Priestess' health didn't drop at all, which meant that she must simply have been hit with some sort of debuff or effect. I couldn't really do anything to help her, since I didn't have any healing skills, but thankfully she recovered within a few seconds anyway.

"I was trying to read your past, but suddenly I lost consciousness. Apparently, someone — or something — is protecting your memory. Still, though, I'm confident you're not an enemy to any of the people in this village."

Task "Speak with the healer" is complete.
Reward: +30 experience.

I already knew what was coming next: I led the Priestess into giving me the task for making the condenser worms, then headed off to see Korn. The Smith didn't recognize me either, but he still gave me the task that involved going to get sand from the river. It felt very weird, heading down to the river and back, because this time around it was easy (actually, it was a source of some vindictive pleasure) to kill the Steel Porcupines. These were the animals that had killed me for the very first time in the game. I could still remember how unpleasant it was — and more than just a little bit humiliating, as well, given that they had fired their quills straight into my backside.

After bringing Korn the sand, I watched him craft a condenser worm, and only then realized that I had killed the porcupines too early. I was supposed to get Lerth to help me take them out. This oversight meant that I would have to make do without the always-intoxicated Archer for the time being. But that didn't seem like a very big deal, at least for the time being; after all, having asked Korn to teach me glassblowing meant that I had access to a forge, and consequently the opportunity to craft a bunch of crappy condenser worms that I could feed to Chaosite. Unfortunately, even with his "sixth sense" turned up to maximum power, he never managed to find any exit or anything anomalous, even after I took him on a long walk around the entire area.

That said, I stopped by Thram's house and received the quest that involved slaughtering the jerboas who were wreaking havoc on his garden. I didn't really know how I was going to kill them, though, since the little rodents would always flee in terror the second they caught sight of me.

It was while thinking about this quest that I suddenly stopped in the middle of the village and... Well, I guess I just snapped out of it. What the hell am I doing, I suddenly wondered? What's the point of completing these low-level quests? Why not simply leave the game, get in touch with Boris, and try to figure out what's going on?

So I opened the menu to do just that. When I did, though, I found that the "Exit" button was inactive for some reason. And when I saw THAT, I started feeling intensely stressed.

"What the hell is this?!"

For a little while, I just kept blankly opening the menu and trying to leave the game, but of course that didn't work any better than it had the first time. When I finally got sick of that, I tried to call out to Hotei, given that this whole experience was obviously his handiwork.

"Hotei!"

"Hotei, you dick, what the hell did you do to me?!"

Alas... The little God completely ignored me. So in the end, I found myself unable either to contact anyone or leave the game and go back to the real world. It gave me the impression that Hotei had basically locked me in the game — and not even Arktania, really, but some sort of two-bit copy.

Come on, I thought as I pictured me giving myself a refreshing little slap on the cheek — get ahold of yourself. If Kelevre-2 is a copy, then how isolated is it from the rest of the world? Teleports don't work, and it would take forever to walk to the next town. As far as I remember, there's an airship that's scheduled to come by in a few days. So what's the plan?

I decided I needed a very clear answer to that question before proceeding, so I went to join Rathmir and Margia for dinner. When I did, I found myself somewhat disappointed: the dishes looked amazing, but they tasted completely bland. This was all the more striking considering that food and drink were absolutely delicious in the original Arktania. What if this version of the game is deliberately inferior, I thought? What if this is Hotei's way of mocking me?

I asked Rathmir for a map, then asked him to show me where Hellscream Gorge and the nearest fort were, as well as asking when the next airship would be coming through.

"The commuter airship will be coming through in three weeks," said the old man. "You can stay with us in the village until then. We actually had a house open up relatively recently."

Of course, I thought. I remember that house.

"So it's a three days' walk to the fortress,

then?" I asked.

The old man nodded.

"Faster on a horse, of course, but they're all in use right now. Why do you want to go there anyway, though? You're too weak."

I certainly was, of course, but how else could I possibly find out what was going on? I knew that I'd be able to get a clearer picture of the overall situation from "Freedom" than I would in Kelevre-2. Most importantly, I wanted to find out if there were any other players there, and just generally learn a little bit more about how expansive this truncated version of Arktania really was.

To be honest, the fact that I couldn't leave the game was starting to make me really nervous. I felt an overwhelming desire to run somewhere and do something — anything, really, as long as it meant I didn't have to stand around doing nothing. Therefore, after convincing myself that these really weren't the same friends I had made in the real Arktania, I decided to borrow a horse from somewhere in the village. I found a nag standing around in the yard of one of the houses, which I had never visited during my first few weeks in the game (although I was pretty sure I could have found some quests there too).

The only problem was that I had no idea whatsoever how to actually RIDE a horse, but I reminded myself that for all its strangeness, this was still a game. I could figure it out somehow.

After walking around the perimeter of the house for a while, waiting for the owners to appear,

I finally ran out of patience, so I opened the gate and walked into the yard. The horse was already saddled up (again — this was still a game), so I wrapped my hand around the pommel on the saddle, slipped a foot into the stirrup, and hopped up onto the animal's back. True, it immediately became clear that she would need to be unhitched before we could actually go anywhere, so I had to jump back down, untie her reins from the hitching post, and jump back up again. We trotted slowly out of the yard, and wound our way through the streets of the village until I finally decided it was time to leave. I actually got to the point where a system communication popped up telling me that I had acquired the ability "Horseback Riding" before I heard a shout from somewhere behind me:

"Thief! He stole that horse!"

Before I had time to react, I felt several arrows slam into my chest and take half of my health away in the blink of an eye. Lerth appeared on the road in front of me.

"Oh. Hi, Lerth," I said (purely by force of habit). Instead of responding, however, the hunter just pulled his bowstring back and fired another arrow. And then another.

I was already falling from my horse when it occurred to me that I had, in fact, managed to make Lerth's acquaintance after all. After that, I found myself swallowed by the rainbow corridor once again.

Strangely, I didn't find myself in the local cemetery when I respawned: I was right back at the edge of the forest.

"Hey, who are you?!" Rathmir asked yet again in the same old hoarse voice.

I whipped around and saw the old man walking toward me from the direction of the village. He didn't seem to be predisposed toward aggression, and... Sure enough, the same old ring was lying in the grass at my feet. Maybe the old man went for a walk and lost it in the exact same place, every single day, or maybe I was back at the start of the game again.

"Hey, I'm Falk, I'm lost," I quickly said. "Here's your ring. You lost it. See you at dinner."

And I took off running toward the village. I wanted to check whether things had actually launched from the start again, and a quick chat with Amina confirmed it: she spoke to me as though we had never seen one another before.

"I don't like this," I muttered to myself as I stood in the middle of the village and looked around. "But I still have to make sure..."

I really didn't want to fight with the locals and catch a bunch more arrows, so I headed down to the river and decided to irritate the porcupines instead. My death was painful, but not nearly as humiliating as the first time, since I stood up proudly and took the steel quill straight to the chest.

And after dying, I found myself back at the edge of the forest opposite the village, where I saw Rathmir coming to meet me. When he was just a few steps away from me, though, he suddenly froze, with one leg just barely elevated off the ground in preparation for his next step.

A little man in a beige suit and vest appeared in midair.

"Ba-ba-ba-BAA! So? How are you liking the place?"

"Hotei!" I tried to grab the little bastard, but he disappeared and then reappeared a few steps away from me.

"Let's keep our hands to ourselves, eh?" He suggested sarcastically. "Isn't this a nice trip down memory lane? You should be thanking me. I could've chosen any location I wanted. Arkem, for example."

I clenched my fists.

"I should be thanking you?! What the hell kind of place IS this?! My tablet doesn't work, my teleports don't work, and most importantly, why the hell can't I exit the game?!"

Hotei just shook his head.

"I told you: every action has consequences. But you didn't listen, and you went out and lost a bunch of levels. How are you going to hold your own against the other Emissaries and get the rest of the swords?"

"I'll get it done," I replied with mounting irritation. "I've certainly been getting everything done up to now."

The little God burst out laughing.

"We can talk later about exactly which of us has been getting everything done. See, in case you've forgotten, I promised the Goddess of Fate that I'd lead you down the Road of Swords without attracting superfluous attention from other players. And not only do I have to hold your hand through every single challenge you face, I also have to account for the fact that almost every Emissary out there now knows exactly who you are and how to interfere with your quest!"

"I'm not doing it all on my own, though," I reminded him. "My friends are helping me."

"It's not enough to keep hiding behind other people. You need to prove that you're at least somewhat competent at fighting your own corner. The Hour is coming, and you're going to need to be at least as prepared as everybody else."

"What the hell is this "Hour" everybody keeps talking about?!"

The little God simply ignored my question.

"Listen very carefully," he said, sounding almost pathetic. "This place is going to be your own personal hell until you hit level 100."

"Level 100?! How?! By killing jerboas?!" I shouted with frustration. "I'll be here forever! I'll definitely miss "the Hour," whatever that is! That'll take WEEKS! I'll fail the Goddess' quest! Not even YOU want that to happen!"

"Every time you die, you'll start back at the beginning," Hotei continued. "And don't worry. You won't fail the Goddess' quest. Time works differently here than in the real world. I sped it up by a factor of ten."

Hold on, I thought — I've already encountered time manipulation in Arktania once before. Eidolon sped up the game clock by a factor of about three, which allowed me to train for ten hours in the game during the space of three real-world hours. I was racked with terrible headaches afterward. And this is going to be a whole new level of desynchronization... I mean, time's going to be TEN TIMES faster? Is that even possible?

"Won't that be dangerous for my health?" I asked hesitantly. "I mean, we're not just talking about speeding up time at a specific location in Arktania here, are we? This is also going to affect my brain."

"According to my calculations, you'll have about three weeks before anything irreversible happens. If you hit level 100 by then, you'll be able to leave the game."

"And if I don't?!" I was getting more and more tense all the time.

"Well, then I'll have to disappoint the Goddess and tell her that her Emissary died of a brain hemorrhage." Hotei waved. "So have fun. Bye bye!"

With a quiet "pop," the little God disappeared, leaving me standing there alone at the edge of the forest.

"Wait!" I shouted with impotent fury. "Come back! What do you mean by "anything irreversible?!" Does that mean there'll be other side-effects, but they'll be reversible?!"

Still in a state of shock, I sat down on the grass, where my eye immediately darted over to the little gleam of light glinting off the headman's ring.

"Hey, who are you?" Rathmir's gravelly voice

The Sands of Eternity

boomed out from behind me.

Okay, I thought... So my life's turning into one big, long Groundhog Day. Actually, there aren't any groundhogs in Arktania. It'll have to be Jerboa Day...

End of Book Eight

Want to be the first to know about our latest LitRPG, sci
fi and fantasy titles from your favorite authors?

Subscribe to our **New Releases** newsletter:
http://eepurl.com/b7niIL

Thank you for reading *Loner!*

If you like what you've read, check out other sci-fi, fantasy and LitRPG novels published by Magic Dome Books:

NEW RELEASES!

The Coming of God of Death
A Portal Progression Fantasy Series
by Dmitry Dornichev

The Hunter's Code
A Portal Progression Fantasy Series
by Oleg Sapphire & Yuri Vinokuroff

Kill to Live
A LitRPG Progression Fantasy Adventure Series
by George Bor & Yuri Vinokuroff

The One Who Changes the Future
A Dystopian Portal Progression Fantasy Series
by Boris Romanovsky

How I Built a Magic Empire
A Portal Progression Fantasy Series
by Konstantin Zubov

The Afflicted
A LitRPG Apocalypse Adventure Series
by Konstantin Zubov

An Ideal World for a Sociopath
A LitRPG Apocalypse Adventure Series
by Oleg Sapphire

Banned
A LitRPG Apocalypse Adventure Series
by Michael Atamanov

The Dark Summoner
A LitRPG Apocalypse Adventure Series
by Andrei Tkachev

The Healer's Way
A Portal Progression Fantasy Series
by Oleg Sapphire & Alexey Kovtunov

The Selected
A LitRPG Action Adventure Series
by Vasily Mahanenko & Yuri Vinokuroff

The Last Portal Jumper
A LitRPG Progression Fantasy Series
by Konstantin Zubov

The Dark Healer
A Historical Progression Fantasy Series
by Alex Toxic & Nadya Lee

The Strongest Student
A Portal Progression Action Fantasy Series
by Andrei Tkachev

A Shelter in Spacetime
A LitRPG Apocalypse Series
by Dmitry Dornichev

The Order of Architects
A Portal Progression Fantasy Series
by Oleg Sapphire & Yuri Vinokuroff

The Village
A LitRPG Progression Fantasy Series
by Dmitry Dornichev & Alexey Kovtunov

Law of the Jungle
A Wuxia Progression Fantasy Adventure Series
by Vasily Mahanenko

Condemned (Lord Valevsky: Last of the Line)
A Progression Fantasy LitRPG Series
by Vasily Mahanenko

Living Ice
A Portal Progression Fantasy Series
by Dmitry Sheleg

Ghost in the System
An Apocalypse LitRPG Series
by Alexey Kovtunov

Crossroads of Oblivion
A Portal Progression Fantasy Adventure Series
by Dem Mikhailov

More books and series are coming out soon!

In order to have new books of the series translated faster, we need your help and support! Please consider leaving a review or spread the word by recommending *Loner* to your friends and posting the link on social media. The more people buy the book, the sooner we'll be able to make new translations available.

Thank you!

Till next time!